THE
PAN-GALACTIC
MISADVENTURES
OF

DICK
BLOWHARD

Copyright T. M. Brenner 2021

Cover by T. M. Brenner

ISBN: 979-8-9850547-0-5

THE
PAN-GALACTIC
MISADVENTURES
OF
DICK
BLOWHARD

This book is dedicated to me,

because without me

I never would have written this book.

1

Unicorns are assholes. People think they're these majestic creatures that grant wishes and shit Skittles, but they're really the biggest douche bags this side of the galaxy. They don't have rainbow hair and white skin like you see on t-shirts and gift bags. Unicorns have black horns, blood red skin, and wear leather jackets like they're in some sort of pan-galactic biker gang. They look more like a bipedal rhinoceros on steroids, if God hated rhinoceroses, and the only wish they've ever granted someone was a quick death.

About a dozen of them have me pinned down behind some barrels of highly explosive malorian ore. I'm not worried about being blown up because my sweet ass is nearly indestructible. What I'm worried about is my suit. It ain't cheap, and it takes weeks to get a new one since they're custom made by the finest tailors on Taliesin-5.

I pop my head up over the barrels just long enough to see where they're positioned. One of them gets lucky with a stray shot and hits me in the face, destroying my shades. I don't really need sunglasses because even staring at a sun won't hurt my eyes but I wear them because they're fuckin' cool.

"You asshole!" I yell. "Those cost me fifty burgmorps!"

More gunfire comes my way as I duck back down. I gotta move now, but before I do I pull out my two trusty space-blasters Irene and Rita (yeah, I named 'em), kiss them, then flip off their safeties. Jumping out from behind the barrels I double-somersault through the air, tagging four of the fuckers before I even land on my feet.

As they try their best to shoot me, I sprint toward the bar and dive over it, knocking a few people's drinks over. Most of the patrons have already run outside leaving their mai-tais, mojitos, and mules behind. And wouldn't you know it, the Unicorns fire at me, sending glass and alcohol raining down all over my new suit.

I pop my head up just to say a one-liner, "I guess drinks are on me!" Unfortunately, I have to laugh to myself because these assholes don't have a sense of humor. A few more shots hit my face but it doesn't matter since they've already ruined my shades.

Ducking back down I notice a woman on the ground next to me, covered in tattoos and with a body to die for. Black hair, mocha skin, and legs for days. She's wearing some kind of leather strappy thing that shows off her molten curves.

"Stay down," I yell at her. "Unless you want your perfect body all shot up."

She rolls her eyes at me, pulls out a power rifle from under the bar, and starts shooting at the Unicorns. What the fuck?

I don't know how to react. First, no woman has ever shrugged off my charm like that. Not one. I lay more pipe than the Mandrells of Barcylon-2. You'd know that's a lot of pipe if you'd read my book on transdimensional pipe installation. And I can't believe she thinks she can take out these Unicorns. But as I watch for a few seconds while getting tagged in the face by laser blasts she's able to nail three of them. Color me fucking impressed.

Before they have a chance to fire back, she ducks down behind the bar which is quickly turning into swiss cheese. Yeah, we got fucking swiss cheese out here in the ass end of space, so what?

I look back at the Unicorns just in time to see a grenade flying my way. Diving toward the woman I cover her with my masculine, hulking frame, feeling the explosion detonate behind me. Goddamn it, that's another suit ruined. My ass is now hanging out the back half. Not that I mind everyone seeing my perfect ass but I hate that I don't have any backup clothes.

Since my suit is already torn to shit, I holster my sidearms, hop over the bar, and run straight for the other five Unicorns who're using some overturned tables for cover. I grab the first one's spiraled horn of death, rip it off, then stab it straight through its eye. Black blood gushes out like diarrhea, coating the bastard's face. It screams out with a horrible, monstrous shriek, and I kick it in the nuts so hard it raises into the air a few feet.

As my clothes get cut to ribbons from blaster fire, I look back at the bar to make sure the hot bartender is watching my every move. I give her a smile and she just shakes her head. I still can't believe it. Can't she see my ass?

Lunging forward, I grab the next Unicorn by the horn. Instead of ripping it off I lift the Unicorn into the air then punch a hole clean through his torso. Glancing back, I see the hot bartender gagging just before ducking behind the bar.

Getting creative, I use the dead body of the Unicorn I'm holding like a baseball bat (yeah, we got baseball too), and start slamming it into the other three. Two of them are knocked to the ground but the third one stays upright. Leaping into the air I head stomp the two on the ground, sending Unicorn brains flying everywhere. Only one more asshole left to deal with.

Just to fuck with him I slowly walk toward the last Unicorn, blaster fire ricocheting off my perfectly formed abs. One of the blasts hits the malorian ore in the corner, detonating it, bringing the ceiling down on top of us. The Unicorn is crushed to death, but I'm still standing, like something out of a goddamn comic book.

Shifting debris around me as I go, I wade my way over to where the bar used to be. Trapped underneath a section of ceiling is the bartender. I pull her free, sling her over my shoulder, and carry her outside.

She's unconscious so I hold her tightly, using my super-deluxe healing powers to try to wake her. After a few seconds she regains consciousness and starts coughing.

"Bleck, get the fuck off me!" she yells, pushing me away.

"Yeah, you're welcome for saving you," I say.

"You didn't save me you asshole! You destroyed my bar!"

"Wait, that was your bar?"

"You're goddamn right it was. And what the hell was the malorian ore doing there in the first place?"

"I was hired to return it to its rightful owner. But now maybe I think it was a set up," I say.

"You think?"

"Yeah, well, work was slow this month so I took what I could get. Anyway, sorry about your bar but I gotta get out of here. I have a score to settle with the little weasel who set me up. I owe him big time."

"If anyone owes anyone anything it's you that owes me a fucking bar."

"Yeah, well I don't own a bar and I don't have that kinda money on me. But I saved your life. Doesn't that count for something?" I ask.

"Not if you're the asshole that put my life in jeopardy in the first place! Seriously, what is wrong with you?" she asks.

"I've just never met a woman who didn't like me before."

"That's a surprise."

"No, seriously, women usually fall all over me. You're… different. Fine, I'll get you your money. Stay here and I'll be back with it in a day or two."

"Do you think I'm stupid? That I'd just let you fly off without paying me? As soon as you're gone you won't come back. I'm coming with you."

"Like hell you are," I say.

"It's either that or I call the space-police on you," she says.

"Goddamn it. Okay, you win," I say, as I walk away from her.

2

She hurries to catch up. "So, who was this guy that hired you? Was he a unicorn like them?" she asks.

"No, he was literally a little weasel. Furry guy. Goes by the name 'Fred'. Should have listened to my gut. Never trust anything cute."

We walk a few blocks to my sweet-ass ride. I call her Bessie. Named her after Bessie Stringfield, the famous motorcyclist. She's got hover and jet capabilities and a zero-to-sixty of 0.1 seconds. She's also armed to the teeth. Black and leather and chrome everywhere, just the way God intended it.

"This? This is your ride?" she asks, pointing to my space-cycle.

"Yeah, what of it?"

"It looks just as douchie as you do. Wait, where are you taking me?" she asks.

"Home. Macho Centauri."

"Wow, even your planet sounds douchie. But you do realize I can't breathe in outer space, right?"

"Actually, I hadn't thought of that because I don't actually have to breathe. But don't worry, you can wear this helmet. It'll keep you alive." I say this while pulling out a helmet from inside the seat.

"Hey, you got a name?"

"Nunya."

"Nunya?"

"Nunya Fuckin' Business."

"Fine. Whatever. Don't tell me your name if you don't want to," I reply.

"No, seriously, my parents thought it was hysterical. They both sell used spaceships and had their last name legally changed to 'Business'. Then when I came along, they thought it would be funny to name me Nunya. Assholes."

"They still breathing?" I ask.

"Yeah, why?"

"Do you want them to stop?"

"Stop what?"

"Breathing."

"Dammit, no! They're assholes but I don't want them dead."

"Hey, up to you. Offer is always on the table," I respond.

5

"No, no it's not! Never! It's totally off the table!"

"Okay, I get it. Damn. Go ahead and hop on my space-cycle in front of me."

"Oh, no way, I'm not falling for that one," she says. "You aren't rubbing your dick against my ass while we're flying, perv."

"That's fine, you can sit behind me and get cozy with my naked ass instead."

"GODDAMN IT! Fine, I'll sit in front. But if I feel anything, and I mean ANYTHING rubbing up against me, I'm gonna cut it off."

"Good luck with that. Like the rest of me my trouser snake is indestructible."

"Gross."

"But I'll try not to rub against you. Okay?"

"Yeah, fine, whatever. Shit, I guess I should know your name. Not that I want to."

"Dick. Dick Blowhard: Pan-Galactic Privates Investigator," I say.

"You mean 'Private Investigator'?" she asks.

"I've heard it both ways."

She shudders, shakes her head, and finally straddles my space-cycle. Getting on behind her I try my hardest not to rub against her.

I kickstart the space-cycle and rev the jet engine a few times. We take off leaving a trail of smoke and dust behind us. As we pull up into the sky I take a look back at her bar. Wasn't much of a bar really; only had three kinds of space-beer on tap. And don't even get me started on the stale space-pretzels. But for the first time I can remember I actually feel slightly bad about something. The feeling fades fast though because why should I feel guilty anyway? This babe is going on an adventure with yours truly instead of running some shithole bar on a shithole planet in the middle of a shithole galaxy.

As we move higher into the air I can see planet Houston grow smaller beneath us. I can make out the dusty desert surrounding the small town that the bar was once a part of, a whole lot of nothing surrounding it. I spit out of the side of my mouth just to let the whole planet know what I think of it. Maybe my super-spit will help them grow crops or something. I don't know, I've never stuck around a place to see what my super-spit did. For all I know it's like acid and can melt all the way through the planet.

In front of me, Nunya's holding onto the sides of my bike, shivering. Oh shit, I forgot things can get cold for people who don't have space-proof skin. Turning on the space-cycle's heater helps her stop shaking. I don't think she likes riding it though because she's gripping the sides like she might fall off and die. I guess that makes sense since she actually might fall off and die. Nah, I wouldn't let her. If she fell off I'd do the superhero thing and swoop down and save her.

I hear mumbling coming from inside Nunya's helmet. Pressing a button on the side of it makes her easier to hear. Not that I really needed to because of course I have super-hearing, I just didn't want to have to focus my powers over the sound of my space-cycle's badass engine.

"How long is this gonna take?" asks Nunya.

"Shouldn't be too long. Maybe a few hours," I yell back.

"What happens if I need to piss?"

"You're shit out of luck."

"And what happens if I have to shit?"

"Uh, you're piss out of luck..."

Suddenly, my space-cycle's force field and inertia arrester kicks in just as we start to reach the upper atmosphere. If it didn't have those it couldn't handle lightspeed travel. I mean I'm sure that my invincible exterior could handle it but my space-cycle would fly apart, and Nunya would fly apart with it.

As the dry, barren, lame-ass planet Houston gets smaller and smaller I turn on the lightspeed drive, sending us hurtling through space as fast as a human being can go. From what I heard when I bought the space-cycle, because of some dumbass laws of physics or some shit, if humans travel faster than light they go back in time and make out with their moms or some shit. Yeah, no thanks.

Even with lightspeed drives planets are too far apart to quickly travel to. To speed things up they invented a freeway system of wormholes. Some egghead came up with a way to basically create holes in space that jump you from one place to another. I call them 'space-assholes' because that's what the energy rings look like: some chick's asshole with glitter on it.

As I slow down and pull up to the nearest onramp a security ship flashes its lights at me. "What is your destination, citizen?" comes over my bike's comm.

"Macho Centauri."

"Macho Centauri... oh, Detective Blowhard, we didn't recognize you! Yes, of course we'll tune the portal for Macho Centauri! Also, we've been instructed to tell you that the President of the Pan-Galactic Space Federation says hello and hopes you have a spectacularly wonderful day."

"Yeah, thanks. Tell him and his wife and daughters I said hi.

Especially his daughters," I reply.

"Will do. Calibrating portal... now."

The portal starts to shimmer and the planets on the other side change from red spheres to a single green-blue planet. I give the engine some juice and make our way through the portal as I see the security ship crew waving at me. I just nod my head back and they wave faster, jumping up and down from the excitement of seeing someone as famous as me.

As we pass through to the other side Nunya turns around and looks at me. "What the fuck was that?" she says.

"What?"

"How the fuck do you know the President?"

"Oh, Bob? Yeah, me and him are old drinking buddies. I also bang his hot wife and daughters sometimes."

"And does the President know you're fucking them?" she asks.

"Yeah, duh."

"Why hasn't he had you killed?"

"First off I can't be killed, as far as I know. And second, Bob's a pussycat. He doesn't give a shit who I stick my dick in as long as I get the job done."

"But why you? Why the hell would you even know the President in the first place?"

"Because I save the galaxy all the time. It's like every ten minutes the President calls me up and asks me to save some planet from some mega-monster, or locusts, or whatever it is, and I take care of it."

"But how? You're incompetent."

"I dunno, I just use my superpowers and shit works out. I don't really think about it much."

"I doubt you think about anything much," says Nunya.

"Hey, look, I'm trying to fix things for you. Least you could do is stop being an asshole to me. Think you can stop?"

"No."

"Yeah, well you suck."

"Yeah, your comebacks suck."

"My ass and your face."

"Still sucks."

I stop arguing with her, and not because I can't beat her in an argument, but because I got bored with arguing. Anyway, it takes us a few minutes to fly to the opposite side of the planet where my home is.

As we approach, I notice that there's smoke coming out of my house. And by smoke I mean a huge fucking fire, and by my house

I mean my 3,000 room mega-mansion. Goddamn it!

"Goddamn it," I say out loud.

"That city's on fire!" yells Nunya.

"That's no city, it's my space-station."

"What?"

"That's my home."

"The whole damn thing?" asks Nunya, clearly not believing me.

"Yeah, the whole damn thing. But it doesn't matter anymore because some fucker destroyed it! What the goddamn fucking-fuck!?!?!"

"Wait a minute, please tell me you keep all your money in a bank."

"Nope. You see that fire? Yeah, that's everything I own burning up. Cash, clothes, everything," I reply.

"Then how the hell are you going to pay me back?"

"I won't, obviously."

"Yeah, that's not okay. I'll make your life a living hell if you don't."

"You already are, obviously."

I hover Bessie over the burning embers of my house. Hopefully my servants, who are all named Ember by the way, aren't burning with it. Otherwise, that'd be really fucking ironic.

"Wait," says Nunya, "Let's track down whoever did this and take all of their money. We can use that to buy me a new bar and you can keep whatever's left over."

"How do you know they have any money?"

"Well, do you have any defense systems in place?"

"Yeah, only the best. Missile systems. Laser systems. Missiles that shoot lasers systems. We even have flying murder-sharks that carry bazookas," I say.

"To get past all of that, and do this much destruction, they would have to have a lot of money. Like, a lot. So who is your biggest enemy?"

"I don't have any enemies. Everyone loves me."

"No, seriously."

"Seriously. You're the first person I've met who doesn't like me."

"What about the Unicorns back at my bar? They seemed to hate your fucking guts."

"They don't count," I reply. "They're just assholes."

"Well, who all do you think is an asshole?"

"Hmmm… well, I think cans with tabs on them are assholes because they never open right. And people who chew with their mouths open. Oh, yeah, and people that like easy listening music."

"That doesn't help. That's too many people," replies Nunya.

"Even one of them is too many," I say.

"Regardless, can you think of anyone you've fought in the past? Anyone who you might have beaten that would hold it against you?"

"Only assholes."

"Well, yeah, we're trying to think of what assholes might be holding a grudge against you. So do you know any assholes who might want to see you dead?"

"Oh yeah, plenty," I reply. "Probably tens-of-thousands."

"Shit, too many of those people too, then."

"Nah, not people, just assholes."

"UNGH! Can you stop being so..."

"Good looking? Sorry, no can do."

"NO! Stop being so... you!"

"Look, I was always told growing up to be myself. Well, myself is fucking awesome. And if you don't like me then you're an asshole. You're not even a person, you're just an asshole."

"Hey, assholes can be people too. In fact, most people ARE assholes. They aren't mutually exclusive, okay?"

"No. I don't know what mutually exclusive means," I say.

"It means either this or that, but not both."

"Then why didn't you just say that?"

"Because it's shorter, fuck-wit."

I do my best to ignore her, setting the space-cycle down in a large open courtyard in the center of what used to be my mansion. The fire hasn't touched this section but smoke still fills the area.

"Oh, shit! There's something I need to get! Stay here!" I say to Nunya.

I take off running, crashing straight through walls, plowing through dozens of rooms, until I finally get to my favorite bedroom. The room is almost entirely burnt to the ground except for one corner, my favorite corner. In my favorite corner is my favorite thing, untouched, except for a fine layer of ash covering it. I pull it off of the wall and run back through the holes I'd made, finding my way back to Nunya.

"Good news! It's safe!" I yell, clutching the object to my chest.

"What, what is it? Is it a painting?" she asks.

"It's not just any painting, it's a one-of-a-kind piece of art!"

"And it's worth a lot?"

"It's literally priceless. I couldn't even get insurance for it because it's so valuable."

"Is it a masterwork? Like from DaVinci, or M'zanzidub?"

"It's a Vivante!"

"I'm not familiar with Vivante," she says.

"He only started painting a few years ago but his stuff is really good. Look!" I say, turning it to show her.

"Oh. My. God."

"I know, right?"

"It's a velvet... you. You had someone paint a velvet version of you. I just can't even..."

"Like I said, it's priceless. Only one of these bad-boys in existence and it's mine. It's worth more than the whole mansion. It could fetch quadrillions on the open market."

"I wouldn't pay ten burgmorps for that piece of shit, let alone a quadrillion burgmorps," says Nunya.

"Well, I guess that just makes you dumb then," I reply.

"It makes me sane is what it makes me. This world is filled with idiots."

"Yeah, and you're one of them."

She ignores my comment.

"Do you really think you can sell that thing for a quadrillion burgmorps? If so, you can just pay me that way."

"Oh, fuck no, I could never sell my painting. It's too damn important to let it just hang on someone's mediocre beige wall. No, this thing stays with me forever."

That's when she screams. And it's not a happy scream like I just gave her the big 'O'. No, this is a scream of frustration.

"Hey, the guys with super-hearing would appreciate it if you could keep it down below 200 decibels, okay?" I say.

"I'm surprised you even know what a decibel is. Seriously, you better figure out who did this to your mansion fast or I'm gonna take that painting and burn it myself," says Nunya.

"You wouldn't dare!"

"Try me."

"I'd like to," I say.

That's when she starts kicking my space-cycle.

"Hey!" I yell. "Stop! If you damage it we'll be stuck here. My vehicle hangar is also destroyed, okay?"

Thankfully, she stops kicking Bessie.

"Wait, don't you have super-flying or something?" she asks.

"Yeah, I do, but I can't fly at lightspeed. So we wouldn't be able to make it to the next planet for several years. You wanna go that long, in space, without food and water and no place to shit?"

"Fine. So how do we even figure out who did this? Don't you

have any cameras in your security system?"

"Oh, shit, yeah. I totally forgot. And they get sent to my PSD, my Personal Space Device."

"I know what a PSD is," says Nunya.

"I was just saying it for the folks at home."

"I wish there was a word that was stronger than 'stupid' so that I could use it on you. Stupid just scratches the surface with you."

"Takes one to know one."

"Yeah, your comebacks are still shit. So use your PSD already to look at the camera footage."

I pull my PSD out of my front pocket and start tapping on it.

"Oh, fuck," I say, as I finally see who was behind the destruction of my home. "Sloths."

3

Okay, I know what you're thinking: how the fuck can Sloths be dangerous? They're cute, they move slowly, and all they do is smile. They're like the stoners of the animal kingdom. Well, although these Sloths look like the ones you're familiar with, they're nothing like that. Their claws are sharper than almost anything in the known universe, they move super fast, and they're agile like ninjas. They're nature's perfect killing machines, and if you get on their bad side they won't stop until you're dead.

These particular Sloths I recognize. They're from planet Beta-Zeta-Zeta, or what everyone calls Buzzworld. Rumor has it that it's covered in bees, and there are rivers of honey and shit. But I think that started because of the name and not because there's any truth to it. No one really knows what's on that planet because it's covered in a mist at all times, and no one's been stupid enough to set foot on their homeworld. Until me.

Yeah, I was screwing around joyriding one night when I decided to finally check out the planet. I don't really remember what happened because I was totally blackout wasted (yeah, I can still get drunk), but I do remember waking up the next day, having been flung back into outer space. My suit was of course torn to shreds because the fuckers did their best to tear me apart but no dice; even their super sharp claws can't penetrate this skin, baby.

I got lucky because a group of space-pirates spotted me and brought me into their ship. I talked them into dropping me off at my space-cycle and the rest is history. So yeah, I'm the only person to ever land on the surface of their planet and live to tell about it. But honestly there ain't much to tell.

So why did the Sloths attack my home? I figure they're still sore from me landing on their planet. I think they took it personally or something. I dunno, maybe I banged their queen and just don't remember. Maybe there's a bunch of little Blowhard-Sloth children running around out there causing trouble. Heh, that'd be awesome. Still, I need to figure out how to pay them back for destroying everything I own. Everything, except of course my prized possession: my portrait.

"Wait, Sloths did this?" asks Nunya.

"Yeah, evil bastards."

"But I thought they were docile and cute. There's no way they did this."

"You've obviously never heard of Buzzworld, have you?"

"No. Don't get a lot of space-news on planet Houston. Why, what's Buzzworld?"

I give her the deets and at first she doesn't believe me until I show her the footage of the Sloths using their ships to blast everything I own to smithereens. You know I never thought about it until now but what the fuck exactly is a smithereen? Sounds like a band name or some shit: The Smithereens.

"Okay, so let me get this straight," starts Nunya. "We're gonna have to go after a group of weaponized Sloths to get my money. That's what you're saying?"

"Yeah, I guess it is."

"This has got to be the stupidest mission that anyone has ever been on."

"Anyway," I start to reply, "first thing's first: I need new clothes."

"New clothes? You're worried about new clothes?"

"Yeah. Would you prefer I walk around naked? 'Cause I can do that if you want."

"Fuck no, ass-wipe. I don't want your gross veiny dick hanging out."

"It ain't gross, it's epic! And you're just jealous 'cause you don't have one!"

"Yeah, no."

"Fine, well at the very least I'm taking what's left of my suit jacket, shirt and tie off."

I start peeling the remaining fabric off my chest which is stuck to my skin from the Unicorn blood I'd been soaked in. My belt thankfully is still holding up what's left of my pants because I always try to spend extra on belts to make sure they're nearly indestructible like me. I notice Nunya pointing at my chest and laughing.

"Mary Sue. You have a tattoo of the name Mary Sue on your chest! Because of course you do," she says.

"Hey, Mary Sue was my mom! What the fuck is your problem?"

"Oh, nothing, never mind." She just keeps laughing at me.

"No seriously, tell me."

"Nah, it's better to keep you in the dark."

"Hey, do you treat everyone like shit?"

"No, just people I despise."

"What did I ever do to you?" I ask.

"You destroyed my bar! That's what you did to me! God, get a fucking clue."

"Yeah, well it was a shithole bar on a shithole planet."

"It may have been a shithole bar on a shithole planet, but it was my shithole bar, and it was on my shithole planet. Anyway, we're wasting time bickering. Let's go find these fuckers. You bust their heads, take their money, and then pay me back," she says.

"Yeah, that's a great plan and all, but we don't know where they are right now."

"Aren't they on Buzzworld?"

"How the fuck would I know? It's not like I have long thoughtful conversations with Sloths where they tell me all their plans and shit."

"Well, you know a hell of a lot more about them than I do. I thought they were just fuzzy and cuddly up until exactly twenty-seven seconds ago."

"I still have no idea where they might be. They could be trying to hunt me down. If they got ahold of one of my Embers and tortured the info out of her they might have headed to planet Houston, but I just don't know."

"Well, is there anyone you can contact?" she asks. "Someone you know that might lead us in the right direction?"

"Oh, yeah, there is someone: the Wise Old Wizard."

"What's his name?"

"As far as I know that is his name. He's the Wise Old Wizard, and whenever I get stuck trying to figure out the next step of an adventure or I need a training montage or something like that he's my guy."

"Montage? What the fuck is this, a movie?" she asks.

"Obviously not yet, but someday I'm sure they'll turn my adventures into movies because I kick ass and my whole life's movie-worthy."

"You really need help. Do you know that?"

"Not what my shrink thinks. He says I'm completely free of any mental anything."

"Now that I believe," she says, snickering. "Can't damage what you don't have."

"Look, stop with the insults or else," I warn.

"Or else what?" asks Nunya.

"Or else I won't help you, that's what else. Seriously, I lost everything I have too. We're in the same boat now and I'm still gonna try and help you. Who's gonna help me? Where's my incredibly handsome, super strong hero that's going to fix all my problems for me? Nowhere, that's where. I have to do all this shit myself. So if you could stop being such an asshole that'd be great."

For the first time she hesitates. She takes a long look at me, nods her head and finally speaks. "Fine, I'll TRY to stop giving you so much shit. And not because you don't deserve it, because you do, but because I'll try to be the better person. Okay?"

"Whatever. I just want to get on with it already," I say.

"So our plan right now is to get you some clothes, because I don't want to be staring at your naked ass anymore, and then we'll go visit your wizard friend."

"You've been staring at my ass?"

"Fuck no! So where are we going to get you clothes?" asks Nunya.

"My tailor. Should only take a week to get a new suit if I ask for a rush job and pay extra for it."

"No way are we waiting a week just so you can get a suit. And how are you gonna pay extra for it when you don't have any money?"

"I'll use my space-credit card, because I master the shit out of those possibilities."

"Wait, you have credit? Can't you just pay me back that way?"

"And pay the 210% interest on it? Yeah, that's not happening. Besides, I couldn't take out that much in cash because I'm sure my insurance company has already told the credit companies that everything I have is destroyed, so they won't let me withdraw that much. Also, before you even ask, I have no collateral for a loan since everything I have is destroyed. So although I can keep us fed and clothed for right now I can't just buy you a damn bar, okay?"

"You have insurance? So you'll get all your money back anyway?" she asks.

"Maybe eventually, but it could take years and I may have to sue them if they decline my claim because I can't remember if there's a clause in my policy that excludes fucking Sloth attacks."

She blinks a few times, just staring at me.

"Seriously, who can plan for that sort of shit?" I ask.

She blinks a few more times.

"I must be having a stroke," she starts, "because it seems like you actually said something that made sense. Shit, I don't know what to do with that information."

"Hey, I'm super smart, okay? It takes some brains to amass the fortune that I have. Or had."

"I guess. Anyway, where can you get clothes where it won't take a week?"

"No idea. I usually have to buy my clothes from the tailor so they fit right. I don't know if you noticed but I have a hulking rock-solid body and a massive pants-python that doesn't like being confined. Pretty much no one else in the galaxy has my muscles so finding something I can wear won't be easy."

"Well, we could always try the Big, Dumb and Ugly store."

"You mean the Bigger and Taller store?"

"No, I meant what I said."

I'm really starting to hate her.

"We can try the Bigger and Taller store," I say. "We'll just have to find one. Should be able to look it up on my PSD and see where the nearest one is." I tap away until I pull up directions to the nearest location. I turn to Nunya and ask: "Are you ready to leave the burning wreckage of my life?"

"No, I'm gonna keep following you until I get my money."

"I didn't mean my life in general, I meant are you ready to leave my home."

"Yeah, let's get the fuck out of here," replies Nunya.

With that she hops back on my space-cycle and puts her helmet back on. I slide in behind her trying not to rub against her. Doing my best to not look at her ass I send the directions from my PSD to my space-cycle which takes a brief moment.

While I'm waiting, I take my one-of-a-kind velvet 'Me' painting and put it in my bag of ultimate wonders, which is a lot less powerful than it sounds. Basically, it's a bag you can put anything into and then pull back out again. Thankfully, it's indestructible like me and it's small enough to fit in a pocket. It magically stretches to fit whatever I'm putting into it. Once the bag is back to its normal tiny size I put it back in my pocket.

Figuring everything's secure I start up Bessie. I hover slowly into the air taking one last look at the destruction of my home. It dawns on me that I don't have a home anymore and it breaks my big hero heart.

And no, I'm not crying. You're crying.

4

Wiping away the tears that were obviously caused by dust getting kicked up from my space-cycle, I steer Bessie around the planet and back to the portal we came through. The security guards at this gate know me really well but still fall all over themselves to help me. This time though I don't care that much. Normally it's an ego boost, which is also the name of my line of energy drinks. Ego Boost, now with 200% extra EGO! (Paid sponsor). But it doesn't make me feel better about myself.

I tell the security crew we want to go to Epsilon-69. I didn't pick it because it had the closest Bigger and Taller store, I picked it because then number 69 is awesome and I thought it was funny. Nunya just looks back at me and shakes her head.

The space-asshole starts sparkling and eventually on the other side of the portal appears a giant planet with a mix of colors. Reds, blues, greens and beige. Four small moons of different colors circle it, one a striking purple color. I nod my head to thank the security crew who wave back and I give Bessie a little extra juice when flying through the space-rectum.

I aim Bessie toward the purple moon because my bike's IPS (Interstellar Positioning System) is telling me that's where the store is. The closer we get the more vibrant the surface's purple hue is. As we approach, I can see fields of purple plants that look like wheat surrounding a lone building seemingly in the middle of nowhere. There aren't many vehicles parked outside, maybe a dozen. An eight-foot-tall panda stands outside the store holding up a sign that reads 'Big Sale on Bigger Clothes!' I have to hope that the panda is just some dude in a panda suit because otherwise that would be weird.

"This place looks okay," says Nunya, taking off her helmet as we land and dismount my ride.

"Yeah, I'm sure it'll be great," I say, trying to sound as sarcastic as possible.

"Just wait until we get inside. Maybe it won't be so bad."

As we step inside a wave of dizziness hits me. It's weird because I never feel dizzy, other than when I drink too much. But seriously, all the jacked-up colors make my eyes hurt. I hate it immediately.

A woman with a squid for a face comes walking up to us. I

assume she's a woman because she's wearing a pearl necklace, blue eye makeup, and bright pink lipstick where lips would normally be, and not just above the weird mass of tentacles that she actually has. She's clothed in a white and blue sundress that seems out of place somehow on this planet. If Cthulhu had a sweet aunt Edna, this would be her.

"May I help you?" she asks.

"Yeah, we're looking for some clothes for him," says Nunya.

"Ah, I can see why you're here," she says, looking me up and down. "Yes, we should be able to accommodate the gentleman. What size are you, sir?"

I give her my dimensions.

"Oh, also" I start, "I need something extra roomy in the nether region."

She looks down. "Yes, I can see that too," she replies. Her cheeks, if you could call them that, somehow turn pink. I shift my hips just slightly to show off the girth of my manliness. Her eyes get very large.

"Are you done, dickhole?" asks Nunya. "Quit sexually harassing this poor lady who's just trying to do her job."

"Oh, no, it's alright," says the tentacle lady, batting her eyelashes at me.

"Like hell it is," says Nunya.

"Jealous much?" I reply.

Nunya kicks me in the shin. Doesn't hurt at all though. Well, for me. Her foot isn't so happy about kicking me though.

"So, are you two married?" asks the saleswoman.

"Fuck no!" I say, a little too loud.

"We're just… acquaintances?" says Nunya, not knowing what else to say.

"Good! I mean, that's fine. Although you too would make a cute couple."

"Yeah, I'm gonna agree with shit-for-brains here: fuck no," says Nunya.

"Well, let me show you what we have that might fit," says the saleswoman. She pulls out a small device, taps on it with her surprisingly human looking fingers, and the lights in the store dim, except for a handful of spotlights that seem to be beaming down at various racks of clothes. We spend a few minutes looking around at the suggestions.

"Hey, do you have anything made out of an indestructible material? I live a life of danger and excitement, and sometimes my shit gets shot up," I say.

"Oh, you want the good stuff," says the saleswoman.

"Yeah, the good stuff," I say, in my deep, gravely, manly voice.

"Perfect. I'll take you to the vault," she replies.

"The vault. Nice," I respond.

We follow her to the back of the store to several racks of pants that are hanging up on the wall. She taps on her tablet and the wall of pants swings open revealing a secret door. The door itself is huge, about twice my size. Maybe there is someone even bigger than me out there. I doubt it, but it's possible. Maybe Godzilla shops here.

There's a keypad on the door that the saleswoman taps on a few times revealing another door. This door has an old-school combo lock like something on a safe. She twists it back and forth a few times, pulls the handle and the door swings open, revealing... another door. This one has a handprint pad and a retinal scanner. The saleswoman places her hand on the pad and her left eye up to the scanner. A second later we hear a series of locks disengaging, and then finally the door sinks into the ground revealing a room about the size of a Denny's. Yeah, we got fucking Denny's too.

We enter the room which is much, much nicer than the main store. Instead, the vault has beautiful dark wood-paneled walls, a strikingly ornate cream-colored ceiling, dim lighting, and the faint sound of jazz playing from nowhere in particular. It makes me feel like fucking James Bond. Wait, I feel like I am James Bond, and not that I feel like fucking him. Not that there's anything wrong with that, but... nope.

We follow the saleswoman to a counter at the back of the vault and standing behind it is a thin robot wearing a glittery bow-tie and trousers.

"Hellllloooo," he says in a slightly high-pitched voice. Where the hair on his head should be is a tiny bonfire that changes colors as he talks, from normal oranges and yellows to purples and greens. "Howwww may I help you?" he asks.

"The gentleman here is looking for something indestructible. He's an adventurer and needs something that will protect him," says the saleswoman.

"Actually, that's not entirely true. I'm indestructible, but I hate having to buy new clothes every ten minutes so I'm looking for an outfit that can keep up with me," I say.

"Interesting," says the robot. "And does sir have a color preference?"

"Motherfucking black," I reply.

"Now, do you mean just the color black, or the actual hue

'motherfucking black'? Because we only have one shirt that comes in motherfucking black, but I don't think we have any matching pants," he replies.

"Uh, just as black as you can get, I guess."

"Ah, that is good as most of our finest indestructible clothes are black. Not many people want indestructible clothes in mauve or chartreuse," says the robot.

"Yeah, fuck mauve," I say.

"Indeed," replies the robot. "Do you have any other parameters that I might use to enhance your decision? Particular styles that sir does or does not like?"

"Yeah, no t-shirts, unless I wear a leather jacket over it. No turtlenecks, because I don't want to feel like a really weak man is strangling me all day long. Also, something that won't get caught in a jet engine, so no capes. Shorts aren't my thing because I try to keep it classy. Anything in a suit or tuxedo or similar is cool. Basically, anything you'd wear shades with. 'Cause shades are fucking cool."

"Hmmmmmmm," says the robot. "I think I know exactly what you're looking for." He wheels around the counter, literally standing on a spinning tire where legs would normally be, and makes his way throughout the vault, gathering a few items. He comes back, looks me up and down, and hands me the clothes. "Try these on, sir, and let me know what you think."

"Here, I'll show you to the dressing room," says the saleswoman, grabbing me by the arm and leading me into a corner. She opens a privacy door, pushes me in, then closes it behind her. "Let me help you try this on." The saleswoman takes the clothes from my hands and sets them down on a counter inside of the small room. I notice that it's actually quite large for a changing room, but I guess that makes sense when your store is called 'Bigger and Taller'.

Anyway, she starts unzipping my pants.

"Oh, uh, I guess you guys really go the extra mile with your customer service here," I mumble.

She just looks at me and pulls my pants down, or at least what's left of them. My meat rocket pops out and dangles in front of her because of course I don't wear underwear. Everything I do is commando.

Before I can even react she gets down on her knees and wraps her tentacle-mouth around my flaccid member. Holy fuck! It feels so fucking good! Damn, maybe I should have gotten with one of these squid women before now. And I have to admit, I've fucked weirder.

I hear a voice from outside the dressing room,"Hey, what is that noise? What the fuck is going on in there?" asks Nunya.

"Oh, uh, nothing. Just trying to get the clothes on," I say back to her.

"Like hell you are. Something's going on," she says. That's when she opens the dressing room door, sees the saleswoman going to town on my love torpedo and yells, "You fucking asshole! What the fuck are you doing?"

"What the fuck does it look like? I'm getting my knob polished!" I say, still thrusting into the saleswoman's mouth.

"Oh, hell no!" says Nunya.

"Look, you don't want to have sex with me, which is fine, so I'm gonna let this beautiful woman suck me off so that I'm not sexually frustrated." I look down and notice the squid-woman's eyes get big at hearing me call her beautiful and she works my shaft even faster.

"GRRRRAAAAAA!" screams Nunya. She leaves the dressing room, slamming the door behind her in anger.

I look down again and grab a couple of loose tentacles so that I can pull her head down on my Staff of Fucking +1 even faster. She squeals in excitement just as I let loose with my man juice, draining a few gallons of goo from my very blue balls. She ravenously slurps down every last drop.

Once she's done cleaning me, she stands up and tries to kiss me. I gently push her away. "No thanks, Babe. I know where those things have been. But damn, you're fucking incredible."

She just smiles and nods knowingly at me. Good as her word though she also helps me try on my new clothes. There are three outfits: a standard black suit, a tuxedo, and a black jacket/t-shirt/leather pants combo. Each of them fit surprisingly well. Maybe not quite as well as my custom-tailored suits, but close enough that I won't have any problems in the flexing and moving departments. Even my magnum sex-cannon has enough room in the pants which is good.

I look in the mirror, checking each outfit for size, and I look damn good in them. Of course, I make anything look good. Actually, that's not true. One time this hot tiger ballerina babe wanted me to wear a tutu while she fucked me and I couldn't say no, especially considering how flexible she was. We were in her studio and there were mirrors everywhere. I could see that I looked fucking ridiculous. But who cares? It was worth it.

"So, this tux is really indestructible?" I ask, staring at myself in the mirror.

"Very nearly," says the saleswoman. "Maybe a nuclear blast would destroy it. It's also wrinkle-free and comes with a one-year warranty."

"Nice! Okay, I'll take all three," I say.

"Wonderful," she squeals. "Oh, and by the way, my name is Sarah."

"Well Sarah, you certainly know how to treat your customers."

"That's very kind, Mr..." she says.

"Blowhard. Dick Blowhard."

"Wait, you're Dick Blowhard, the Private Investigator? You're famous! I can't wait to tell all of my friends and family that I sucked off Dick Blowhard! They'll be so jealous! Especially my dad!"

"Uh, your dad wants to suck me off?"

"No, he's just a big fan! Well, I dunno, maybe he does. Anyway, can I get your autograph?" she asks.

"Sure, Babe," I say.

She pulls a pen out and hands it to me.

"What do you want me to sign?" I ask.

"What do you think I want you to sign?" she says, pulling her dress up and over her head. Apparently, she likes going commando too. Her face might look like seafood but the rest of her body looks 100% human. Not only that, but she has a totally banging body! Perky tits, slender hips, and a round juicy ass. I can feel my love lance getting hard again in my tuxedo pants. Thankfully, the material stretches to accommodate my growth.

"On your knees," she commands. She points to her clean shaved snatch. "But first, before you sign it, it's your turn," she says, pulling my head into her wetlands as I go to town.

After what feels like hours of licking, but was probably more like twenty minutes, I let her back down off my face. She deliriously lies down on the ground with a tired look of happiness. At least I think it's happiness. Hard to tell with the tentacles. I give her a moment to calm herself then I bend down and put my autograph right above her love hole, followed by 'Dick was here'.

"Thank you," she says.

"No, thank you," I say, winking.

I drop the pen on the ground and walk out of the dressing room with the clothes. The robot wheels up to me.

"Is everything satisfactory?" he asks.

"More than," I say.

"Cash or credit?"

"Credit," I say, pulling my bag of ultimate wonders, wallet and card out of what's left of my old pants.

"Would sir like us to dispose of your old pants?"

"Sure, that'd be great. Also, if you could throw in a few pairs of shoes and socks to match the outfits that'd be great too," I say.

"Certainly sir," he replies.

"Oh, and have you seen that woman I came in with?"

"I believe she left, sir."

"Shit, really? Man, she's got no patience."

"Indeed."

I wait for the robot to grab the shoes and socks for me then I put on a pair of formal dress shoes to match the tux. The robot is kind enough to place everything else in bags. He runs my card and hands it back to me. I put it along with my wallet and bag of ultimate wonders in my new pants pockets.

"Thanks," I say, shaking the robot's hand.

"It's been a pleasure, sir," says the robot.

5

I walk out of the vault, out through the store, and see Nunya sitting on my space-cycle, obviously still angry at me.

"What the fuck is wrong with you?" she yells.

"What, can't a guy have a sex life?" I ask.

"Not when you're in the middle of a mission! Especially when you still owe me a shit-ton of money!"

"Hey, I'm always on a mission. If I could only get some when I'm not on a mission, I'd never get some!"

"And I'm sure that'd be a huge loss for the galaxy," says Nunya.

"Actually, it would. I'm helping improve the gene pool," I reply.

"Do you even realize how horribly ridiculous you are?"

"No, and I don't plan to."

She screams, pulls out Rita from one of the pouches on my space-cycle, and shoots me in the chest. Amazingly, the material absorbs the laser blast, glows blue for a brief second where she shot me then fades back to black. I guess it works. Good to know sooner rather than later while I'm still at the store and have my receipt.

Nunya, still frustrated, keeps shooting me. Shot-after-shot gets absorbed by my tux. She aims upward, shooting my face a bunch of times. I just keep looking at her while she does it.

"Are you done?" I ask, once it seems like all the rage has left her system.

"Yeah, fine," she says. She looks tired. Instead of saying anything else she puts Rita back in the pouch she took her out of. I walk over to Bessie, lift the back part of the seat and place the bags of clothes inside. Putting down the seat I hop back on. I look over at the front door and standing there is the saleswoman, still naked, waving at me. I nod back at her. She yells "I'm never washing this!" pointing to her exposed lady bits.

"Yeah, I don't agree with that," I yell back.

"Then I'll get this tattooed on!"

"Sounds like a better plan!" I respond. "Stay perfect, angel!"

"You too, you miraculous mound of man-meat!"

"Oh my God," says Nunya, "can we get out of here before I vomit all over your bike?"

Without responding to her I fire up the space-cycle and get us airborne again. As I turn us back toward the space-asshole I wave goodbye to the saleswoman. She blows a kiss back at me. I'll always remember… what's her name again? I think it started with an 'S'. Susan? Samantha? Oh, well.

Pulling up to the portal gets the usual response but this time I'm feelin' great. This time I fly a few loop-de-loops to show off for the security crew. They scream and jump up and down and dance. Damn I love being a celebrity. Nunya hits my chest after the second loop so I pull out of it.

"What's your destination, Detective Blowhard?" asks the security ship over my comm.

"We're heading to planet Merlin," I reply.

"In the Vegas Constellation?"

"That's the one."

"Certainly, sir! Right away!"

The space-asshole starts to sparkle and I'd be lying if I said it wasn't making me tingle. I steer us through the poop chute and we end up on the other side, but not quite as close to planet Merlin as I'd hoped. Normally I get dropped off a few minutes away. This time I have to fly through the united downtown casino planets. Some crazy bastard connected most of the planets together using space-bridges, which allow for fast and safe travel between the planets, so people have more time to gamble.

Because of how close we are to the planets we're not allowed to fly at lightspeed. I think it's a bullshit rule to get people to slow down and look at the casinos, but they say it's some dumbass thing about not wanting people to collide with each other. It's really too bad everyone isn't indestructible because then I could fly whatever fucking speed I want.

Since we have some time on our hands I try to talk to Nunya.

"Hey Nunya," I start to say.

"Fuck off," she replies.

"Hey, I just want to talk to you, alright?"

"Don't care."

"Seriously, we've got like an hour before we get there. Can't you just drop the attitude for five minutes so we can bullshit a little?"

It takes a couple of minutes for her to respond. "Fine."

"Cool. So how the fuck did you end up living on planet Houston?"

"Next question."

"No, seriously, why would a hot-ass babe like you be living on such a shithole planet?"

"It's a long story."

"We got a fucking hour before we reach Merlin. You don't think you can tell the whole story in under an hour?"

"Fine. Before I bought the bar I was a smuggler, and before that I was a soldier in the Asteroid Corps," says Nunya.

"You were a soldier? That's fucking hot," I say.

"Shut up and don't interrupt."

"I can say whatever I want."

"You want me to finish? Because if you keep talking, I'm done."

"Okay. I'll try."

"Anyway, yeah, I was a soldier, and a damn good one too. I was awarded the Pan-Galactic Allegiance Army's Medal of Distinguishment and Valor. Twice."

"Shit, what for?"

"First one was for killing 117 enemy combatants in one day. Just found their base, snuck in, found a nice choke point, and let the bodies pile up."

"And the second?"

"Running back into our base which was on fire and saving 43 people," says Nunya.

"Damn, that's a lot."

"Oh, and I took out another 15 enemy combatants while doing it."

"So that's why you know how to shoot a gun. It all makes sense!"

"No, I know how to fire a gun because my mom taught me how to shoot growing up. She taught me how to protect myself, how to survive in hostile environments, how to handle pretty much anything that comes at me. Seems like she knew what kind of life I was gonna have and wanted to make sure I survived it."

"She sounds like a goddamn badass! Is she single?" I ask.

"No, dildo-breath, she's married to my dad! And I thought you said you wouldn't interrupt," says Nunya.

"No, I said I would try."

"Anyway, I spent my first twenty-eight years just surviving and I needed a change. I didn't want to smuggle anymore. I didn't want to kill anymore. I was burnt out. So me and my crew of smugglers pulled one last job. It was a suicide mission, but whoever survived would get so many burgmorps they'd be set for life. Well, I was the only one who walked away. Thirteen of my friends died. They knew the risks, so I don't really blame myself, but I still miss them."

"Did your team have a name? Every team has to have a cool-ass name."

"Nah, we didn't have any name. Harder to track a team of

individuals if they don't have anything that ties them together."

"Huh, never thought of that," I say, impressed.

"Yeah, well thinking ain't your strong suit."

"You want me to hit the eject button?" I ask.

"You don't really have an eject button," replies Nunya. "Do you really want to take that chance?"

"Alright, I'll try to stop with the insults."

"So, what were you smuggling on your final mission?"

"Does it really matter?"

"It might. Was it something cool like a super weapon? Drugs? Was it drugs?"

"Nah. It was a box of golden lotus petals."

"I don't even know what that is."

"It's a plant that only flowers once every three-thousand years, and supposedly when you ingest the petals they make you immortal and invincible," says Nunya.

"Kind of like me," I say.

"Are you immortal?"

"I dunno, I haven't died yet. But the older I get, the more it seems like my aging has slowed down."

"Maybe that's how you got your powers then. Maybe someone fed you a golden lotus petal when you were a baby."

"Nah," I say. "I know exactly when my abilities started to develop. Not sure why though."

"So, your origin story is still a mystery?" she asks.

"Sure. I mean, my life is like a fucking comic book. I guess I won't find out until later, when some bad guy taunts me with the knowledge of my past and I defeat them to get the information I've been looking for my whole life."

"Yeah, that would be pretty cliche," says Nunya. "So, when did your powers first develop? Maybe that'll help us figure it out."

"They started the first time I had sex. I was fifteen, and it was with my mom's best friend."

"Uh, that's not okay," says Nunya.

"Why? It was awesome!" I reply.

"Because that's illegal and gross. No wonder you're so fucked up. Hey, Dick, I'm sorry that happened to you."

"I'm not, she was fucking hot! She had big titties and a nice juicy ass!"

"I don't need or want the details. But what happened to you is probably at least part of why you're fucked up in the head."

"Hey, I ain't fucked up in the head! I'm totally fucking fine. I like being me and being the way I am. I'm fucking awesome! And am I telling you how you should live your life and who you should be? No. Other than you should really get that stick out of your ass."

She gets quiet, like she's thinking about something really important. I don't like where the conversation was going anyway so I don't say another word to her. I just stare at the casinos as we pass by them. It makes for a long hour of waiting but I don't care. I'm used to being a lone wolf with no sarcastic assholes insulting me all the time. How the hell did all this happen, anyway?

Eventually we make our way to Merlin, a tiny dark-blue planet with clusters of lights that look like stars. It's almost as if the surface was painted intentionally to look like outer space, as if it were some strange form of camouflage. I know though it's just the Wise Old Wizard's love of theatrics. He tries to keep everything mystical.

I steer the ship toward what looks like a small town, but in reality is the Wise Old Wizard's castle. Yup, he really loves castles. He even has a moat filled with alligators to scare away invaders.

We hover down to a patch of grass just outside the gate of the castle. Normally I could just set the space-cycle down in the middle of his castle's courtyard, but he likes to do this whole formal thing at the gate when greeting people.

"Hark, who goes there?" I hear coming from a parapet to our left.

"Tis I, Dickus Blowhardius of the planet Macho Centauri, arriving with a guest. We are here to seek your counsel, oh wise one," I reply.

"Hmmm, how do I know that it's actually Dickus Blowhardius of the planet Macho Centauri and not some crooked-nosed knave? Prove yourself or face my mighty wrath!"

"How would you like me to prove myself, oh wise one?"

"By reciting the poem."

"Really, Wise Old Wizard? Is there no other way? No other way that I can prove who I say I am?"

"I am sorry, traveler, but there is no other way," he responds.

Sigh.

"Fine. Roses are red, violence is too. If you get lippy then I'll pummel you," I say.

"Nope, not that one," he replies.

"Well, that's the only one I know!" I respond.

"No, it's not. Recite the other one."

"Ohhh, the other one. Right. There once was a man from Nantucket…" I start.

Nunya interrupts, "Okay, let me stop you right there. Wise Old Wizard, I am Nunya, Queen of planet Houston. We have come to gain your counsel on matters of great import. Obviously, you can tell by my cohort's lack of intelligence that he is most definitely Dickus Blowhardius, and that he is also a crooked-nosed knave, as you put it. I, however, am neither. I politely and with great humility request your permission to enter your gates so that we might learn from you and your awe-inspiring wisdom."

The Wise Old Wizard thinks for a moment.

"Queen Nunya, although we have never met before I can see that you are pure of intention and character. You may both enter. And please beware the moat as it is filled with alligators. You would not enjoy taking a dip in that pool."

"Thank you, wise one. We will tread carefully," replies Nunya.

As the Wise Old Wizard disappears, I turn to Nunya.

"Wait, are you really the Queen of planet Houston?" I ask.

"No, moron. I just thought it'd be fun to pretend."

The drawbridge in front of us begins to lower and the portcullis begins to rise. It takes a moment for the drawbridge to be brought down as the Wise Old Wizard insists on using old-school cranks and pulleys instead of motors. He isn't a fan of modern technology; he thinks it ruins his aesthetic.

As we walk across the drawbridge, I see familiar sights: the moat that is most definitely filled with alligators (how does he feed them?), a few statues of knights that flank the opening of the castle, and a few banners with dragons, lions, and pointy wizard hat drawings on them. To me it always feels like going to the Castle of Enchantment at Mouseyland, only somehow more and less realistic at the same time.

We walk into the main courtyard and are greeted by our host the Wise Old Wizard. He's on the smaller side, being only five foot tall, but he wears a pointy hat that makes him look a little taller than he really is. The Wise Old Wizard also wears matching blue robes with silver stars that remind me of a children's wizard costume, which is what it might actually be. His beard is white and fluffy, much like Santa Claus (dude, of course we have Santa Claus), and he holds a magical globe that I'm pretty sure is just a snow globe he picked up at a gift shop. The oddest part of his appearance is his addition of a spatula in a holster attached to his belt. I have no idea why he keeps that thing there and I've never asked.

"Why do you have that spatula?" I blurt out.

"I'm glad you finally asked that!" says the Wise Old Wizard.

I just look at him, but he doesn't say anything else. I keep waiting, but he keeps not explaining the need for the spatula.

"But seriously, why?" I finally say.

"Yes," he responds, knowingly.

I wait another moment.

"Are you just messing with me?" I ask.

He turns to Nunya and bows. "It is a great pleasure to meet you, Queen of Houston."

"And you as well, Wise Old Wizard," she replies, curtseying.

"Come! Come to my kitchen and I will fix you a feast worthy of two travelers such as yourselves," says the wizard.

6

As we follow behind him the gate starts to close by some unseen force. I have to assume it's just one of the Wise Old Wizard's imps cranking the gate back down into place. He's hired a few imps from planet Tabasco to take care of some of his more menial chores. They don't seem to mind it much. The imps are a bit shorter than the Wise Old Wizard, maybe three feet tall. They have dark purple-gray skin, spindly arms and legs, and small wings that don't actually work. I think they look a bit like gargoyles, with tiny fangs and pointy ears. They're creepy but likeable.

Nunya turns to me as we're following behind the Wise Old Wizard. "Have you been in his kitchen before?"

"That's a negative."

"I wonder if it'll look like a wizard's laboratory, filled with vials and flasks of different colors, with bubbling cauldrons and walls of books."

"Maybe," I say, wondering why she's suddenly become slightly nicer.

We follow the Wise Old Wizard down a dark stone hallway dimly lit by torches along the walls. After a few twists and turns we arrive at the kitchen. It isn't anything like what I expected. It has a beautiful blond wood floor, gas stove, center island, and granite countertops. Pots and pans hang from the ceiling. The well-polished cabinets are a beautiful mahogany color. It looks like a completely modern kitchen and it's blowing my mind a little. He even has a professional-grade espresso machine.

"What the hell, dude?" I say.

"What?" asks the Wise Old Wizard.

"I thought you were all about being old-school and medieval and shit."

"I am, but I'm also about food. So, you know, there's exceptions," he says, giggling. "Is there anything you'd like in particular?"

"Pizza. No, burgers," I say.

"Steak, lobster, and wine," says Nunya.

"Wouldn't you both prefer sloppy joes?" asks the Wise Old Wizard.

"Uhhhh," I start to say.

"I'm just fucking with you," says the Wise Old Wizard. "Steak, lobster, and burgers it is!"

He pulls out his spatula, waves it around a few times, and things start moving by themselves. The stainless-steel refrigerator opens up and food starts floating out. Pans come hovering down from the ceiling and land on the stove which magically turns itself on. A carving board floats out of a cabinet and over to the center island, followed by a large knife from the butcher's block. Meat and vegetables are being cut; things are mixing in bowls; it's a whole lot of craziness just to make a meal. It's like something out of a cartoon, only in this cartoon everything seems to be working out okay.

I look over at Nunya and she looks like a kid again. I don't mean that she suddenly shrunk and grew pigtails, I mean the look of wonder on her face is kind of... nice.

It takes about twenty minutes for all the food to be cooked. During that time we just kind of watch the Wise Old Wizard do his thing. The whole time he whistles, but it isn't an annoying whistle that makes you want to murder someone. It's more the whistle of someone who is happy and enjoying themselves so I don't mind it so much.

Once the meal is finished cooking plates and silverware float down the hall, as does the food. We follow the enchanted edibles to a large dining room, and by large dining room I mean it looks like something out of Game of Thrones. There's a main table at one end for important people like me to sit at.

We walk down the length of the hall, passing long tables and benches that look just like the real thing. Not that the real thing was the real thing, being fiction and all, but... whatever. We go around to the main table where our food has already floated down into place, sit down, and start chowing down.

After a few bites I turn to the Wise Old Wizard. "Holy fuck this is good! What do you put in this shit, crack?"

"Yes," says the Wizard.

Nunya and I both choke on the food.

"I'm kidding," said the Wizard.

"Oh, okay. Not that I, uh, judge crack-doers," I try to mumble.

Nunya turns and looks at me. "I don't think you need to defend crack. It's horrible stuff that hurts people."

"Yeah," I reply. "How's your steak?"

"It's the best thing I've ever eaten," says Nunya.

"Mine too," I say. "What are you eating?" I ask the Wizard.

"Oh, my favorite meal: macaroni and cheese with fried hot

dogs."

"Wait, what? You made us burgers and lobster and shit, and you're eating dorm food?"

"Yes, well, it reminds me of my childhood. And what is food about if not about good memories. So tell me, Dickus, what brings you two here?"

Before I can start to explain Nunya jumps in.

"We're trying to track down some killer Sloths who blew up all of Dickus' shit."

"Oh, oh I see. Killer Sloths. I've tangled with them a few times myself. Horrible creatures, at least the killer kind. I would own a regular one as a pet but the ones from Buzzworld are indeed complete and utter assholes," replies the Wizard.

"That's what I'm saying," which actually is what I'm saying.

"So, what can we do about them?" asks Nunya.

"Well, what's your main goal? Your end-game?" asks the Wizard.

"We need to get Dickus back his money so he can pay me for my bar that he destroyed," says Nunya.

"Ah, so you want to find where they keep their treasure and take it for yourselves. Well, that's going to be very difficult as they usually have quite diversified portfolios with investments around the galaxy, and no single unified pool of currency," says the Wizard.

"Wait, seriously?" I ask.

"No, I was fucking with you again. They usually keep all their money in one of their secret bases. You'll just have to figure out which secret base it is."

"Can you tell us where that might be?"

"Sure, but what would be the fun in that? It'd make for a pretty boring adventure if I just told you exactly where they were and how to get your money back, wouldn't it? I mean you're just starting out, right?" says the Wise Old Wizard.

"Wait, you know exactly what we need to do, and where we need to go, and you're holding out on us?" asks Nunya.

"Oh, I'm not holding out on you. I will definitely aid you in your quest. But I'm not going to just hand it to you," replies the Wizard.

The look on Nunya's face right now is priceless.

"Look, no offense Wizard, but I'm here for one reason and one reason only, and that's to get money for a new bar. I don't care about the adventure aspect of this. I just want to get paid and go back to my very boring and depressing life, okay?" says Nunya.

"Did I mention I was going to send you on a quest to procure some magical armor and robes for yourself?" asks the Wizard.

"Magical robes?" she mumbles, her eyes huge with wonder.

"Yes, magical robes."

"And they're beautiful?"

"Made from only the finest materials."

"And I'd get to keep them?"

"Yes, you'd get to keep them."

It takes her a moment to respond. She swallows hard. "Fine, fuck it. Let's do this," says Nunya.

I was a little surprised that magical robes would be so exciting for her, but I guess since she doesn't have any superpowers of her own it's probably cooler for her than it would be for me. I don't think I'd look good in robes anyway, so I'm not jealous. I mean, the wizard has never sent me on a mission to get anything magical, and I've been his friend for a long-ass time. And I have three sets of nearly indestructible clothes now, and she'll only have some dumb robes. Yeah, fuck those robes.

"So, what do I need to do to get the robes?" asks Nunya.

"You must travel to The Dragon's Black Hole. There you will ask for someone named Phil. He will say something cryptic to you and you will respond with 'but the lasagna has no cheese'," says the Wise Old Wizard.

"Really?" asks Nunya.

"Yes, really. Phil's a foodie like me, which is why that's the code phrase, but he also knows things. Wondrous, dangerous and scary things. He should be able to tell you how to procure the robes."

"Okay. Wow, The Dragon's Black Hole. That place is super dangerous from what I've heard," says Nunya.

"Don't worry, Babe, I'll protect you," I say.

"First, I'm not worried. Second, never call me 'Babe' again. Third, I don't need your protection. I can handle myself in a fight just fine," replies Nunya. "That does bring up one thing though: I don't have any weapons of my own right now. Do you have anything you can lend me? Maybe a power rifle or space-blaster or something? Mine got trashed when El Stupido here destroyed my bar."

"Hmmm, I know it may not be as cool as a space-blaster but I do have a wand you could use," says the Wise Old Wizard.

"A wand? Really? What does it do?" asks Nunya.

"If you flick it sideways it casts fireballs. If you flick it up and down it shoots lightning."

"That's awesome! Yeah, I want the wand!"

"One bit of warning though," starts the wizard. "Under no

circumstances should you ever twirl the wand. There's no telling what will happen."

"Why, have you ever tried it?" asks Nunya.

"No."

"Then how do you know it's dangerous?"

"Because I read the instruction manual that came with it."

"Oh," says Nunya, not knowing what else to say.

The Wise Old Wizard claps his hands and a wand poofs into existence, floating right in front of Nunya. She reaches out and takes it but then starts gagging. I quickly cover my nose and mouth.

"God, I'll never get used to the rotten egg smell that happens whenever you make something magically appear," I say through my hand.

"Side-effect of the brimstone, I'm afraid," says the wizard.

"Can't you cast a spell that makes us unable to smell for a while?"

"Sure."

"Well then why don't you?" I ask.

The Wise Old Wizard smiles like he just stole the last piece of chocolate cake.

"Oh, you're one of those guys who likes to fart around people then laughs when they smell it, aren't you?" I say.

"Maybe," says the wizard, proudly grinning.

Sigh.

"Okay, well, I'm gonna finish this burger then we're outta here," I say.

"Wait, so you're not going to stay for the night? I haven't even done the puppet show!" says the Wise Old Wizard.

"Yeah, sorry, but we really need to find the Sloths before the trail goes cold. Nunya here is in a big fuckin' hurry to get her money and I don't want to stand in her way," I reply.

"Dickus, it's okay, stand in my way. I would love to see the puppet show," says Nunya.

"Nope, we really need to go. But thank you Wizard for your help," I say, even though he didn't do much more than make me a burger. I mean, it was a really great fuckin' burger, but still, didn't do a lot for me personally.

I pop the rest of the burger in my mouth then turn and shake the wizard's hand. He squishes and shakes it happily until he realizes my hand was coated in ketchup, mustard and bacon grease. Once I let go he stares at his messy hand, debating whether to wipe it off on his robes or not. After a brief moment he pulls a handkerchief out of his pocket then keeps pulling and pulling until he's pulled seventy or eighty feet of handkerchief out, finally wiping his hands on the big wad he ended up with.

"Hey Wiz, that's something I've been meaning to ask you: if you can do real magic then why do you do the kid's birthday magician shit too?" I ask.

"If everything I did was serious, life wouldn't be very fun, would it?"

"Uh, sure..." I reply.

"Come now, Dickus, you really need to learn how to be more fun," says the wizard.

"Me? I'm hella fun! I've partied with the triplets from Galaxian-6, thrown back space-beers with the band Einstein-Rosen Bridge to Nowhere, and even did a keg stand at the top of the Waffle Tower on the Intergalactic Home of Pancakes Planet (IHOPP). No one has more fun than me!" I say.

"Are you sure you're doing those things for fun and not just to feed your ego?" asks Nunya.

"Yes, I fucking love it, okay! Get off my back!" I say, walking away.

As I walk between the benches and long tables, making my way to the other end of the hall, I hear Nunya talking to the Wise Old Wizard. I could listen in on what they're saying with my super-hearing but instead I just block it out. I was kind of done with them. The wizard didn't really want to help me, and instead he just kept giving gifts to Nunya, Queen of planet Asshole. Maybe it'd be better to just leave her here and get her the money.

The imps must have seen me coming because the main gate starts moving up and the drawbridge starts going down. Probably better that way because otherwise I would have just walked through them. I think the Wise Old Wizard would have been pissed if I'd done that. Not that I care, because that guy was being a jerk, and because he could just use his magic to repair it. It really sucks because we used to be good friends. I don't know if I should add him to my list of assholes or not.

Nunya's ruining everything. Before I met her I had a killer home and a really great wizard friend, sort of. Now I have neither. She's even making me start to question who I am and why I do shit and I don't like that feeling. I'm a hero, I don't need to get lectured every ten seconds.

I get on my space-cycle and before I can take off Nunya comes running up to me, seemingly out of breath.

"Hey, wait up asshole!" she yells.

I just turn and stare at her and the look on my handsome,

chiseled face lets her know that her words have actually been hurting me a little. Yeah, I may be indestructible on the outside, but even I accidentally have feelings sometimes. Not that I would ever tell anyone that because feelings are for wussies.

"Dickus? I mean Dick?" she starts to say.

"What?"

"I… I apologize."

"About fucking time."

"Hey, look, you act like a fucking asshole…"

I start to rev the engine on the space-cycle to interrupt her. Every time she tries to talk I rev the engine until she finally gives up. I'm still angry at her and I don't feel like getting insulted when she's trying to fake-apologize to me.

"Just shut up and get on," I say.

Nunya puts her helmet on, climbs on top of the space-cycle in front of me, and we hover slowly into the air.

7

The flight back to the space-asshole is a tough one. I don't want to talk and I definitely don't want to listen to what Nunya has to say. So instead of talking we drift silently past the casinos. Usually they make me happy, with all the sparkling lights and excitement, but somehow their bright glowing signs just make me sadder. I feel lonely, which is something I don't normally feel. I like being a lone wolf. It's hard to be a lone wolf with people around. This is different, though, and I fucking hate it.

When we're about three-quarters of the way to the gate Nunya breaks the silence.

"Did you name your guns?"

It takes me a moment to decide whether to respond or not. I'm worried that if I admit it she'll just make fun of me. Hard to tell from her voice whether she's setting me up for a joke or not.

"And what if I have?" I ask.

"I named my power rifle back when I served," she admits. "Gladys. I named her Gladys."

"Any reason?"

"I dunno, just liked the name. She seemed like a Gladys: dangerous, tough, and a bit hard to handle."

"Sounds like a Gladys, alright," I mumble.

"So, what are your blasters named?"

"Irene and Rita."

"Any reason you named them that?"

"Well, Rita Hayworth and the Shawshank Redemption is my favorite story, even if I like the movie a little better. So that's why one's named Rita."

"And the other?"

"When I use my blasters, I'm saying 'goodnight' to people. Permanently."

"I don't think I get it."

"Goodnight, Irene. It's a song by Lead Belly."

"Who?" asks Nunya.

"And you think I have a lot to learn? You need some culture, that's what you need."

"Hey, sorry if I'm not super fucking old, okay."

"You don't have to be old to appreciate things from the past," I say.

"No, but you have to have time to be able to appreciate things. I haven't had a whole lot of time where I wasn't either killing people, smuggling shit, or running a bar."

"What about when you were a kid?"

"I was being a goddamn kid. What kid do you know that listens to Lead Belly, whoever that is?"

"The kinda kid I'd want as a sidekick, that's who," I reply.

"Yeah, well good luck with that."

"With what, finding someone who has good taste in music?"

"No, with finding someone stupid enough to be your sidekick."

"Well, you're stupid, and so far you're doing a 'great' job of being my sidekick," I say.

"I ain't your fucking sidekick," says Nunya. "If anything, you're my sidekick."

"I'm no one's sidekick. The hero is always the hero, and the person without powers is always the sidekick. How could you even think that I'm your sidekick?" I ask.

"Because I'm the brains of this operation, obviously, and because so far you've been doing exactly what I've told you to do. So you gotta be the sidekick because I'm the boss of you."

"Bullshit. I can throw you into space or leave your ass on any random planet I want."

"Well then why haven't you?"

I grit my teeth.

"C'mon, why haven't you?" asks Nunya.

"Because I'm a fucking hero, that's why. And heroes are defined by the bullshit they have to deal with and how fucking hard their life is. Putting up with your bullshit makes me the biggest fucking hero in the universe. Not that I wasn't already, but you're helping me prove it."

"Well then I'm an even bigger fucking hero because I've had to put up with you!" says Nunya. "You're the most egotistical, self-absorbed moron that the universe ever created. I'm sure that if there is a hell, and there was one place inside it that was worse than all the other places in hell, it would be a small room with you in it. So go ahead and eject me from your space-cycle because I'd rather be dead than deal with your bullshit!"

I stare at the eject button on Bessie. It's a big red button labeled 'Eject'. I stare at it long and hard and dream of what it would feel like to send Nunya hurtling through space, freezing to death almost immediately. That's when something surprising happens: I feel bad about the thought of her dying. She's one of the biggest assholes I've ever met but something inside of me knows if I launched her into outer space to die it would really bother me. I've killed thousands of bad guys, maybe tens-of-thousands, and I don't feel bad about any of it. I mean, they were bad guys. But her, for some reason, it would hurt. I'd feel emotions, and I fucking hate feeling emotions, so I don't push the button.

"Coward," she says, finally noticing the button. She pushes it.

8

"What the fuck!" I yell, as Nunya is launched out of the safety bubble on my space-cycle.

I steer my ride toward the direction she was propelled. Her exposed body starts to ice over. I'm just glad she still has her helmet on because it might buy her a few seconds. I fly as quickly and carefully to her as I can, and as soon as she hits the space-cycle's shield she bounces off. I realize what's happened, turn off the shield, fly toward her and grab her then quickly turn the shield back on. I also turn the bike's heater on full blast, trying to thaw her out.

She shivers in my arms. Her skin is pale blue and her eyes are closed. I stop my space-cycle and put my hands on her exposed back, trying to use my powers to heal her. It doesn't work very well because her entire body is still coated in ice. I can heal her, but until the ice is thawed it's going to keep hurting her. I start to rub up and down her body, trying to shake the ice off. It seems to be helping as her skin starts going back to its normal color.

I try healing her again and this time it starts to work for real. Her color fully returns and she starts breathing again but she's shaking uncontrollably. Eventually, after a few tense moments, she opens her eyes.

"Why the fuck did you do that?" I yell.

She closes her eyes again and looks away from me.

"Did you really want to die or were you just trying to fuck with me?" I ask.

It takes her a long moment to respond.

"I don't have to explain myself to you," says Nunya.

"Like hell you don't! You just tried to kill yourself! You had no way of knowing if I would or even could save you. I need a goddamn explanation, now!"

She just stays quiet.

"Tell me!" I yell.

Nothing.

I think about it for a moment. Think about what little I know about her. She was a smuggler and she pulled one last mission to get the money to buy a bar out in the middle of nowhere. Why would she risk her life on a suicide mission if the payoff was to go live away from everyone she knew and have to scrape by just to survive? What happened to her that could cause her to not care whether she lived or not, and even if she did somehow live, punish herself by having to live in the ass-end of space? It doesn't make any sense and I want to know why but I don't think she'll tell me. Maybe not now, maybe not ever. So instead of yelling at her, I decide that I'll let her have her quiet. It's up to her if she's going to tell me or not.

I give Nunya a while longer to thaw. Once she seems warmed up, I turn her around on the seat so she's aimed forward again. I reach down for the eject button and rip it off my bike to prevent her from trying that again. We spend the rest of the flight travelling to the space-asshole in silence.

When we reach the gate, security is waiting there like usual. Thankfully, this time I think they can tell something's up so they don't get all excited about seeing such a huge celebrity like me. Instead, they just ask us our destination.

"The Dragon's Black Hole," I say.

"Uh, are you absolutely sure you want to go there?" asks one of the security crew over the comm.

"Yeah. Why, is there something wrong with going there?"

"Oh, no, nothing. It's just that I figured someone as prestigious as you wouldn't be going to a place like that."

"Yeah, well I go where the work takes me. Sometimes it's dangerous places, sometimes it's seedy places. Sometimes it's both."

"Well, The Dragon's Black Hole is certainly that, Detective. Permission granted. We'll have the gate re-aligned in just a second," says the security crewmember.

"Thanks."

The space-asshole shimmers and does its changey thing. I can now see off in the distance a lone planet, and behind it, even further, a real black hole. It's weird because it kind of looks like a reverse sun. The center is impossibly dark and light around it seems to get sucked into it instead of being pushed out of it. I've never seen one before, mostly because they aren't safe to be around. I don't know how they've done it but the planet floating near the gate must have something powerful keeping it from getting sucked in. Maybe it's just far enough away from the black hole that there isn't enough gravity to pull it in.

I turn and nod at the security crew. "Thanks."

"No problem, Detective Blowhard. And... safe travels," says the security officer.

"Yeah, I don't see too many safe travels in my future."

I steer us through the gate and out the other side.

Because the planet is far enough away and there's no law here

I gun the engine, quickly closing the distance between us and the planet. The planet is a lot larger than I'd thought it would be and it's almost entirely black. The biggest surprise isn't that the landscape is dotted with volcanoes, it's that they somehow form the shape of a dragon, as if someone had worked very hard to make the volcanoes line up into that specific shape.

Anyway, the view is a bit shocking because whoever set this place up has worked very hard to make it look intimidating. Thankfully, I'm never intimidated. Why would I be when I'm the best there is? That's the confidence you get when you know you're God's gift to the universe.

I set the IPS for The Dragon's Black Hole and it gets confused. Apparently, the entire planet is called The Dragon's Black Hole, and there's also a bar named The Dragon's Black Hole somewhere in the massive city of Vore that rests inside the volcano dragon's eye. I choose the bar on my IPS device and steer us toward the city.

As we approach, I look down and see super tall skyscrapers, all shiny black like really classy pianos. I'm sure this place would be some pianists wet-dream. Heh, I always thought pianist was a funny word because it sounds like penis. Anyway, I'm surprised at how many people must live here for the city to be so big. Unless of course this is the only city on the planet. I figured this place wouldn't have many inhabitants but I was totally wrong.

I bring the hover bike lower and start to see streets where puddles reflect all of the neon lights that line the walkways. It's also raining, which is odd, because I didn't see any clouds at all when we flew in. Either way it reminds me of the movie Blade Runner which is one of my favorites. (Yes, we have Harrison Ford, too).

Now that I think about it, there's a lot of things going on here that don't make any sense. Maybe these are the things that can happen when you're parked next to a black hole. Maybe they have strange properties no one knows about and can warp reality, not just matter. Not that I understand any of that stuff because I'm not a goddamn egghead.

Anyway, I find us a decent place to land at the far end of the bar's parking lot. I decide to change into my t-shirt and leather jacket, figuring I'll fit in better than with my tux. I also make sure to turn on the space-cycle's security system as we get off because in this type of place I wouldn't be surprised if someone tried to steal it.

I look up at the bar and a giant neon dragon sits on top of it glowing red and yellow and green. It's ass droops down the side of the building, and as we walk up to it I realize we're walking into the dragon's asshole. It's a nice touch that adds to the classiness of the joint.

Walking inside, however, shatters all my expectations of the place. Everything is very elegant and refined. Hell, even the little mint tray at the front is ornate and expensive looking. Off to the right is the bar area which looks like a really nice lounge, dimly lit and well furnished. There are also pictures of dragons scattered throughout. Instead of looking old-school and cheesy, though, it looks more like something out of an article in GGQ (Galactic Gentleman's Quarterly). The main restaurant is equally beautiful and expensive looking, with wine glasses, white napkins, and fancy silverware lining the tables.

Nunya turns to me, "Boy, bot you wish you'd kept your tux on."

"Too late now," I mumble. I probably normally would have made a snarkier comment, but after she tried killing herself I figure I'll let things slide a little.

The restaurant's host comes up to us, clad in a black tuxedo with a large gold dragon on the front. He looks us up and down, noticing our street clothes, and asks "table for two?"

"Actually, we're supposed to meet someone here," I say.

"And may I have their name?"

"Phil."

"Phil?"

"Phil."

"And does this Phil have a last name?" asks the host.

"We don't know his last name," interrupts Nunya. "But we were told we would know him when we saw him."

"Interesting. Is this a blind date of sorts?" asks the host.

"Something like that," I say, trying not to give away too much.

"Well, you're welcome to look over the restaurant and lounge to see if your mysterious stranger is here."

"Thank you, we will," replies Nunya.

We both take a step forward to get a better view of the restaurant. Looking over the tables, no one seems to be sitting alone. I listen in and hear people talk about bullshit like politics, their new spaceships, taxes; basically anything that makes you want to fall asleep. They eat their steak tartare and escargot, their caviar and bone marrow, and seem to be enjoying their boring selves.

I turn to Nunya, "I don't think I see him."

"Me neither. Must be in the lounge if he's here at all," she replies.

We nod at the host who scurries away to the kitchen.

I turn and look off to our right where the lounge is, which isn't currently as busy as the restaurant. Only a few people sit in booths, most of which are wearing clothes that look like they were quite fancy thirty years ago when they bought them. They sip at mixed drinks that have super high alcohol content such as AMFs and

45

Long Island Iced Teas. I figure those people are 'regulars'.

In the middle of the lounge is a large table with a single occupant. He's mostly bald, wears simple black framed glasses, and has a broom style moustache. He's also wearing a cheap, gray flannel suit. He looks like an accountant which is not a good thing. I also notice that he's sipping on a vodka cran, one of the most boring drinks out there. Definitely an accountant. I don't think he could have looked more like a 'Phil' if he tried.

He notices us staring and waves at us to come toward him. Standing up as we approach, he reaches out a hand which Nunya shakes. "I'm Phil," he says.

"Uh, good to meet you Phil," says Nunya. I just nod my head.

"Oh yeah, right, I almost forgot: the secret words!" Phil seems really excited about saying them, so I'm guessing he must be a total newb at this spy shit. "The spaghetti is missing its sauce."

Nunya replies, "but the lasagna has no cheese."

Phil giggles in excitement. I do my best not to roll my eyes for like a fraction of a second then I let them do their thing. Phil either doesn't notice or doesn't care.

"Sit down," he says. "You guys want something to drink? The vodka crans are really good here and super cheap!"

"Sure, I'll have a drink," says Nunya.

"Yeah, why not?" I reply.

The bartendress thankfully was already on her way over to take our order. When she sees me she recognizes me immediately and blushes. It's sort of amazing I could even tell under the thick layer of makeup she's wearing that she'd blushed, but again, superpowers. I can easily tell when a chick is into me. I apparently have a harder time telling when a chick isn't into me because in my defense it's only happened once.

"What would you like, sir?" she asks in a very flirtatious tone.

"I'd like a bottle of The Macallan 50 and an empty glass," I reply.

The bartendress seems super impressed which is why I ordered it. A bottle of The Macallan 50 goes for about 90,000 burgmorps which is about the same as a decent spaceship. Not that I have 90,000 burgmorps right now, and my credit card might not work, but if it gets me a shot at this bartendress I'm game. She's hot, wearing fishnet stockings, a short black skirt, and a white dress shirt with black bow tie. As near as I can tell she's human, unlike Phil who looks like an accountant. Her dark roots show through her slightly frizzy bleach-blonde hair, and she wears bright red lipstick that accentuates her pouty lips. Yup, I'm definitely gonna have sex with her.

"I'll have a Dark and Stormy," says Nunya.

The waitress quickly glances over at Nunya, and for a fraction of a second she frowns then nods her head in understanding of what Nunya had just ordered. The bartendress turns and walks back to the bar.

"Did you really just order The Macallan 50?" asks Phil. "Good lord, I could put a down payment on a house for that much!"

"Yeah, well a down payment won't get you drunk," I reply. "Besides, I usually make a lot of money saving the galaxy so I ain't too worried about it."

"Except you still have to buy me a bar," says Nunya.

"Workin' on it," I mumble.

"Anyway, Phil, our mutual friend told us you could point us in the direction of some magical robes and armor that might fit me," says Nunya.

"Oh, yes, I can definitely do that," replies Phil. "But first I'd like to get to know you before I help you out. I refuse to dispense with pleasantries. Tell me all about yourselves."

I look at Nunya and frown, and she shoots an angry glance at me then kicks me under the table. It doesn't hurt, obviously, so I just shrug it off. Nunya turns back to Phil and tries her best to pretend that she's friendly.

"Well, I'm a Capricorn," starts Nunya.

"That makes sense," I blurt out.

"What?" she says, staring at me, her jaw rigid.

Sigh. "Nothing."

"Anyway, I was going to say that I used to be in the military, although I've been out for a long while. I own, or owned a bar on the planet Houston, and I spend my free time playing the piano," says Nunya.

"You play?" I say in surprise.

"Yeah, I play. Is there a problem with that?" she asks.

"Nope, no problem. Just surprised is all."

"Well, when my mom wasn't teaching me how to kick ass and take names, she also taught me how to play piano. I think she thought it would be good for me to learn something more than just survival skills," replies Nunya.

"Huh," is all I say.

"Do you have a favorite song you like to play?" asks Phil.

"Yeah, actually I do. Moonlight Sonata. It's easy to hit the right notes but difficult to make it sound beautiful. I've heard professionals who've played all their lives not do it justice. I also think it should be played slightly slower than most people play it."

"Interesting," replies Phil. "I'm more of a Brahms fan myself."

"Makes sense. This conversation is putting me to sleep," I say, under my breath.

"I'm sorry, I didn't catch that," says Phil.

"Nothing. Nothing," I say.

"Oh. Well, how about you, Mr. Blowhard?" asks Phil.

"First of all, it's Detective Blowhard. I didn't go to detective school for three weeks to be known as 'Mr. Blowhard'. But my life in a nutshell is one of adventure and action. I basically save everyone's ass all the time. I'm like Superman, but not a goody-two-shoes like him. I have tons of superpowers, some I probably don't even know about yet, and if I have one superpower that's more impressive than the rest, it's scoring. I've had more sex than any living being and that includes the space-bunnies from planet 23. Like seriously, if I wasn't immune to disease I'd probably be a walking encyclopedia of sexually transmitted infections."

I look over and notice the disgusted look on Nunya's face.

"She's just jealous," I say, pointing my thumb at her.

I notice out of the corner of my eye Nunya shaking her head. That's when the bartendress walks up and sets our drinks down. The bottle of Macallan 50 is unopened so I nonchalantly remove the wrapper, pull the cork, and pour myself a nearly full glass. The waitress pauses a moment, winks at me so the others can't see, and motions her head slightly away from the bar and toward the entrance. I look behind me and notice that's where the restrooms are. Perfect.

I cross my arms so that Phil and Nunya can't see my hand and flash five fingers at the waitress letting her know I'll meet her in the restroom in five minutes. Her smile brightens and she nods her head then walks away. I take my first sip of The Macallan like a champ, downing half the drink in one gulp.

"Don't you want to be able to taste that?" says Phil.

"Nah, I'm not a fan of Scotch," I reply.

"What?" says Nunya. "You buy the most expensive Scotch in the galaxy and you don't even like it?"

"I only drink the best because I can afford the best," I say.

"Only you can't, dumbass, because you're fucking broke," says Nunya.

"Do you have to blurt it out like that?" I say, looking around the room. "And I'll get my money back one way or another."

"You better," says Nunya. "But so far you're literally writing checks that you can't cash. Aren't you worried about it?"

"Nah. I never worry about money."

"That's pretty much all I worry about," says Phil.

"I know, Phil. I know," I reply in a condescending manner.

I take another gulp of The Macallan.

"Hey, if you're gonna drink it like that at least let me have a taste," says Nunya.

It takes me a moment to relent.

"Fine, you can have what's left in my glass," which admittedly wasn't much.

She takes my glass, probably a finger's worth, swirls it around then takes a small sip. Her eyes get big but then she closes them, savoring the flavours. "My God that's amazing," she says. It takes her another few moments of joyful sipping before she hands me back the empty glass.

"Hey, at least I finally made you orgasm," I joke. Of course, Nunya throws another angry look at me. What's new?

We talk for another few minutes then I say "gotta drop a deuce, if you know what I mean," and stand up.

"Gross, and yeah, we know what you mean, Dick. Just don't take forever," says Nunya.

"It takes however long it takes," I say.

"Just go," she replies.

I turn and walk back to the restrooms.

9

First, I knock on the door to the ladies room, not knowing which restroom she might be in. I don't hear anything so I walk to the men's room. I open the door and inside waiting for me, wearing only her thigh-high fishnet stockings and bow tie, is the bartendress. My God she has an amazing body. Large, well-rounded tits with soft pale nipples. A small thatch of dark brown hair covers her pink cadillac. Curvy hips, long legs...

She leans back against a sink, her legs spread out. The bartendress licks her lips sensually, giving me a fake innocent look that drives me crazy. I walk up to her, and just as I'm about to kiss her she pushes my head down to her rose bush.

I hungrily lick her love button as her thighs tighten around my head. It doesn't take long for her to reach her first 'O', gliding her wetness up and down the length of my face until she has to cover her mouth to stop from screaming. I keep at it, quickly slurping her to a second orgasm.

Once she hits her third, she pushes me away for a moment. Turning around, the bartendress bends over, holds onto the sink and waggles her ass at me. "Fuck me," she says. "Fuck me hard."

I walk over to her, unzip my pants and let my massive meat missile fall out. Her eyes get huge in the reflection of the mirror as she sees it grow. I have to use both hands to guide it into her, but when I do she reacts like it's too much for her to handle. She scrunches her face in pain but only for a second, as she eventually opens her eyes and flashes the most evil grin I've ever seen.

I rock back and forth against the bartendress, as hard and as fast as I can without accidentally splitting her in half. She covers her mouth again as I give her orgasms four through thirteen. Her legs start shaking involuntarily. She looks tired and weak and finally says, "stop, fuck, you gotta give me a moment."

Pulling out of her I keep my fishing rod hard because I haven't gotten mine yet. It takes her a couple of minutes to catch her breath but eventually she stands back up. Placing her hands up against the mirror, legs still spread, she says the words, "I want you between my cheekies."

I move up to her again and very slowly guide my space-thruster into her naughty girl pucker. It's even tighter than I could have imagined. Of course, for me every hole is tight. But this is one of the greatest feelings I've ever had in my life. I look down at her cheeks and watch as my baby-maker slides in and out between them. Reaching up, I cup her breasts, holding them tight as I move in and out of her. I stare into her eyes in the mirror and she stares right back, excited by the naughtiness of what we're doing. The bartendress starts pushing her ass back at me, moving me faster inside her until I eventually send ribbons of hero juice deep into her keister.

After a few more strokes, making sure everything that is gonna come out of me has, I pull out. She turns around and finally kisses me, licking some of the girl goo off my face that she'd put there. It's hot, and sexy, and I want to go for round two but she stops me.

"That's all you're getting for now," she says. "It'll give you a reason to come back again."

"Oh, I definitely will, beautiful."

She blushes again.

We spend a few minutes cleaning ourselves up. Thankfully my t-shirt is easy to clean because some of her juices made their way down to my chest. It was almost like the people who made the outfit knew that this exact situation was going to happen and created fabric that wouldn't hold onto stains. Either way I give her one last kiss then wash the lipstick and woman-wetness off my face.

I check myself out in the mirror and I look exactly like I did before I came into the men's room. Hopefully Phil and Nunya don't notice. The last thing I need is for Nunya to hate me more than she already does.

"So, what's your name?" I ask the bartendress.

She thinks for a moment. "You know, I don't think I'll give it to you."

"Why not?" I ask.

"Because it's more fun for me if you don't know," she replies. Damn, she has the sexy thing down cold.

The bartendress leaves the restroom.

10

I wait a few minutes then make my way back to our table. Nunya and Phil are both talking and don't seem to notice me sitting down. Eventually, Nunya turns to me and says, "took you long enough. Wait, what's that smell?"

"What smell?" I ask.

"That smell."

"It's probably just the smell of shit," I say.

"You're disgusting, and no. Wait, you smell like sex!" says Nunya. "Why do you smell like sex? Did you bang some random broad again? Is that what took you so long?"

"I didn't bang a random broad, okay," I say.

"Good," says Nunya.

"It was the bartendress," I say, trying not to laugh.

"You, disgusting, piggish, irritating asshole! Can't you just keep your prick to yourself for five minutes?"

"Apparently not," I say, pouring myself more of the Macallan, which is now magically more than halfway gone. "What the fuck happened to my Scotch?"

"Drank some of it," said Nunya.

"I said you could have a little."

"Yeah, well, you were back there for like two hours. See, the ice in my drink melted and everything you self-absorbed sonofabitch!"

"I'm the sonofabitch? What about you? You literally just drank the same amount in Scotch as it would take to buy you a new shitty bar! You stole from me!" I say.

"Hey, you know a new bar is gonna be more expensive than that. And I couldn't have stolen the Scotch from you because it's not really yours in the first place. You can't even afford it!" says Nunya.

That's when the bartendress comes walking up. "Oh, drinks are on the house," she says, smiling at me.

"Wait, but he got a super expensive Scotch! No offense, but how can a waitress cover that?" asks Nunya.

"First, I'm not a waitress. Well, not just a waitress; I'm a bartendress. And don't worry about the Scotch, I'll just fill it with some Macallan 18 and no one will notice."

"But the Macallan 18 is still 300 burgmorps a bottle!" says

Nunya.

"Well, the Dick was worth it," she says, beaming at me.

"Oh. My. God." says Nunya.

I smile back at the bartendress who winks, turns and walks back to the bar. I catch her looking back at me every few seconds and she catches me looking at her.

Nunya smacks my shoulder. "Why do you have to be such a... dick?"

"Hey, I'm not trying to be a dick, okay? I'm just being me. If you don't like it you can fuck the right off for all I care."

She gets even angrier, stands up, knocks her chair over in the process and storms off.

Phil just looks at me, not knowing what to say.

"So Phil, did you tell Nunya where the fancy robe and armor are?" I ask.

"Uh, yeah. Yeah, I did. You know, Detective Blowhard, just a bit of advice: I wouldn't keep provoking her like that. I don't know if you can tell, but from talking with her the last few hours I learned she's a really unhappy person. She's had a rough life. Some bad things have happened to her and she's done some bad things. Things she's ashamed of. She may look and act tough like an amazonian warrior-princess, but inside she's still a human being. And she seems to be a decent human being at that," says Phil.

"Yeah, I'll take it under advisement," I say.

"Seriously, Dick, maybe cut her some slack."

I think about it for a moment.

"Okay, I'll... try to do better."

"I think that's a good plan."

"Oh, and did she say she's into me?" I ask.

"No, she didn't say that."

"Not even a little?"

"In all the stuff we talked about there was zero indication that she's interested in you. Not even the tiniest bit," says Phil.

"Her loss," I say.

"Sure. Anyway, I'm off. And I guess I should thank you for your indiscretion with the bartendress. First time I've ever had a free drink."

"Yeah, you're welcome," I mumble as I get up and walk out of the Dragon's Black Hole.

11

I make my way back to the space-cycle. As I walk up, I notice Nunya already has her helmet on and she's sitting on the seat, ready to go. Without saying anything I climb on behind her. As I start the engine and we lift up into the air I realize something else crazy happened.

"How the hell did you get past Bessie's security system? It's top of the line," I say.

It takes a long while for Nunya to finally respond. Her voice sounds dead and monotone. "You know how I used to be a smuggler?"

"Yeah."

"Well, part of what I did was crack security systems. If I had a superpower, it would be the ability to hack into almost any computer."

"Seriously? There's been plenty of times I ran into a lock or keypad I couldn't open," I say.

"If I'd been there I could have gotten you in no problem," says Nunya.

"I don't really let doors stop me anyway. I just punch them open."

"Of course you do, because brawn over brains, right?"

"Hey, I'm still not as dumb as you look," I say, trying to get her to laugh but she doesn't.

"Well, I look pretty dumb hanging out with you," quips Nunya.

For the first time she insults me and it doesn't really hurt. I mean don't get me wrong, I'm not used to being insulted and I really don't like it. But this time it doesn't seem as much like she's putting me down, like it was more of a friendly thing. That's a weird thought, what if after all of this Nunya becomes my friend? I've never had a friend. I've always done the lone wolf thing. Even the Wise Old Wizard isn't really my friend, he's just a guy I know that helps sometimes. It's not like we throw back beers and reminisce about the good 'ole days.

Anyway, Nunya may not have sex with me, but maybe, just maybe... I hang my head. There's no way she'd want to be my friend. She hates me. Even when I'm doing things that don't affect her they piss her off. Never mind, I guess.

I finally shake off my thoughts and ask Nunya the big question,

"So where the fuck are we going?"

"You mean for the armor and robes?" asks Nunya.

"Yeah."

"The Riegel Cluster."

"But that's where…"

"Yup."

"And you're sure you want to go there?" I ask.

"I don't think we have a choice. I mean, I need some sort of armor to protect myself. Without it I'm a liability," says Nunya.

"Are you sure the armor and robes are even worth it? Did Phil tell you what they do?" I ask.

"Apparently the armor is like your new clothes: they're nearly indestructible. And the robes grant the wearer some magical powers, like flight, super-strength and a shield that just appears and you can use to block attacks. You still have to aim the shield because it doesn't do the blocking for you."

I think for a moment. "Fuck," I say.

"What?"

"I've never been a fan of magical shit."

"Why not?"

"Because my powers don't work with it. Magic seems to disrupt my abilities."

"Wait, seriously? So, you do have a weakness? And isn't that the same weakness that Superman has?"

"His weakness was kryptonite," I mutter.

"Kryptonite was one of a few weaknesses he had. But he also had a problem with magic. It's why magic users always got the drop on him."

"So you're saying I'm Superman?"

"Fuck no, if anything you're Super-annoying-man. But I think it's funny that David Copperfield could kick your ass."

"Hey, fuck you and fuck David Copperfield, whoever the fuck that is! My powers have saved the galaxy a bunch of times. What's so great about magic anyway?" I ask.

"Well, once I get the robes and armor, and with my wand, I should be able to kick your ass myself."

I get really angry about that. She's probably right, she probably could kick my ass if she got her hands on the new outfit. Fuck.

"So then why should I take you to get them if you're just going to use them on me?" I ask.

"I never said that I would kick your ass just because I could kick your ass," says Nunya.

"How do I know you won't turn into some evil supervillain as soon as you get them? Maybe they're cursed and you'll turn all veiny and emo. How do I know you won't try to kick my ass even if it isn't cursed?"

"Because I'm a good guy!" says Nunya.

"How do you know? I mean, you tell me I'm not a good guy all the time and I'm pretty sure I'm a good guy. I even have the trophies and medals for saving the galaxy to prove it. What makes you think that you'll be a good guy and only use your magic for good?"

"Because I know, alright. Now quit asking stupid questions."

"Hey, look, you've questioned everything I've ever done and I think it's fair to question whether you should have the robes and armor. Convince me. What would you use them for?"

"To save people."

"And what happens when you make a mistake and someone dies? And maybe it's your fault because you didn't use your powers, right?" I ask.

"I don't know. I never really..."

"And what happens when it's not just one person, what if it's an entire planet of people. And they all died because you misunderstood what was going on and destroyed the one atmosphere machine that was keeping their entire planet alive. What then?"

"That's oddly specific. Wait, Dick, did that happen to you?" I don't respond.

"Dick, my God. If that happened to you, I'm so, so sorry." I still don't respond.

"Of course it never happened," I say, my voice cracking. I swallow hard. "I'm fucking perfect, and I have a perfect body and face, and perfect superpowers. And I never fucking make mistakes."

Nunya makes me stop the space-cycle. She turns around in her seat and does something I never thought she would do in a million years: she hugs me.

"Hey, what the fuck?" I say, tears leaking into my mouth. "Get the fuck off me!"

"No," she says.

"Look, I don't want your pity."

"Yes, you do."

I don't know what to do. I don't want to feel like crying anymore so I will myself to stop leaking all over my face.

"Can you just let me go," I ask.

"Nope."

This is the worst. I hate feeling like this. Why can't these feelings just go away?

"Fine, I'll take you to get your stupid magical robes and armor if you just let go of me," I say.

"Not happening."

I just sit there, waiting for her to give up. She'll have to eventually, otherwise she'll starve herself to death. But it takes an uncomfortably long amount of time for her to finally let go.

"Do you feel better?" she asks.

"Fuck no," I say. "I don't want to feel my pain, okay? I just want to ignore it."

"But you'll never get better if you don't face your pain," says Nunya.

"Maybe I don't want to get better. Maybe I already am better, did you think of that?"

"You're not, Dick. You've got to process this trauma or you'll never be okay again."

"No, I need to swallow my feelings. That's what real men do. We bottle everything up."

"That's the stupidest shit I've heard come out of your mouth yet," says Nunya.

"I don't care," I reply. "And how about you? What was it, twenty fucking minutes ago that you tried killing yourself? How about you and bottling up pain? You think I'm not smart enough to understand that you have demons too? Maybe I'm less of an idiot than you think, and more of someone who can understand what you've been through."

She looks hurt. Like really hurt. She doesn't cry, but I can see that my words really cut her. It's not anger in her eyes right now, it's defeat.

"I... I'm sorry," I say.

"No, it's okay. You're right," she replies.

"No I'm not."

"You actually are, Dick. It's the smartest thing you've probably ever said. Maybe I am wrong about you, and maybe I'm wrong about myself. Shit."

"Still, I shouldn't have said that."

"I'm glad you did. Maybe I need someone calling me out on my bullshit just as much as someone needs to call you out on yours," says Nunya.

"So does this mean we're friends?" I ask meekly.

"Fuck no, motherfucker. I still hate your guts."

"I hate your guts too," I say. We both smile. I take the opportunity to ask her, "You wanna fuck?"

"Goddamn it, Dick! No, I'm not gonna fuck you. You're ruining a perfectly good moment, okay?"

"Yeah, sure, fine."

"So how long will it take to get us to the Riegel Cluster?" she asks.

"Eh, not too long. Just need to make it back to the space-asshole. I'm sure they can send us there," I say.

"Space-asshole? What the fuck is a space-asshole?" asks Nunya.

"Oh, it's what I call the space bridges that let us teleport across the galaxy. To me they look like a stripper's asshole covered in glitter."

"Wow, that's both disturbingly gross and, now that I think about it, disturbingly accurate."

"So you've stared at strippers glittery assholes before?"

"Maybe," she says, smiling to herself.

"Hey, you better cram it with that bullshit, otherwise you're gonna have to deal with getting poked in the butt with a boner on the way there."

"You do and I'll cut Dick Jr. off."

"Yeah, others have tried and died."

"Well, I'm not like the others," she says.

"Yeah, no shit."

With that, Nunya turns back around and I fly us toward the space-asshole.

12

As we pull up to the space-asshole both of us are actually in a better mood. I think it may have helped yelling at each other. Let out some of the sexual tension we obviously feel toward each other.

"I know what you're thinking, and no, there is no sexual tension between us. Okay, Dick?" says Nunya.

"What the fuck! Get out of my thoughts!" I say. "I thought you didn't have superpowers!"

"I don't, but your mind is so simple I can't help but read it. It's kind of like an old shitty pulp book where someone stuck the pages together with bubblegum, pissed on it, then left it in a gutter."

"Gee, thanks," I say.

Anyway, we look over at the security crew at the gate and where I would normally be greeted with waves and all that, the crew looks super serious.

"Who are you?" they ask.

"I'm Detective Dick Blowhard and this is my side-kick Nunya Business."

"I'm not your fucking side-kick!" yells Nunya.

We watch as they type some stuff into their computer.

"The cost for passage is ten million burgmorps," says the security guard.

"Oh no it's not. It's free for everyone after the Kennedy law of interstellar travel was passed four-hundred and twenty years ago."

"Well things have changed. If you want to pass, you'll need to pay us ten million burgmorps. Otherwise, if you don't like it, I believe the next closest gate is only ten lightyears away. Should take you twelve years to get there so you don't disintegrate along the way," says the security guard.

"Look, you obviously don't know who I am. I'm Dick Blowhard! I'm friends with the President! I have superpowers and shit!" I reply.

"And?"

"And if you don't let me through, I'll go through anyway!"

"You can certainly try," says the security guard.

Nunya pushes the button on my space-cycle to turn off the comm. "Dick, I don't think that's a real security guard. I think they're space pirates trying to extort people for money."

"Nah, they can't be space pirates. They don't even have eye

patches!"

"Wait, Dick, do you think that all space pirates have peg legs and parrots and say 'arrr'?"

"Don't they?" I ask.

"For fuck's sake, no! I mean, I guess there used to be people like that thousands of years ago, back in the old days of Earth Uno. But no, they're just like everyone else, only they like to take advantage of people. Stealing shit, smuggling shit, pillaging and plundering. That kind of thing," says Nunya.

"So, you're saying you were a pirate?" I ask.

"Uh, no, I don't think so."

"But you were a smuggler," I point out.

"Yeah, but not that kind of smuggler. Pirates are more..."

"Charming?" I say.

"Hell no! I'm plenty fucking charming. I'm as charming as that motherfucking pig Arnold on Green Acres."

"What the fuck are you talking about?" I ask.

"I was paraphrasing a movie line. Shit. So what should we do?" asks Nunya.

"How should I know? You're the brains of the operation," I say sarcastically.

"Well, I dunno. Can we just fly through the gate?" she asks.

"If we do that they could change where they're sending us. Could shoot us right into some kind of trap or something. Maybe open a gate straight into a star. We don't know what would be on the other side," I say.

She thinks for a moment.

"Can you get me on board their ship?" she asks.

"Fuck yeah, I like where you're going with this!"

"Let's give them a warning first," says Nunya.

"Sure, why don't you go ahead."

Nunya turns the comm back on. "Hi security guards that obviously aren't real security guards. You have ten seconds to comply with our request or we're going to board your ship. If we do that, my friend here will not only rip each of your heads off in alphabetical order, but he'll shit in your mouths while doing it. And he's had a big lunch. Lots of garlic."

We wait eight seconds. They finally respond, "Five million burgmorps?"

I turn Bessie toward the security ship. It only takes a few seconds to get to their airlock. I steer the bike so Nunya can reach the controls, and while she hacks into their door I use my space-cycle's near field tractor beam to anchor us to the ship. It takes her hardly any time to get the first door open.

"You ready?" she asks.

"Yup. Keep your helmet on. It'll help you breathe until we can get the second door open."

"Roger."

"No, I'm Dick. Who the fuck is Roger?"

"God you're dumb."

With that I disable the space-cycle's shield. We hop into the airlock and I turn my ride's security system on just in case someone tries to flee the hijacked security ship. As soon as Nunya gets across the small airlock she starts hacking the second control panel. It takes her hardly any time to get the outer door closed. Air rushes into the room and only a half-second later the inner door opens.

"Okay, you stay here while I take care of this," I say.

"Yeah, that's a big nope. I'm going with you," replies Nunya.

"Here's the thing: I need someone to stay here and guard Bessie just in case any of them slip past me. It's not a huge ship but I don't want to take chances. Not only that, but you don't have any armor. You also don't want to use your wand because casting fireballs and lightning bolts in a place like this will destroy it and you might end up dying from the vacuum of space. So here, take Rita and Irene. They'll keep you company. I'll just use my superpowers to take care of these guys. Make sense?"

"Yeah, makes sense."

"Good. Be safe," I say, handing her my blasters.

Nunya nods her head at me.

I turn the corner and run down the hallway toward where I think the ship's bridge is. Suddenly, an alarm rings out and the lighting changes. Instead of white light everywhere things are much darker. The safety lights seem to be the only ones on right now which is better because I look even more intimidating in the dark.

I keep going down the hallway, making a few twists and turns, before I finally reach the ship's bridge. In front of me is a door with a small round porthole window. Looking inside I see about fifteen 'security guards' dressed in their standard issue maroon outfits, pointing guns at the door and looking nervous. I just smile at them.

Tugging at the door handle I realize it won't budge. I could rip the handle off but I decide it might be better to use as leverage. Holding onto the handle firmly with my left hand, I make a tiger claw with my right and shove my fingers into the metal door. Clamping down, I rip out some of the metal then use both hands to pry and split the door like I'm tearing a piece of cardboard.

A couple of energy blasts hit me and I just shrug them off. After a few seconds of being hit with blaster fire I decide to talk to them.

"Hey, I don't have to kill you. I can if you want. I'm really, really good at it. I'm super strong, super fast, and super willing. But I'll make you a deal. If you all drop your guns and follow me to the mess I'll seal you in there with all that food so that you might have a chance at surviving this. Otherwise, I really will rip your heads off."

One guy, who I'm guessing is their leader, walks up to me.

"We will never submit to you! We will fight to the death! We will…"

That's when I grab the little guy by the head and squeeze. A gross squishing and cracking sound echoes in the metal-walled room, like someone sticking an M-80 in a frog's butt and throwing him into a bucket. Not that I've ever done that. Don't be cruel to animals, kids.

"Next?" I say.

The rest of the 'security guards' drop their weapons.

"Thanks guys for making my life easier. Go ahead and start heading toward the mess. I'll be right behind you. If any of you try anything so help me I will snap, crackle and pop your head, just like this guy," I say, pointing at the corpse.

I wait until the last one leaves the door, following behind them to make sure they actually reach the mess. Once they're inside I close the door then punch it just hard enough to get it to deform and jam into place. Should keep them from getting out anytime soon.

Running back to the airlock I wave Nunya to follow me. I lead her to the bridge and she gets to work immediately hacking the computer system.

"Oh, good," she says.

"What?"

"They didn't log out. So I can just go ahead and set up the gateway to take us to the Riegel Cluster."

"That's lucky," I reply.

"Nah, it would have been easy to hack into the system. Only take a couple of seconds. It's a government ship, and they're usually the least effective when it comes to security."

"I wonder why that is."

"Oh, it's easy. Anyone actually good at security would never take a low-paying government job. And you know the old adage that you get what you pay for? Since the government doesn't want to spend much on quality developers they hire from the bottom of the barrel, not the top. If there was one place the government should spend its money it's on security. Thankfully for us they're too stupid to realize it," says Nunya.

"Yeah, thankfully," I say, now worried about how unsecure government security systems are.

"It's all set. Let's get the fuck out of dodge," says Nunya.

We run back down to the airlock and Nunya messes with the

door controls as I disable the security system on my space-cycle and near-field tractor beam. After a few seconds we're back on board and flying toward the gate. I take one last look at the security ship just to make sure no one has made their way back to the ship's bridge. As near as I can tell the coast is clear.

Just before we pass through the gate Nunya asks, "Do you think the rumors about the Riegel Cluster are true? Is it as crazy as they say?"

"Crazier."

"Oh shit," says Nunya.

"Yes, oh shit," I reply.

13

A few hundred years ago the Riegel Cluster was a group of five planets that manufactured all kinds of kids toys for the entire galaxy. Apparently, one of the manufacturers had stolen a mad wizard's design for a 100-in-1 magic kit. The wizard wanted revenge and blew up the manufacturer's planet, named Willingham, sending toys floating around the other four. Now it's like an asteroid belt made of stuffed animals, toy soldiers, and really creepy dolls.

To make matters worse the mad wizard cursed the toys to attack anything that came too close, which made shipping toys from the other planets impossible. A small group of survivors made it out alive to tell the tale, but not many. Ever since, the Riegel Cluster has been assumed to be abandoned because of the danger of the evil automated toys.

As we drift out of the gate I look over and see an abandoned security ship. The lights are still on but it seems that nobody's home. I can't blame them for leaving it abandoned because who would want to protect a gate that no one is using in an extremely dangerous section of space? Thankfully, the gate is far enough away from the mass of toys that we aren't in immediate danger. But I'm telling you these toys are like fucking gremlins. They'll tear your ship apart, have their way with you, and don't care if they die in the process. You can't talk them down. You can't intimidate them. They just keep on coming.

"So which planet are we heading to?" I ask Nunya.

"Planet O'Brien," she replies.

"Which one is that?"

"How should I know? Just use your IPS."

"Do you know where we're supposed to land on planet O'Brien?" I ask.

"There's supposed to be a temple there. A big, purple temple shaped like a…"

"Like a what?"

"Penis."

"Wait, what?" I say, laughing.

"A dick, alright? It looks like a dick," says Nunya, clearly not happy about it.

"Okay, so let me get this straight. We're headed toward a temple that looks like a giant penis in the middle of a planet system famous for making children's toys. Is that what you're telling me?"

"Yeah."

"And old Phil back there said that?" I ask.

"Yup."

"This is too awesome! Did he say why it looks like a giant man-salami?"

"Yeah. Apparently, the mad wizard who cursed this place lived there. It was kind of their way of giving the middle finger to anyone that showed up. I guess they were a bit of a weirdo."

"I dunno, I think most places built by egomaniacs look like penises. Fuck the patriarchy," I say.

"Wait, what? You're like the epitome of the worst parts of the patriarchy," says Nunya.

"Fuck you! No I ain't! I'm like progressive and shit."

"You're about as progressive as dog shit."

"Your mom is dog shit," I mumble.

"Don't make me use my wand on you!"

"Don't threaten me with a good time," I say.

"That's not what I meant, asshole."

"Uh-huh, sure."

"Just shut the fuck up already and steer us toward the giant purple dick, okay?" says Nunya.

"You're the boss," I say.

"Goddamn right I am," she replies.

Whatever.

"Anyway, we gotta be super careful. My space-cycle's shield should keep us safe until we get there, but if there are any of the plastic bastards in the temple we may be fucked. Remember, I'm vulnerable to magic and that's what makes the toys work," I say.

"That's fine, just stay behind me," says Nunya.

"Hey, I don't need your protection," I say.

"Sounds like you do."

"I don't."

"You do."

"Nope."

"Yep."

I'm starting to get irritated again. Why did I break the damn eject button?

I type the information into the IPS and it plots a course straight through the belt of floating toys. Great. And by great I mean 'oh fuck'.

I let the autopilot steer the ship so that I can stay alert in case I need to take evasive action. I've got my blasters in my hands and Nunya's pulled out her wand.

"Hey, Dick?" starts Nunya. "Is your space-cycle's force field 'one way'?"

"What do you mean?" I ask.

"Can I shoot shit with my wand that's outside of the force field without messing with it?"

"I have no idea but I wouldn't try it. If it isn't, you could damage or destroy the only thing keeping us safe right now."

"So, you've never used your blasters on stuff outside the force field while it's up?"

"Never needed to," I reply.

"I guess we'll just have to hope they can't get in," says Nunya.

"Yup."

With that we reach the belt of toys. At first, nothing happens. A seemingly lifeless teddy bear bounces off of the shield, then a toy tank. A few seconds later a speak-and-spell bumps into us. I guess not all of the toys will be able to attack us, which is a good thing. Just as the speak-and-spell harmlessly deflects off the force field, it blinks to life, both displaying the message and saying out loud in its disturbing, synthesized voice: "Intruders! You will die!"

"I guess we woke them up," I say.

"Shit," replies Nunya.

I realize I'm holding my breath, which is weird. I can actually hold my breath pretty much forever, which is why I can survive being in space without a spacesuit. I couldn't breathe in outer space if I wanted to, because no air. But I can just ignore the need to. It's like my body makes its own oxygen. But I still instinctively take in air anyway. I must be even more worried than I thought.

In the few seconds it takes to think my thoughts about a dozen toys start drifting toward us. The first to reach us are a couple of really freaky looking dolls and they seem like something out of a scary movie. Pale skin, dark frizzy hair, and evil glowing red eyes. Somehow, instead of bouncing off the force field they're able to stick to it. We watch in horror as the dolls try to chew through the force field. It shocks them as they munch hungrily like stoners on a bag of Doritos. So far the force field seems to be holding. So far.

I also want to say that I completely deny screaming like a little girl just now, and fuck you if you thought that sound was me. It was just my space-cycle, which probably needs a tune-up. Yeah, that's all it was: a squeaky belt.

The next few toys that reach us are a teddy bear, a toy robot, and a Mr. Potato Head. I've never seen anything scarier. It has extra arms, eyes, and noses, and all of the eyes are glowing red. It even has several mouths that are trying to eat their way through the force field. I wonder if it's even worth it to be here.

More toys attach themselves, chewing at the bubble separating them from us. So far they haven't been able to make their way through, but I genuinely don't know if that'll last. One of the toys stuck to the shield is an action figure and he tries to cut through the forcefield with his laser rifle.

"Hey, do you think if you speed the space-cycle up that it'll shake some of them off?" asks Nunya.

"Nah, I've tried stuff like that before. For that to work you gotta have air pushing against them or some other external force. Out here in space though there's nothing to rub them off. Heh, I just said 'rub them off.'"

"Dick, knock it the fuck off. This is serious. Maybe if we speed up then less of them will be able to attach to us."

"I dunno. Maybe," I reply.

I holster Rita and Irene and turn the autopilot off. Speeding the space-cycle up I use the IPS to guide me toward planet O'Brien. Doing my best to avoid the larger groups of toys we still end up bumping into more and more until we're flying blind. The entire shield is now covered in toys trying to break their way in. We're surrounded by a mass of teeth and glowing red eyes and lasers trying to cut through the bubble and it's making me sick to my stomach. That's when the shield starts making sparking noises and blinks.

"Shit," I say.

"What? Is the force field going to hold?" asks Nunya.

"I hoped it would but they've done a lot of damage to it. It's not invincible like me."

"Are you saying you think this is the end?"

"It might be. Do you want to use our last few moments alive having sex?" I ask.

She thinks for a moment.

"Sure," she replies.

"Wait, really?" I say.

"Fuck no, asshole! And fuck you for even asking right now," says Nunya. "I wouldn't have sex with you if the entire human race and all the other races depended on it! Except Bloopnarps. Those slimy fuckers can die."

"Bloopnarps? What's wrong with Bloopnarps?" I ask.

"The giant slug people? Have you seen them? They get their gooey snot substance everywhere and smell like rotten meat."

"It's not their fault they're born like that! Some of the best people I know are Bloopnarps!"

"Can't they just wear rubber pants to hold in all their goo?" asks Nunya.

"No, because they use the slime to move around. They don't have any legs. How would you like it if someone glued your feet to the floor just to feel less repulsed by you. I don't think you'd like it very much," I say.

"Don't care. They're still gross," she mumbles.

"Well, I think your speciesist attitude is gross!"

"Still don't care. And hey, do you really want to waste our last few seconds arguing over space-slugs? We're gonna die!"

"No, I don't wanna argue with you, and yeah, maybe we'll die, but at least we'll die together. At least I'll die with my... wait, I have an idea!" I say.

I find the button that turns the force field off and on.

"I hope this works," I yell. I press the force field button once then quickly a second time. The bubble disappears for just a moment, letting some of the toys inside. The second button press catches the toys as they're part way through, cutting them in half. We watch as a lot of red glowing eyes dim and die.

"Huh, that was sort of brilliant," says Nunya.

Unfortunately, a couple of the smaller toys made it through including one of the laser soldiers.

"Crap," I say. I turn the autopilot back on and pull out my space-blasters. I hand Irene to Nunya. "Whatever you do, don't hit the shield," I say.

"I'll do my best," she replies.

We start lining up our shots. I take out a couple of Barbies while Nunya shoots what looks like a G. I. Joe figure. Thankfully, our first few shots hit their targets, destroying the toys. Unthankfully, a couple of the action figures start shooting their laser guns at my space-cycle's energy cells. Brightly glowing white-blue goo starts oozing out of Bessie, floating out of the force field behind us. I shoot the two soldiers but they've already done enough damage that we're completely fucked.

"Oh shit, oh shit, oh shit!" I yell.

"What is it, Dick?"

"We're losing energy! We're gonna have to crash-land her!"

"Oh fuck!" yells Nunya.

I turn off the autopilot and aim straight at the coordinates that are still faintly showing up on my display. Putting as much energy as I can into firing a quick burst of speed toward planet O'Brien I reach forward, wrapping Nunya in my arms.

"The fuck are you doing?" yells Nunya. "Why the fuck are you hugging me?"

"Because we're about to crash-land and I'm trying to protect you. Now shut the fuck up and hold on!"

The toys that are still trapped inside the shield continue damaging Bessie, and if I wasn't so worried about what was going to happen next I'd probably be crying right now. Not that I ever cry, but Bessie and I have been through thick-and-thin and she's gotten me out of some tight spots. I've always been able to trust her with my life. I feel like I've let her down. She's the best goddamn space-cycle in the galaxy and doesn't deserve to go out like this.

Most of the chopped up toys have drifted away from the force field so I can finally see what's in front of us. Planet O'Brien is mostly green, with a few large blue spots that must be oceans. I also see several sections of white, which I can only guess are snowy regions. The planet actually reminds me of pictures of Earth Uno from thousands of years ago before the entire thing was paved and converted into parking for the other seven planets.

Keeping Nunya as protected as I can, I turn us backwards on the seat so that I can keep her from burning up as we enter the planet's atmosphere. Just as we start to enter it the last of Bessie's energy goo drips out and the engine whirs down, making a dieseling sound like an old truck. Poor girl.

"Hold on!" I yell as the force field bubble blinks one final time and disappears. I can feel the toys that were trapped inside with us attacking, and a few that were still clinging onto the outside of the bubble shoot at me. It hurts, because the back of my leather jacket does little to protect me from the blasts and I realize that the fine folks at the Bigger and Taller store never said it was magic-proof. Dammit.

A few of the toys are able to work together, holding hands so they can anchor themselves to me. Normally I'd punch them, or grab them and throw them, but my arms are currently wrapped around Nunya, protecting her. I let the toys laser me and chew at my skin, sending blood droplets and chunks of stringy flesh dripping behind us. I do what I can to ignore the pain because if I let it distract me Nunya will die.

Bessie starts getting warm; really warm. I'm getting warm too. It's kind of like taking a really hot shower that isn't getting you wet while sitting on a heated car seat in the middle of summer with the AC turned off.

Chrome pieces start ripping off Bessie. First small ones, like the mirrors, then trim pieces and sections of exhaust come off. Black panels and dull metal chunks start breaking away too. Eventually, my poor girl just starts disintegrating in the atmosphere, burning up and scattering into the air behind us. Some of the toys that are anchored to me catch fire and burn. I see a couple of dolls and a teddy bear burst into flames, like something out of a post-apocalyptic Schwarzenegger film. It's the stuff of nightmares.

The few toys still connected to my arms continue to chew and laser me with no regard for their own safety. I guess it makes sense since they're just soulless creatures bent on killing anything they come into contact with.

That's when something really important pops in my head: if I don't figure out a way to slow us down, Nunya's gonna die anyway. As soon as we hit the ground she'll squish against my abs of steel and man-pecs of iron, liquifying instantly.

Shit, I need to think of something and I need to think of something quick! But the pain from being chewed on is distracting. It's taking all my concentration just to keep Nunya wrapped up inside of my arms. C'mon Dick, ignore the pain and figure this out, because you probably only have seconds before you're smashed into toothpaste.

Fuck. One of the toys, I think a Furby, has latched itself onto my face and is chewing my nose. I freak out, scream, then remember that I have super breath. I suck in as much air as I can in the thin atmosphere and blow, sending the toy flying off behind us. It takes a chunk of my nose with it which hurts like a bitch. I twist my head just enough so that I can see the ground coming rapidly closer to us out of the corner of my eye. That's when I finally remember I can fly.

I twist a bit in the air so that my feet are pointed toward the ground and I put everything I have into flying against our momentum. Even with my powers weakened by the magical damage that's been done to me I'm able to slow our fall. Not enough to stop completely, but there's a chance we might survive. That's when we crash into planet O'Brien, skipping like a stone, and I pass out.

14

Suddenly, I'm in this weird room. It has white walls, a white ceiling and a white floor. That's not what's weird about it, though. What's weird is there are no windows and no doors yet I'm still somehow inside of it. And I'm not the only one who's inside of it. On the other side of the room sits a woman at a desk, looking at me expectantly.

She's hot. Like, flawlessly hot. God, I hope I get to bang her. And it's strange, because her hair is brown, and also blonde, with some red and black as well. Her eyes somehow are brown and green and blue and gray all at the same time, shimmering with color. Her dark yet light skin glows like something out of a wrinkle-cream commercial. And her body. Oh wow, her body. Curvy in just the right way; not too little, not too much. The white flowing robe she's partially covered in reveals the outline of her nipples. If I asked God for the perfect woman this is who she'd be.

"Actually, you're right," says the woman, "because I'm God, and I made myself in the image you'd find most pleasing."

"Wait, you're God?" I say.

"That's right," she replies.

"God's a chick? And a super hot one to boot? Holy fuck!"

"Yes, holy fuck," replies God.

"But why are you a hot chick?" I ask.

"I literally just explained it to you a second ago. Basically, everyone has their own image of what God is, whether it's some old bearded guy like Santa Claus or a dude with a few extra appendages. Some people even see a monstrous flying plate of spaghetti. Your mind conjured the hottest woman you could think of."

"Oh, I guess that makes sense. So, I think God's a woman? Wow, maybe I'm not as piggish as Nunya thinks I am."

"No, you're still a pig, which is why I look like this. If you'd made me look like Mother Theresa or Susan B. Anthony or Marie Curie you probably would have scored more points."

"Wait, there's a point system? Do I have a lot of points?" I ask.

"No, there's no point system. I was just using a metaphor," says God.

"Oh. So if you're God then I must be in heaven!" I look around. "You know, honestly, I thought it would be much nicer than this.

Like, fountains of liquid chocolate, naked women everywhere, all-you-can-eat buffets. Maybe combine them and have chocolate covered all-you-can-eat women. Shit like that."

"To be honest, you aren't in heaven."

"Wait, so this is hell?"

"Nope. This is just a room where we talk for a bit and I decide where you go."

"How are you gonna decide?"

"We're gonna talk. Like I just said."

"Shit, I hate talking," I say. "How about instead of talking we fuck?"

"Dick, you're hitting on me?"

"Yeah."

"I'm God, Dick."

"So? You're fucking hot!"

"Dick, do you truly think you're God's gift to... God?"

"You know it, Baby," I say.

God just stares at me.

"Fine, we can talk," I say. "Just hope it doesn't get boring. So what do you want to talk about?"

"Well, why do you think you should go to heaven? Or for that matter, you can always make an argument to go to hell. Do you have a preference?"

"Is there still sex in heaven?" I ask.

"If that's your idea of heaven, then yes."

"Does it have cussing and beer?"

"Sure, why not?" says God, somewhat annoyed.

"How about burgers the size of my head?"

"Yes, those too."

"And what's hell really like?"

"You know how there's people that really annoy you? They chew with their mouths open, or cut you off in traffic, or troll people on the Intergalactic Information System?"

"Yeah, they're called assholes!"

"Well, you're stuck in a room with them. All of them. And you can't get out."

"Shit, that does sound like the worst," I say. "Can I kill them?"

"No, they're invincible."

"Can I make them stop being annoying?"

"No," says God.

"Hmm, hard pass. You know, it's funny, a lot of people think hell is a burning inferno where you're pushing a rock up a hill and it keeps crushing you and rolling back down. Shit like that."

"No. It turns out that the thing people can't stand the most is annoying people. Nothing gets them more riled up."

"But what happens to the annoying people? What's their version of hell like?" I ask.

"It's the same thing. Everyone has people who annoy them. It's how I designed it. It keeps things interesting."

"So what you're saying is the universe is basically just your personal reality TV show?"

"Yes."

"But why would you create all that? I mean, are we just entertainment to you?"

"Well, you've probably heard that I can see everything that's going on, and I know everything, and I live forever and all that?" says God.

"Yeah," I reply.

"Well, if you have eternity all to yourself you get kinda bored. Just hanging around in space with nothing to do is the worst. So I decided to create people so that I'd have something interesting to watch. I gave people free will to do what they want to make it more exciting. That way I wouldn't see things coming. Even though, technically, I could if I wanted to. But I block that out of my mind."

"So you're saying the meaning of life is that we're all self-absorbed schmucks? You just like to see us bump into things and make mistakes and act like assholes?"

"Pretty much."

"That's kinda fucked up. I mean, it makes sense. But shit."

"Well, I like to watch existence because it makes me feel better about myself," says God.

"You know, I guess I would probably do the same thing if I was you," I admit. "So have we talked enough?"

"Normally I'd spend quite a while talking with someone before I make a determination. But in your case, I know what I'm going to do."

"You're sending me to heaven?" I ask.

"No."

"Hell then?"

"Nope."

"So, then what?"

"Well, here's the thing: you're a bit of a fuck-up to put it in terms you can understand. Yes, you save lives and help people but it's because it fuels your ego. It doesn't really make you a good guy. It also doesn't make you a bad guy, because despite your selfishness and general lack of empathy and understanding you usually manage to do the right thing, and you aren't actively trying to hurt people. Also, since you started spending time with Nunya, you've become a little… better. Your story is fairly interesting and I really want to see how the rest of it plays out so I'm sending you back."

"Wait! Nunya! Is she okay? Did she survive?" I ask.

"Yes, Nunya survived. In fact, she's trying to revive your corpse right now."

"Is she giving me mouth-to-mouth?" I ask, an evil grin on my face.

"No."

"Damn. Okay, well, that's fine. Send me back I guess."

And with that I disappear from the white room.

15

"Dick? Dick?" I hear a female voice say.

My eyes are closed and I hurt like hell. I start to cough and realize that even my throat hurts.

"Dick, are you alive?" It's Nunya.

"Uh, (cough) yeah. I think I need mouth-to-mouth, though," I say.

She smacks me in the face.

"Asshole! You don't need mouth-to-mouth if you can say you need mouth-to-mouth. You're breathing," says Nunya.

"Weird. I don't really need to. Anyway, are we safe?" I ask, finally opening my eyes.

"As near as I can tell. The toys that came down to the planet with us were all burnt to a crisp. All except a Furby. But I shot it with Irene."

"Thanks, that fucker chewed off part of my nose."

"I was wondering," says Nunya. "You look like hell."

"I feel like it."

"Well, why don't you use your healing powers on yourself?"

"Because it doesn't work on magical damage. I'll still be able to heal eventually, but damage from magical things takes way longer to heal from. I hate magic."

"Yeah, you've said that before. Looks like your clothes are fucked up again," says Nunya.

"I should have asked at the Bigger and Taller store if they were magic resistant. I would have paid extra for that," I say.

"Well, I guess you're in luck, because the part of your space-cycle you kept stuff in survived. It's not far from here. I already grabbed your shit and brought it back."

"Thanks. Yeah, I remember reading the pamphlet for Bessie when I bought her. It had a tagline that said 'you may not make it to your destination but your shit will.' Still my favorite ad slogan."

We both chuckle.

"Hey, I'm sorry about your loss," says Nunya.

"Bessie? Thanks. I honestly have no idea how we're gonna get off this planet without her."

"Me neither."

It hurts like hell when I sit up. Nunya starts doing the best she can to clean up my wounds using some of my torn up t-shirt. She has me tear it into bandage strips since she isn't strong enough to rip through the near indestructible material herself.

Once she has all the holes I wasn't born with patched I glance around to see what we're up against. We're in a grassy field next to a forest. Surrounding us on all sides are snow-capped mountains. The sky is a beautiful blue color, the air is crisp and warm from the sun that hangs overhead. So far planet O'Brien looks like paradise. Off in the distance I see the giant purple penis. It looks like it's a few hours walk to get there.

"Think you'll be able to make it to the cock tower?" asks Nunya.

"Eventually. It might be good to take a short rest to heal a bit," I say.

"You mean one hour?" asks Nunya.

"Wait, you play D&D?"

"I used to. When I was a smuggler we had a bunch of down time when we flew from place to place so to keep everyone's energy up we'd play. Unfortunately, my crew died before we got to finish the campaign."

"TPK."

"Yeah," says Nunya, looking off into space.

"Hey, I, uh… just want you to know that… I'm sorry that happened to you," I say.

Nunya looks at me for the briefest of moments then looks away.

"Thanks, Dick."

"Sure. And if you ever want to talk about stuff…"

"I'm good."

"Okay." I give her a moment then try talking to her again. "Hey, so are you having fun on our adventure so far?"

"Uh, not really. I mean you're banged the fuck up and I had problems breathing while we entered the atmosphere. And thank you for protecting me by the way," says Nunya.

"Hey, if I didn't keep you alive then who else will follow me around and treat me like shit all day?"

She chuckles half-heartedly.

"Yeah, I guess that's true," she says. "I'm doing a public service."

"Hey, you wanna hear something crazy?" I ask.

"Uh, sure."

"I met God."

"Wait, what?" asks Nunya.

"I actually met her. And she was so fucking hot! Like, even hotter than you," I say.

"Hey, there's no bitch in this universe that's hotter than me," says Nunya.

"Yeah, I think that's still true because when I was with God we were in this white room and I don't think it was in this universe."

"That sounds like a million other bullshit stories of people going into the light."

"Yeah, but this room was weird. It wasn't like what you'd expect the afterlife to be. It wasn't a blinding white light or whatever, it was just a normal room with normal walls and no windows or doors. And there's God, sitting at a desk, wearing some see-through robes."

"Alright, let's say I believe you and that this actually happened. Why is she super hot and mostly naked?"

"She said that she appears to everyone in the form that makes the person the most comfortable. Whatever works best for them. Apparently I worship hot women," I explain.

"I guess that makes sense. So what did she say?"

"Well, she thought I was kind of a pig, just like you said," I admit.

"That tracks," says Nunya.

"And she said that I wasn't a good guy because I did things to feed my own ego."

"Also tracks."

"But she said I wasn't a bad guy either because in spite of my selfishness or whatever that I still usually try to do the right thing."

"Huh."

"She also said that you're helping me become a better person. Not a lot, but some."

"Damn, maybe it was God. She sounds pretty smart," says Nunya.

"Maybe. Anyway, she sent me back to the land of the living so that you could help me be a better person."

Nunya seems genuinely surprised. I can see the gears turning in her head.

"Dick, since you had the chance to talk to her, did you ask her about anything important? Like the meaning of life? Like why do we exist and everything?"

"Actually, yeah," I say, smiling.

"And?"

"And what?"

"And what the fuck did she say?"

"Oh. Yeah, so she gets bored easily being all super-super powered and shit. So we're like entertainment to her," I say.

The look on Nunya's face is totally priceless.

"So what you're saying is that God told you we're on some sort of fucking reality TV show? That's what you're saying?"

"Yeah."

"That is so fucked up but makes so much fucking sense. No wonder my life seems so crazy all the time. Sometimes it's drama, sometimes action/adventure. We're on fucking TV all the time!"

"Pretty much," I admit.

"Damn. I dunno, maybe you did meet God. Well, if you meet her again, put in a good word for me," says Nunya.

"Will do. Oh, and she said one more thing. She told me that you need to stop masturbating. You masturbate way too much. She was really specific about it. Said something about it doing permanent damage to your soul."

"Wait, really?" asks Nunya, completely shocked.

"No dumbass, we didn't talk about your masturbating habits. But based on how you reacted it sounds like I'm right."

"Hey, I don't masturbate!" she says, blushing.

"Are you a rotten liar!" I say. "I can tell you get 'cooter claw'."

"Cooter claw? What the fuck is that?"

"It's where your hand cramps up and you can't uncurl it because you masturbate too much. That's what you have," I say, laughing at her.

"What-the-fuck-ever," says Nunya.

"Seriously, it's amazing you can even work a gun considering how mangled your fingers are. They look like they belong to a geriatric pianist with arthritis whose hands got slammed in a car door."

"They do not!" she says.

I'm surprised, because she's actually laughing a little at my teasing her and she hasn't hit me yet. Maybe my charm is finally working on her.

I look up at her and smile. She smiles back and after a brief pause I can tell she instantly regrets it.

"Dick, before you even start, no, I will not have sex with you. Okay? Seriously, just because I went from hating you 110% down to 109% doesn't mean I want to have sex with you. So keep it in your pants."

I look down in disappointment.

"Dick, I really need you to understand that we're never going to have sex. Okay? I really need you to be okay with that," says

Nunya.

"But why? I mean, look at me! Even my muscles have muscles! I'm strong, and good looking, and I have a huge locomotive in my pants!"

"Because I'm gay! See, now you made me say it!"

"What do you mean?" I ask.

"I'm a lesbian! I like chicks!" says Nunya.

"So?"

"What do you mean, 'so'?"

"I've had sex with plenty of women that like women. It's fucking hot!" I say. "Two chicks goin' at it? Yes please!"

"Dude, not okay! But can't you see now why I don't want to have sex with you?"

"Nope," I reply. "Seriously, women, and I mean all women, fall all over themselves to be with me. Even the women that only like women. It really is a superpower I have. But for some reason you seem immune. I wish I knew how."

"It's because my bullshit meter is super sensitive and it goes off every time you open your mouth," says Nunya.

"Nah, that's not it."

"It's the only thing that makes sense."

"Maybe you have secret superpowers you don't even know about."

"I don't think so," replies Nunya.

"Seriously, think about it! You shoot blasters better than pretty much anyone I've seen, you were the only one that came back alive from your smuggling group, and you somehow survived falling from outer space down to a planet's surface. That sounds to me like you probably have some sort of luck power or some shit."

"A luck power? How would that even work?" she asks.

"Well, maybe it just affects probability. Like, if two things could happen, maybe the random thing that happens is whatever is more favorable to you. I mean, maybe you don't have perfect luck all the time, like when your bar blew up, or when your parents named you, or shit like that. But it does seem like a bunch of strange things have happened that point to it."

"If I have a luck power then why would it have anything to do with not having sex with you?"

"Because maybe it's how the universe keeps your power in balance. Like, because you have a gift, your punishment is that you don't ever get to know just how really really good I am in bed."

"Do you realize how ridiculous you sound?" asks Nunya. "Have you seriously never been turned down before?"

"Never."

"Wow. That must be super damaging to your ego. Like, you must feel like much less of a man than you thought you were," says Nunya.

"Hey, that's just plain mean!"

"Well you kind of deserve it, you dirty slut-bag."

"You're the dirty slut-bag," I mumble.

"Yeah I am, but you'll never know about it because I won't ever have sex with you!"

Nunya suddenly grabs the back of my head, pulls my face close to her's and kisses me, all hot, and wet, and with tongue.

No, not really. I'm just fucking with you. She apparently really doesn't want to have sex with me. Maybe I do have to be okay with that. It just really sucks because I actually kind of like her. Even more than just someone to fuck. But I do want her to be my friend. Maybe that's enough. I wonder if a guy and a girl can even be friends. Has that ever actually happened?

"Okay, I'll work on not wanting you so bad," I say. "Seriously."

"Thank you," says Nunya, still grumpy.

"I think I'm gonna need an actual rest. I lost some blood and it's making me feel a bit woozy. You cool watching over me? Just in case bad guys show up?"

"Sure, I can do that."

"Oh, shit," I start to say.

"What?"

"Rita! What happened to Rita? Did you find her?" I ask.

"You mean Rita, your blaster? I haven't seen her," says Nunya.

"I… I think that maybe I let go of her when I held onto you. I lost both Bessie and Rita. Fuck!!!" I yell.

"I'm sorry, Dick. I know how emotionally close you get with inanimate objects."

"Well if your only friends were your possessions I don't think you'd be joking about it if you lost them."

"You're right, I probably wouldn't. But you still have Irene. I kept her safe for you."

"Thanks, I guess," I mumble.

"Do you want her back?"

"Nah, keep her for now. Use her if you need to. I'll just use my superpowers or whatever."

I lie down, curl up into a fetal position and try my best to sleep.

16

I wake up and look around and Nunya's nowhere to be seen. Standing up I still hurt like hell but not as bad as before. I'm also tired but feel better than I did. Having a rest helped some. But now I'm worried because I have no idea where Nunya is.

"Nunya! NUUUUUUUUUUUUNYA!" I yell.

Nothing.

"NUUUUUUUUUUUUNYA!"

"What?" I hear someone yell from the trees.

"Where are you?" I ask.

"I'm behind a tree taking a shit! What's it to you?" yells Nunya.

"I just wanted to make sure you weren't lost or dead or something," I say.

"Well, just give me a minute."

After she's done taking her dump I see her come around a large brown tree full of broad green leaves. It's a beautiful tree and I think it's kind of a shame that Nunya shit on it.

As she approaches, I ask "Hey, why'd you shit on that tree? What did that tree ever do to you?"

"Ha-ha, you're so funny. I didn't shit on the tree, I just used the tree for privacy. I dug a hole and shit in that. Not that it's any of your business."

"And what'd you use to clean yourself?" I ask.

"Also none of your goddamn business is what," says Nunya.

"Well, I'm not eating any sandwiches you make, that's for damn sure. No high-fives and no handshakes either. And I'm gonna start calling you Poo-fingers."

"You are not!" says Nunya.

"Yeah I am, Poo-fingers. I'm gonna tell everyone how you constantly have poo on your fingers and no one should go near you because they'll have poo-fingers too!"

"That's gross, Dick. I didn't use my fingers, alright? Just drop it."

"Fine. But you can definitely keep Irene because I don't want to touch her now. Gross," I say.

"Oh I definitely will, especially because you don't know how to treat a lady with respect. Irene is too much woman for you to handle," says Nunya.

"Hey, I've treated Irene with a lot of respect, okay? I keep her clean and I protect her, and I take her out and use her for practice just so she knows I still love her. So you can suck it."

"Sounds like you treat your guns better than you treat real women," says Nunya.

"Hey, just because I like to have sex doesn't mean I don't treat women well, okay? I mean it's not like I call them the next day or anything, or listen to them complain about shit. And relationships really aren't my thing. I'm kind of a one-and-done man. But it's not like I'm mean to them or anything. I don't insult them or shit on their feet or anything. Unless they're into that."

"Dick, that's super gross!"

"Calm your tits, it was just a joke. I swear, hand to God, that I've never shit on anyone's feet."

"So they've shit on yours?"

"NO! There's been no shitting involved!"

"Whatever you say, Shit-foot," says Nunya.

Grrrrrrr.

"Alright, fine," I say. "I won't call you Poo-fingers, you don't call me Shit-foot. Deal?"

She hesitates but finally agrees. "Deal." She reaches her hand out to shake on it but I respond, "Fuck no! I still ain't touching your hands."

"Dude, aren't you immune to disease? And you're scared of contracting what exactly?" asks Nunya.

"I dunno. Maybe if you have magical luck powers you have magical shit, too. Maybe your great-grandma fucked a leprechaun and now you have glittery shit that kills superheroes. How the fuck should I know? I just don't want your shit on me. Boundaries!"

"If you're done being such a pussy do you think you're ready to start walking toward the giant purple erection?"

"Walk? Why would we walk?" I ask.

"How else are we gonna get there?"

"I'll fly us," I say.

"Are you sure that's a good idea, being banged up and all?"

"No, I'm sure it's a terrible idea but it might save us a few hours."

"Well since we're in the middle of nowhere with no vehicle and no real medkit, I don't want to risk breaking my neck just to save a couple of hours. If I get hurt or sick we don't know if there's anything we can do to get me help," says Nunya.

"Seriously? Have you already forgotten I can just heal you?"

"That's true, but if I die before you can heal me then I'm dead, right? Like, you can't reanimate people, can you? Because I really don't want to be a zombie."

"Yeah, if you die you're dead. So please, for both our sakes, try not to die."

"Right. So let's just walk. Besides, it's beautiful here. Taking a long walk might be nice," says Nunya.

"Okay, I'm fine with walking, but how do we know there aren't any bad guys waiting in the bushes for us? There could be landmines everywhere. Hell, we could be standing on some right now and we wouldn't even know it until we started walking."

"Well shit, Dick. I wasn't paranoid before but now you've got me freaked out. Thanks a lot for that."

"Good, paranoia keeps you alive. You were a soldier, you should know that. Just make sure that you're constantly looking around in every possible direction at all times and we should be fine. I tell you what, if you're worried about mines I can just hover a foot off the ground and carry you there. That way we won't trip them and you won't die from falling if something were to happen. Does that sound like a plan?" I ask.

"We can try it," says Nunya.

"Cool. Anyway, I need to change," I say, as I take off my damaged leather jacket, t-shirt, and pants.

Nunya looks away.

"What? Are you shy or some shit?" I ask.

"No."

"Then why are you looking away?"

"Just trying to give you your privacy."

"I have no problems with people seeing me naked. Seriously, I don't care. You can look all you want. Maybe you'll change your mind."

"I won't, but fine."

Nunya turns toward me. "Holy fuck!"

"Yeah, it's huge ain't it?" I say.

"It's like the size of my arm!"

"Now you know why I have so much 'big dick energy' and why women can't control themselves around me. Sometimes I wonder if my superpowers don't come from my enormous schlong. It would explain a lot."

"Yeah it would," says Nunya. "But my guess is your superpowers come from your asshole. It'd be more fitting."

"And fuck you too," I reply.

I leave the bandages in place as I can tell my wounds are still healing but I put my suit on over the top of them, making sure not to get any blood on my outfit.

"How do I look?" I ask.

"Like a two burgmorp burrito stuffed into a thousand burgmorp suit. You're oozing beans and hot sauce everywhere."

"Wow, what a colorful description that was. Thank you for that," I say sarcastically. "You know, come to think of it, I've always wondered why money is called 'burgmorps'."

"Oh, that's easy. It's because of Burgmorp, King of the Pengwings. He was the ruler of the galaxy about a thousand years ago," says Nunya.

"What the hell is a 'pengwing'?" I ask.

"You know, they're those little birds that can't fly, and they're black and white and look like they're wearing tuxedos. And they like cold climates and waddle in a really cute way."

"Wait, you mean penguins?"

"What's a penguin?" asks Nunya.

"It's what you just described. Tuxedo birds!"

"No, they're called pengwings!"

"According to who?"

"According to everyone I've ever talked to!"

"Then the people you've been talking to are stupid," I say.

"Yeah, well you're stupid too," says Nunya. "Regardless, that's who our currency is named after. He was a benign and benevolent ruler, and was so beloved that burgmorps were branded with his byname."

"Nice rhyming," I say.

"It's called alliteration, not rhyming," replies Nunya.

"Anyway, I need you to carry my stuff while I carry you. Can you handle that?"

"Yeah, fine."

I make sure to take out my bag of ultimate wonders and put it in my pocket then stuff my torn up clothes into one bag and keep my clean tuxedo in the other. Nunya's able to hold the bags in one hand while holding Irene in the other. I wrap my arms around her waist as we start to hover.

"Wait, hold up," says Nunya.

"What?"

"Why don't we just put your shit in your magic bag or whatever. Isn't there enough room?"

"Oh, duh. Yeah, hadn't thought of that."

I set her back down then quickly stuff my clothes bags into the bag of ultimate wonders which I then place in my pocket.

"By the way, do you still have that magic wand that the Wise

Old Wizard gave you?" I ask.

"Yeah. I keep it in my pants."

"Good. You may want to pull it out now. We don't know if there's anything else magical out here and it could be our only defense."

"On it."

Carrying her wand in her left hand and Irene in her right, I lift Nunya back up and we start to hover away.

17

It helps that we can see the purple penis tower looming in the distance like some phallic castle rising above the trees. There isn't a path to follow because there doesn't seem to be any people on this planet as near as I can tell. No signs of civilization other than the tower.

"Hey Nunya, have you noticed that there aren't any animals around?" I ask.

"I hadn't, but now that you mention it.... I mean, as much as animals need plants, plants need animals too. They help spread seeds and pollen to keep things growing. But here there are trees and plants, and it doesn't seem like there are any creatures to spread them. It's almost like this is a fake ecosystem."

"Do you think it's the Mad Wizard's doing?"

"Probably. And it would make sense, I guess. Hey, just in case everything around here is magical I wouldn't go fucking any tree holes. Your dick might fall off," says Nunya.

"I'm not gonna fuck any tree holes! What do you take me for?" I ask.

"A guy that fucks tree holes."

"Not cool, Nunya. Not cool."

"Hey, if the tree hole fits…"

"I can drop you here and let you walk the rest of the way," I say.

"Not really much of a threat when we're already halfway there," says Nunya.

"Are we living on a prayer?"

"Take my hand, we'll make it I swear."

"God, as if this trip wasn't going bad enough we're quoting 'Bon Jovi'."

"What's wrong with Bon Jovi?" asks Nunya.

"If you need to ask, explaining it to you won't make any difference."

Nunya seems a little pissed that I'm not a huge fan of Bon Jovi. Honestly, their music's fine, but I think that's why I don't like them that much. It's just kind of bland. They're the white bread of hair bands. Sure, it makes for a decent enough sandwich but it doesn't add anything new or flavorful. And since there are dozens of other types of much better breads out there why would I even bother? I mean there's the dark rye of Def Leppard, the sour dough of Van Halen, and even the pumpernickel of Scorpions to name a few.

As we get closer to where we can finally see the base of the purple penis, something makes me stop in my tracks.

"Can you hear that?" I ask Nunya.

"Hear what?"

"That purring."

"No, I don't hear any purring."

"Maybe it's my super hearing that's picking it up. God, I hope it's not what I think it is. Stay sharp. Make sure your wand and Irene are ready," I say.

"Uh, sure."

Just as we crest over a small hill I see it, a few hundred feet away. It's furry, about the size of a human child, with cute fuzzy ears, big sincere eyes and tufts of whiskers. It's on all fours, looking at us expectantly, as if it wants to play with us.

"Fuck, I was right. It's a Meow," I say. "Shoot it."

"What the fuck is a 'Meow'?"

"It looks like a large, sweet kitty cat but I promise you those things are vicious. It'll just as soon rip off your face as cuddle with you. Whatever you do, don't make any sudden moves, and for God's sake don't pet it, unless of course you don't like having arms."

I set us on the ground just in case things go down. The Meow starts sauntering up to us, acting all sweet and innocent, but I know better.

"Shoot it!" I yell. "It's charging us!"

"But it's so cute!" says Nunya. "I couldn't possibly shoot something so cute. And I think it likes me!"

"Yeah, for lunch," I mumble. "Fine, if you won't do it I will." I start walking toward the Meow, ready to punch it into oblivion.

"Stop, Dick! You'll do no such thing or I'll use my wand on you!"

I'm frustrated by her not taking this seriously enough. "Your funeral," I say, as I start walking back behind her. Far behind her. Sometimes you just gotta let people make their own mistakes I guess.

The Meow walks right up to Nunya and flops onto its back, making it obvious it wants its tummy rubbed.

"Oh my God, he's so cute!" she screeches. Nunya bends down and starts to rub its belly. It seems to enjoy it and his purrs become louder and louder. "Who's a sweet kitty? You are, that's who!" She keeps petting it and the Meow keeps purring. Eventually, she turns to me and says "See, you were wrong. He's a sweethea-OUCH!!!"

That's when all hell breaks loose. The Meow latches onto her right arm, burying its teeth deep into her skin, which sends up a spray of blood that coats Nunya's face. A dozen other Meows jump out from behind some nearby bushes and start charging toward us. As Nunya freaks out she not only drops Irene but accidentally points her wand at me and hits me with a magical lightning bolt, knocking me back fifty feet. I take the full impact of the lightning bolt and my suit now has a big black spot on it. It knocks the wind out of me and I'm stunned briefly. I look on in horror as the other Meows start circling around her, ready to pounce on their delicious snack.

Nunya turns and points the wand at the Meow attached to her arm and hits it with a fireball. Thankfully, the Meow ignites in a super creepy looking ball of blazing fur. The smell alone is horrible but the image of a burning kitten will haunt my nightmares. Unfortunately, the fireball also singes Nunya, burning away some of her hair and damaging some of her flawless skin in the process.

I try to recover but I'm in so much pain from the magical lightning I was struck with that it's hard to move. Willing myself upright I try to use one of my powers to help out, my super blower. I take as deep of a breath as I can, aim and blow. A few of the Meows that had just appeared from the bushes are hit by the air which only ruffles their fur slightly and does nothing more than annoy them. Great, that was helpful.

Nunya is screaming, both from the pain and from the terror of being surrounded by a pack of evil kittens. She casts a few more fireballs, burning three Meows in the process, but instead of retreating they pounce. Blood starts squirting here and there as the Meows rip at her flesh, biting and tearing at her. I realize I have to act fast but what can I do?

That's when it hits me. I flop onto my stomach, my head pointed at Nunya and the pack of killer cats, and use my flying ability to launch myself like a torpedo toward them. Scraping against the ground my suit gets even dirtier but I make it to Nunya. I reach out and grab her, pulling her up into the air and away from the Meows. A few stay latched on and I do my best to punch them off of her. I fly us way far away from the Meow's to a clearing where I'm hoping we won't get ambushed again.

I start to cry because there isn't much left of her. Dozens of bloody bite holes cover her body, and where she isn't bitten she's burned. One of her eyes is gone, blackened from the fireball, but the other one can see clearly. That is until it starts rolling up into her head like she's losing consciousness.

I do my best to heal her but it doesn't work very well as I'm still recovering from all of the magical damage I've suffered. It takes a long time, and her pain is so intense that she holds my hand, gripping it tightly. It's like a sick torture that's meant to fix her and there's nothing I can do to make her feel better. Normally when I heal people it doesn't seem to hurt them. But since my powers aren't what they normally are they just can't block out the pain.

I'm so glad when her eye finally regrows. As cool as eyepatches are, I'd rather have Nunya keep her depth perception. The burned and scarred flesh starts mending, and after at least an hour of her writhing in pain she's almost back to her normal self. A patch of hair on the right side of her head is missing but it doesn't look that bad. It's almost as if she shaved it on purpose to make it look cool.

Nunya finally smiles at me, realizing the horror is over. "Thank you, Dick," she says.

"You can thank me by listening to me in the future, okay? I've been around the galaxy for a long time and I've seen a lot of crazy shit. When I tell you something's dangerous you need to believe me."

"Yeah. Sorry," she says.

"Hey, people make mistakes. That's why you gotta not be like normal people, okay?"

"Sure, I'll get right on that," she says sarcastically.

"Shit, it's too bad I healed your sense of sarcasm along with the rest of you," I say.

"And here I thought you liked it."

"Nope. Oh, shit, I think you left Irene and your wand back where we were attacked."

"Yeah, I dropped them. Again, I'm sorry."

"It's okay. I'll just need to go back for them, otherwise we may never see them again."

"Just be careful," says Nunya.

Shit, never thought I'd hear her be concerned for my safety. Anyway, I take off into the air but I can't really fly that fast because I'm still completely wrecked. I do my best to follow what I think was my path when I flew off with Nunya but it isn't easy. Thankfully, I have the big purple penis as a landmark to know where I've gone and where I've probably been. The huge dick is actually useful for something.

After a fair bit of searching I find the spot where we had our battle. Some of Nunya's blood is still there but all of the burnt dead Meow bodies are gone, as well as Irene and the wand. Shit, so far this isn't going so great.

I try to focus my super hearing, thinking I might catch a sound that will lead me to them. Seconds go by then minutes. I try to use my super-vision too, looking as far as I can, but I see nothing. After what feels like ten minutes I hear a gentle purring off in the distance. Bingo.

Turning in the direction of the sound I fly as quickly as I can. It's coming in the opposite direction of Nunya, which I'm glad to hear because I was worried they might find her in the meantime. I try to fly low so they don't see me until I'm right on top of them, but I still have a hard time steering because of my wounds and exhaustion. Just as I come up over a small hill I see the remaining Meows and notice them in the process of burying the four that Nunya had fried. Apparently, the few that I'd punched off of us somehow managed to survive.

I'm not too worried as I approach because I should be invincible to their attacks, until I remember they have Nunya's wand. I just have to hope they have no fucking clue how to use it. Unfortunately, my hope is immediately demolished as a group of three fireballs start rocketing my way.

I fly up into the air, doing my best to dodge and swerve out of the way of the fireballs, until I finally see which Meow is firing at me. I dive toward him, or her, or whatever the fuck it is, and narrowly avoid a second barrage of fireballs. It feels like the trench scene in Star Wars only even fucking cooler because I don't have a douchebag smuggler in an old-ass spaceship covering me. I left my douchebag smuggler several miles away.

Left, right, up, down I move, trying to make an impossible target. Just as I'm about to hit the Meow it dives out of the way.

"Shit!" I yell. I do my best to spin in the air, reverse direction, and ram the Meow. This time though I actually slow down as I get closer to make sure it can't duck out of the way. As soon as it realizes what I'm doing it's too late. I grab it by its scrawny neck and I start pounding the pussy. I hit that pussy hard, pushing my fist in and out of it. I can barely hear over the sound of the screams. It keeps screaming and I keep fisting. After one final scream the pussy stops writhing. It's now totally soaked in pussy goo from me fisting it so hard. I feel pretty satisfied.

I pick up the magic wand and start rubbing it against the pussy, poking deep inside just to make a point, and the other Meows freak out and scatter. Thankfully, they also leave Irene behind. Picking up my gun and Nunya's wand I fly back to where I left her.

When she sees me she's a bit grossed out.

"Dick, you're coated in goo!" says Nunya.

"Yeah, well it was hard for only a few seconds but once I pounded the pussy it was all over. There was goo everywhere. You wouldn't happen to have a wet-wipe, would you? Maybe a hanky or something?" I ask.

"No, definitely no handkerchief. Those things are gross."

"Yeah, I think they're nasty too. Who wants a reusable tissue? Here, blow your nose on this thing that I've already blown my nose on a few thousand times," I say. "Of course, who am I to judge? I have pussy goo all over me and I can't even get it off."

"Not getting it off does seem to be your problem," says Nunya. "Maybe you were just doing it wrong."

"Hey, I've pounded thousands of pussies and I've never had a mess like this. Seriously."

"Fine, you know how to pound pussies. Maybe next time just breathe on it really hard instead. That's one of your superpowers, right?"

"I tried it earlier and nothing happened. It just seemed to make the pussies angry," I explain. "I think I'm just too tired and my head hurts. It made my performance suffer. You know, I just realized that back when you were being attacked by the Meows that pussies were eating you. Isn't it normally the other-way-around?"

"Ha-ha, very funny. But yes," says Nunya.

"Well, here's your wand back. It has pussy goo on it too. You might wipe it off in the grass. At least Irene didn't have any pussy goo on her. I try to keep her as clean and respectable as possible. Anyway, I guess I'll have to find a stream or lake or something nearby to wash off in."

"Yeah, you should get cleaned up. Fly away, Dick, pounder of pussies."

Turning away from Nunya I fly upward.

18

Spotting a nearby pond I'm glad to see there isn't anything living in it or near it. I slowly fly down, peel off my clothes and soak in it. A huge blob of gross floats off my body as I enter it, and as soon as my chest is submerged it starts hurting like hell. I knew that the lightning bolt had really hurt me but didn't realize just how much damage it had actually done. Thankfully, the suit had absorbed some of the blast but not enough as my chest looks like someone spilled a half dozen sloppy joes on me. And even though it stings like a motherfucker I stay in the pond until I'm sure I've cleaned out my wounds. Once I finish, I get out of the pond and fly back to Nunya, letting the air and suns dry my skin.

"Oh, for fuck's sake, Dick, couldn't you have kept your pants on?" says Nunya as I approach.

"Story of my life, am I right?" I say jokingly.

"Now that you mention it, yes."

"Sorry, snakes gotta eat," I reply.

I slowly and carefully put on the tux. It takes a little time for me to get the shirt on because it hurts so much. Thankfully, cleaning out the wounds seems to have helped keep me from bleeding all over myself.

"Do you think you should rest again?" asks Nunya. "You seem even more fucked up than before."

"Yeah, I think that would be a good idea," I say. "I'm just glad I don't have some whiney ass DM telling me I just rested a little while ago and I can't rest again because it's too soon. It's not like I have any healing potions I can use instead."

"Are healing potions even a real thing?" asks Nunya.

"I'm sure they probably are but I'd never thought to ask the Wise Old Wizard for any. I probably should though."

"Would they even work on you since you have a weakness for magic?"

"Don't know. Either they'd work better than usual or they'd kill me. Probably not worth risking it. If it did work, and worked stronger than normal, maybe extra shit would grow on me, like a third arm or leg or something. No thanks," I say. "Anyway, I'm gonna catch some sleep. Wake me if there's trouble."

"Yup, will do," says Nunya.

This time I pass the fuck out. It's a good thing too because I needed it badly. By the time I finally wake up it's dark out. Nunya has actually fallen asleep next to me, still clutching her wand and Irene. She looks so tiny compared to me. She also looks peaceful like she doesn't have a care in the world. I'm glad she's getting some rest for herself and even more glad that we didn't get attacked by anything in the meantime.

I touch my chest and it feels a lot better. Not perfect, but way better than it was. It doesn't sting anymore; it just has a soreness that feels like a really deep bruise. Probably exactly what it is.

I sit upright and spend some time lost in my thoughts. Wondering what the giant purple penis is gonna look like on the inside, thinking about the fact that God is actually watching me right now, interested in what I'm doing. It was cool to know that maybe the universe did sort of revolve around me. I'd always assumed that. I look up into the sky and wave at God but nothing waves back. I guess she wouldn't do that because she's sort of hands-off.

I just spend the next several hours thinking about dumb shit, waiting for Nunya to wake up. Eventually she does, once the suns start coming up, and she looks surprised as she opens her eyes.

"Oh shit! Dick, I'm so sorry. I fell asleep," says Nunya.

"It's okay, we survived anyway," I say. "You needed the sleep."

"Yeah, you too. How are you doing?"

"I'm better. Chest still hurts but the rest of the wounds seem to have healed. Do you need anything? Food or water?"

"Water would be good. I can wait for breakfast. That meal the Wise Old Wizard made was really filling," says Nunya.

"I'll need to find a place to get you water," I say. "You don't want to drink the pond water I took a bath in. It was super disgusting by the time I was done with it."

"Agreed."

"Okay, give me a few minutes."

I fly up into the air using my super-vision to try to find a place with water. I know that fast moving water is the safest from my time in the Space Scouts. It takes a couple of minutes but I finally see a waterfall off into the distance. Swooping down, I carefully land near Nunya.

"Found it. Grab your stuff, we're heading to the sky," I say.

Nunya picks up her wand and Irene and turns around, waiting for me to hold onto her. I fly us into the air and head straight for the waterfall. It's only a few miles away, thankfully, and now that a lot of my strength has returned I can fly us there faster.

Once we touch down, Nunya starts to take off her clothes. She notices me staring at her.

"Turn the fuck around, perv," says Nunya.

"Oh, come on, you've seen me naked a bunch!" I say.

"Seriously, quit staring at me. It's making me feel uncomfortable."

"Fine, whatever," I say. I wait a few minutes then turn around anyway. Nunya is washing herself off in the waterfall and she seems to really be enjoying it. My God she has a beautiful body. Everything is perfect. She seriously gives God a run for her money. That's when she turns and looks toward me.

"Goddamn it, Dick! You're getting a boner! I fucking told you not to look at me!" yells Nunya.

"Sorry, sorry," I say, turning back around. And yup, she's right, there's a huge bulge growing in my tuxedo pants. Not that there's anything I can do about it. I figure rubbing one out in front of Nunya would bring a shitstorm of trouble for me and I don't want to ruin my chances of finally having a real friend. I'll just have to let it calm down on its own.

So I wait, and I wait, and it's not going down. Eventually, after what feels like twenty minutes, Nunya tells me I can turn around. She has her clothes back on, which look freshly washed. She has Irene in her right hand, her wand in her left, and her wet hair looks amazing. She also looks like she's still angry.

"Dick, you still have a fucking boner!" she yells. "Can't you do something about it?"

"Like what, cut it off?" I ask sarcastically.

"Yes!"

"Yeah, ain't gonna happen."

"Seriously, make it calm down."

"I tried. I tried thinking about everything I could that would make it calm down but nothing worked. I hate to say it but you're just too fucking hot. I kind of wish I hadn't looked now. I can't get your naked body out of my mind."

"You asshole!" she yells. "If you can't respect my wishes, you obviously don't respect me."

"I do respect you though," I say. "At least I'm trying to. I think you're tough, and cool, and you're good in a fight. I really am... sorry."

With that, my hard-on starts to go back down. Nunya notices but quickly looks away.

"Glad you finally got your shit under control," she says.

"It usually doesn't go down on its own. Usually doesn't have to," I say.

"Okay, can we stop talking about your meat tube for like five

seconds please?"
"Sure."
We just stand there in awkward silence.
"Are you ready to go to the purple tower?" asks Nunya.
"If you are," I reply.
"Then let's get over there."

19

Flying down to the base of the giant purple penis I notice it has a moat surrounding it. Creatures that look like mutated sharks swim in the gross murky water. I set us down a few feet away from the moat, in front of what looks like a large drawbridge door.

"Here, I've got this," says Nunya. "Hey! Is anybody home? Can you lower the drawbridge for us?"

We wait for a few moments but don't hear anything.

"Hello? Can you even hear me?" yells Nunya.

Nothing.

"We've come to retrieve some magical robes and armor, and I'm willing to go through some trials or whatever to get them," she says.

Nada.

"Open up or we'll burn your stupid giant penis down and you with it!" she yells.

Still nothing.

"Fine." She turns to me, "Dick, you know what to do."

"On it."

I fly across the moat to the top of the drawbridge and pry the drawbridge door open, pulling it down into place so that Nunya can cross. Once she's inside I let go and the drawbridge doesn't close on its own. I feel a little weird leaving it open because who knows what assholes might show up unannounced?

The inside of the base of the penis isn't what I'd imagined. It's dimly lit and set up like a museum, featuring magician paraphernalia from Earth Uno back before real magic existed. It's kind of cool if you're into that sort of thing. Pairs of old handcuffs, crystal balls, posters, magic hats; you name it. It would make a good gift shop if the Mad Wizard ever wanted to sell their stuff.

In the middle of the room, in a large glass case with a spotlight aimed at it, seems to be the most important piece: an old straightjacket, worn apparently by some guy named Houdini. I'm not sure who the guy was but he must have been pretty crazy if they put him in a straightjacket. Makes sense that someone named the Mad Wizard would be into crazy magicians.

"This place is making me feel a little uncomfortable," says Nunya.

"What, you don't like magicians?" I ask.

"It's not that. I feel like we're being watched."

"Did the cameras in the corners give it away?"

"That and I hear some quiet, creepy breathing through the loudspeakers."

"Funny, even with my super hearing I hadn't noticed," I say. I look around and see at the back of the room an overly ornate elevator. It fits the theme of some of the posters and magic devices in the room; red and gold with ornate creatures from the Chinese zodiac around the frame.

As we wander to the elevator it opens for us.

"Hey, to whoever's watching, how do we know that this elevator isn't some sort of deathtrap?" asks Nunya.

A few seconds of silence make me tense.

"Because I could have killed you the moment you set foot here," says a deep, garbled voice over the speakers.

"Oh really?" replies Nunya.

"Really. I was able to blow up an entire planet. Do you think I'd have a hard time killing two people such as yourselves? Especially since your muscle-bound friend seems particularly susceptible to magic?"

"Okay, so if you're so powerful then why didn't you kill us when we landed?" asks Nunya.

"Because everyone's so scared to come here that I never have any company. Do you know how horrible it is to be all powerful and have no one to talk to?" asks the Mad Wizard.

"Yeah, actually I do," I say. "And so does God. But I don't know how a chick as hot as God could ever be lonely."

"Wait, did you just refer to God as a 'hot chick'?" asks the Mad Wizard.

"Yeah, I met her and she was a total babe. I would have fucked her if she'd been into it but she just kind of ignored me."

"Well, isn't that special for you," says the Mad Wizard. "So you've come here to procure the Mercerian Robes and Platemail of Justice? I mean I'm just assuming since I can't think of any other reason you'd come here."

"Yes," says Nunya. "I don't have any superpowers and I need some sort of protection against the Sloths of Buzzworld."

"That makes sense," says the Mad Wizard over the loudspeakers. "Evil fucks those Sloths. They're like really adorable death ninjas."

"Kind of like the Meows you sicked on us," I reply.

"I did no such thing. They attacked you on their own. I have no reason to kill you, honestly. And again, I could kill you if I wanted to, and already would have if that was my inclination. So please, get on the elevator so we can have some tea together."

I look at Nunya and we shrug at each other. A few seconds go by and I get tired of just waiting around so I get into the elevator. Holding the door, Nunya follows me inside. The elevator cabin is covered in brass, polished to a high sheen that reflects our images. I turn around to the doors as they close.

For a second it feels like we're in free fall then suddenly we're rocketing toward the top of the dick. Hopefully we don't go shooting out of it like a couple of sperm because that really would be the icing on top of the humiliation birthday cake. Thankfully, as we get closer to the top, we slow down. We come to a stop on the forty-second floor which seems like an excessive number of floors for someone who lives by themselves.

The elevator doors open, and as unprepared as I was for the lobby of this place, I'm even less prepared for what I see. The top floor of the penis palace is decorated like the living room of an eighty-year-old woman who likes the color magenta a disturbing amount. Shelves stacked with creepy dolls and knick-knacks line the walls, and in the gaps between decorative plates are framed portraits, proudly displayed. The furniture matches the odd decor; crazy magenta floral patterns and brown wooden ornate tables covered in a barrage of doilies. It's starting to give me a headache.

"What... the... fuck?" whispers Nunya.

I just shrug.

"Come in." The words waft from a cream and magenta fabric wingback chair that is turned away from us, centered in the bizarre room. "I already have our tea ready."

I walk in front of Nunya, just in case, but she doesn't seem too worried at the moment.

"Please sit," says the voice.

I move around the chair and opposite it are two more of the same white and magenta wingbacks. Nunya and I both sit down on them. I have to say, what I'm seeing is a bit confusing. Instead of an angry looking man with a pointy hat and beard I'm confronted with an elderly woman who looks like she could be someone's great-grandma. And even though she looks ancient, with gray hair, wrinkles, magenta robe and matching bunny slippers, she has a twinkle in her eye that lets me know she is still very much with it mentally, despite her eccentricity.

"Not what you expected?" asks the Mad Wizard.

"Well, I thought wizards were only men. And women who

practice magic are called witches," I admitted.

"Young man you very much are ignorant to such things then. There are of course female wizards, just as there are male witches."

"Male witches? Who'd want to be a male witch?" I ask.

"Seriously? You really need some lessons about sexism," mumbles Nunya.

"So, then what's the difference between wizards and witches?" I ask.

"Wizards derive their power from gods and demons whereas witches derive their power from nature," says the Mad Wizard. "Also, the types of spells differ. I for one cannot reanimate corpses or brew love potions or curse human beings. But I can cast fireballs and make things teleport, and charm inanimate objects into doing my bidding.

"Ohhhhhhh," I say. "Kind of like the Wise Old Wizard."

"You mean Steve?" asks the Mad Wizard.

"Steve? Steve who?" I reply.

"Oh, he hasn't told you his name? So you just call him the Wise Old Wizard then? Yes, Steve was his name when I was married to him."

"Wait, the two of you were married? Why didn't he ever tell me?" I ask.

"Who knows. The man loves his secrets. It's why we didn't work out. That and he thought I was a bit crazy. I do have a temper, admittedly," says the Mad Wizard.

"You think?" says Nunya.

"So did the manufacturer on planet Willingham really steal your plans for a 100-in-1 magic kit?" I ask.

"Oh, is that the rumor that went around? No, it wasn't anything as mundane as all that. The owner of the company was having an affair with Steve and I took umbrage to it. Especially since she was a Bloopnarp."

"Gross," says Nunya.

"Hey, who's the judgemental one now?" I say.

"Me, and I don't care," says Nunya.

"Anyway, I blew up the planet once I was sure I'd scared everyone away. I didn't want to kill anyone, I just wanted the universe to know not to fuck with me," says the Mad Wizard.

I choke back my laughter at her use of the word 'fuck'.

"So why did you curse the toys to attack people?" I ask.

"I just wanted everyone to stay away from me for a while. Oh, and it was a charm I used, not a curse. Unfortunately, I never figured out the counterspell to turn off the charm so I've been stuck here all alone ever since. I can't leave the planet otherwise they'll attack me too," says the Mad Wizard.

"Well, why don't you just put a second charm on them that overrides the first charm and makes them nice instead?" I ask.

"Oh."

"Oh?"

"Oh. I hadn't thought of that," says the Mad Wizard, sheepishly. "That might actually work."

The little old granny walks over to the window and opens it. We watch as she waves her arm arounds and starts speaking in some weird language I don't recognize. After a brief moment a bright flash of purple fills the room and her body projects a massive cone of energy out into the sky.

"There, that should do it. Thank you for the idea..." starts the Mad Wizard.

"Dick. My name is Dick."

"Of course it is, Dear. And my name is Maggie," says Maggie the Mad Wizard. "And you are?"

"Nunya. Charmed."

"No, not yet, but we'll just have to wait and see," says Maggie, giggling.

Nunya looks both worried and puzzled.

"Sorry, just a little wizard humor," says Maggie. "So let's get down to the matter at hand. You've come for the robes and armor, correct?"

"Yes," says Nunya.

"Okay, well I have three challenges for you. If you accomplish all of them I'll give you the robes and armor. And if you don't..."

"I'll die?" asks Nunya, worried.

"No, nothing as horrible as that. You'll be turned into a Bloopnarp," says Maggie.

"No! I'd rather die," says Nunya.

"I'm sorry, but I do my best to not kill people. It's not in my nature," says Maggie. "I hope you can understand."

Nunya turns to me. "Dick, there has to be another way! I don't want to be a Bloopnarp!"

"Well, how hard are the challenges?" I ask.

"Hmmm, on a scale of one to ten I'd say thirteen," says Maggie.

"Hard pass," says Nunya.

"Look, we've made it this far and I think it's fair for you to go through this since I've been chewed on by toys and hit by stray lightning bolts trying to get you your money," I say.

"Money I wouldn't need if you hadn't destroyed my bar," replies Nunya.

"You're kind of beating a dead horse up a tree."

"Wait, you destroyed her bar? Why did you do that? Did she cheat on you?" asks Maggie.

"No, we definitely aren't a couple," says Nunya. "He demolished it when he was fighting with some Unicorns."

"Oh. Unicorns are assholes," says Maggie.

"I know, right?" I reply.

"So, when do we start?" asks Nunya, clearly still concerned.

"Well, I can administer the first challenge right now if you think you're ready."

"Uh, sure. May as well get it over with," replies Nunya.

"Good. First, you must pass the Bechdel test," says Maggie.

"What's the Bechdel test?" I ask.

"The Bechdel test is a test to see if a piece of fiction, whether it be a movie, book, etc. represents female characters a minimally acceptable amount. Essentially, two women who must be named have to have a conversation about something other than a male," says Maggie.

"So what you're saying is we need to have a conversation and it can't be about guys," says Nunya.

"Unless you brought another female along with you to talk to," replies Maggie.

"Sorry, fresh out," says Nunya. "Alright, what should we talk about?"

"It's your challenge, dear. A better question is: what do you think we should talk about?"

"Um, do you know much about military stuff?" asks Nunya.

"No, I admit that I do not."

"Running and owning a bar?"

"I don't."

"Street hockey?"

"No."

"Books?"

"Why yes, I love books! Do you?" asks Maggie.

"I'm not much of a reader," admits Nunya. "More of a movie woman myself."

"Ah. Well it seems that we don't have a lot in common, unfortunately. Maybe if we just talk about life in general we can come up with something."

"Maybe. How about what was your magical training like? Did it take you long? Did you go to a fancy school for it? Being a wizard sounds really cool."

"Oh, you don't want to know about that," says Maggie.

"No, I really do! I've always wondered what it would be like to have magical powers," says Nunya.

"Well then where do I start? I guess I'll start at the beginning. When I was a young girl I lived in a small cupboard under my evil aunt and uncle's stairs."

"Wait, isn't that Harry Potter?" asks Nunya.

"Oh, that's right. What I meant to say is that I was apprenticing for this wizard and he wanted me to clean up his workshop so I enchanted some brooms to help me clean up and I lost control of them," says Maggie.

"That was the Sorcerer's Apprentice," says Nunya, dryly.

"Sorry, my memory isn't what it used to be. What if I told you that I helped my tiny friend who had a magic invisibility ring destroy it in a volcano?"

"Nope, that was Gandalf."

"A flock of flying monkeys helped me capture an annoying teenager and her dog?"

"Wicked Witch of the West."

"These aren't the droids you're looking for?"

"Obi-wan Kenobi."

"Shit. Okay, then I guess I can't fool you. I'll tell you my actual, real, and one-hundred percent accurate backstory," says Maggie. "When I was a teenager I started exhibiting special abilities. Abilities that happened around the same time my monthly visitor came."

"Monthly visitor? Who was that?" I ask.

"Dick, shut up. It was when she got her period, okay?" says Nunya.

"Geez, I've never had one. Sorry I don't know your weird secret women lingo."

"Anyway, as I was saying I started being able to do things, but most of them were accidents and I couldn't control them. So my parents had me tested and found out I have innate magical abilities. They sent me to the Wanda Trussler School of Magic where after eight years of studying I received my bachelor's degree in spellcasting with a minor in potion making. Once school ended I went out on my own to become a private practitioner for hire. It was kind of exciting at first; casting spells on cheating husbands, hunting down magical criminals, surveillance, that sort of thing. Eventually, though, I grew bored. Thankfully, that's when I met

Steve," said Maggie.

"Wait, sorry, you'll have to skip the Steve part since we aren't allowed to talk about guys," says Nunya.

"Right, good catch. Anyway, my life took a turn and we started travelling the galaxy, meeting new species, seeing new worlds. It was all very exciting. They really were my best years. How I miss them. But then the thing happened with the Bloopnarp and I blew up a planet."

"So then how long have you been here by yourself?" asks Nunya.

"I'd say maybe fifty years, give or take," replies Maggie.

"Holy shit that's a long time! I'm sorry that most of your life was taken away from you."

"It's okay, dear. It was of my own doing. Just wish I'd thought of recharming the toys sooner."

"What will you do now that you can travel again?" asks Nunya.

"Well, I'm not really sure. Maybe go back to places I've been to before and see if they've changed, visit friends and family, things like that."

"That sounds really nice."

"It does, doesn't it? Anyway, you have now officially passed the first test," says Maggie.

"Awesome!" says Nunya, who turns to me and tries to give me a high-five. I just shake my head 'no' at her but don't mention anything about her poo-fingers. "So what's the second test?" she asks.

"Now I will challenge you to a battle of wits! I have placed poison in one of our teacups. You choose which teacup you'll drink from and you'll also choose which teacup I drink from," says Maggie.

"Maggie?" says Nunya.

"Yes Dear?"

"Did you put poison in all three teacups?"

"Why, whatever do you mean?"

"I mean, did you put poison that you're already immune to in all three teacups?"

"Uhhhhh..."

"I knew it! I've seen the Princess Bride too. One of the greatest movies of all time. Does iocane powder ring a bell? You fell victim to one of the classic blunders. Never go in against a Sicilian when death is on the line!"

I was fairly proud of Nunya for outsmarting Maggie the Mad Wizard. Hopefully Nunya's taunting doesn't make Maggie angry because I don't think we want a repeat of planet Willingham.

"Fine," starts Maggie. "You've seen through my second ruse. Congratulations. But the first two challenges were child's play compared to what you'll find on... the thirteenth floor!"

"What's on the thirteenth floor?" asks Nunya.

"It's where the Mercerian Robe and Platemail of Justice are being kept. And you won't be able to just walk in and take them, you'll have to make your way through a gauntlet of dangers where traps and creatures are around every corner. If you're careful and cunning then you might just make it out of the labyrinth alive!"

"Anything else I should know before I go down there?"

"Oh, yes, one last thing," says Maggie, and then she starts mumbling something that neither Nunya nor I can make out.

"I'm sorry, what was that?" asks Nunya.

"Good luck, and may the odds be ever in your favor," replies Maggie.

"Hunger Games," mumbles Nunya.

With that Nunya gets up from her comfy chair, walks to the elevator, and makes her way down to the thirteenth floor.

20

I realize it's just me and Maggie now, alone. She gives me an evil little smile.

"So, uh, what do you want to do while Nunya's busy?" I ask.

"Well, to be honest I was hoping that maybe you'd have sex with me," says Maggie.

"Uhhh, aren't you a little old to be having sex? Haven't the pipe's dried up and stuff?"

"Oh, you're never too old to have sex. And I've actually kept my body in very good shape, not that I've been able to share it with anyone. In the last fifty years I've had nothin' twixt my nethers weren't run on batteries."

"You know if I do that Nunya's gonna kill me," I say.

"I thought you two weren't an item," replies Maggie. "Besides, she probably won't survive the gauntlet so what does it matter?"

"That is a fair point but I'm still injured. Yeah, that's it, I'm too injured to have sex."

Maggie pulls out a wand, says 'bippity-boppity-boo', and hits me with a ball of energy. I start to tingle then realize I'm healing rapidly like when I get hurt with non-magical things. My chest feels a hell of a lot better.

"Uh, thanks," I say.

"Oh, it wasn't for you, it was for me. I want you in top physical shape for what I have planned for you," says Maggie. That's when she gets up out of her seat and starts to undress.

"Um, okay, so let's say this happens. I need you to promise that you won't grow attached and that you understand I'm going to be leaving after this. And you have to promise not to blow up any planets because I'm leaving. Do we have a deal?"

"Deal!" she says, launching her naked body at me.

I'm actually surprised because she's right: her body looks extremely good for a woman her age. She's thin, her boobs are ample but not saggy, and her bush has been carefully trimmed into the shape of a heart.

She starts kissing me like a tornado, licking my gums, twirling her tongue around in my mouth. It's very… passionate, and it scares me a little. We kiss for several minutes and I'm just not quite feeling it. Maggie can tell when she reaches down and my tube of man-paste is only a quarter full.

"I was a little worried about this," says Maggie. "You know, I can charm myself to look like anyone. I have an idea!"

Maggie stands up and pulls out her wand. I wonder where she hid it since she's naked. Anyway, she twirls it in a circle above her head and streamers of glowing sparkles surround her until she transforms into a much, much younger woman.

"This is what I looked like when I was young. Do you like it?" she asks.

I'm stunned. She's now a beautiful blonde with long flowing hair, perfect skin, perky breasts and a small thatch of hair on her love mound. My god she's hot. My boner starts pushing hard against my tuxedo pants so I quickly pull my clothes off.

"Hot fucking damn!" I say.

Maggie leaps on top of me and lands herself squarely on my beanstalk. I lose myself to the feeling of having her wrapped around my body. It feels so incredible I wonder if she's using magic to make it feel even better than normal.

We go at it hard for what must be thirty minutes. I keep thrusting inside her chunnel, she keeps rocking against my cocking. A few more deep thrusts and she goes quiet, then explodes with sound, her scream nearly blowing out my eardrums. Magical fireworks start going off in the room, sending sparks of color everywhere. It's like the goddamn fourth of July only even better. As soon as she relaxes slightly, basking in the glow, I blow my hot load, filling her toaster oven with alfredo sauce.

We kiss for a while, just enjoying the warmth of each other's bodies. God, she was so hot when she was young. Why the fuck would Steve the Wise Old Wizard cheat on this hottie? Especially since she could change into whoever he fucking wanted her to look like. I'm gonna have a long ass talk with him the next time I see him.

"I love you, Dick Blowhard," says Maggie.

"Uh, yeah, right back at ya," I say, starting to get worried.

She smiles at me, a mischievous grin. "Ready for rounds two, three and four?"

Fuck, she used the 'L' word but I told her up front this was a one-time deal so she knows not to fall for me. Ah, what the hell, maybe if I sex her enough she won't be angry when I leave. Sore, yes. Angry, hopefully not.

So we fuck, and I mean we not only do everything in the Kama Sutra, we also do all of the things in the Kama Sutra 2, the Sequel. I completely lose track of the time and pretty much everything else until a ding comes echoing from the elevator as if it's spelling out my impending doom, which it does. The doors open wide and inside is Nunya, wearing her new armor and robes, holding a helmet and her wand, but looking torn the fuck up. A gash on her head is bleeding badly and she looks pissed. As soon as she sees Maggie, who is currently dangling from a love swing, and me with my spaghetti noodle buried deep inside her meatball maker, she gets downright hysterical.

"WHAT THE ABSOLUTE FUCK IS GOING ON, AND WHO THE FUCK IS SHE?" yells Nunya.

"It's me, Maggie," says the Mad Wizard, who whips out her wand and turns back into her old self, complete with her old lady clothes and all. My meat thermometer is still buried in her pork smoker so I pull out real quick and accidentally unleash a blast of hot sauce all over the old lady's dress.

"Uh, sorry," I mumble.

"Oh, no worries," says Maggie. "It was worth it."

"Wait, so you just fucked an old lady?" says Nunya.

"Hey, I didn't want you to hate me for being an ageist," I reply.

"Oh my God, Dick. Seriously? That's what you're going with?"

"Look, you can fuck whoever you want and I can fuck whoever I want. If that happens to be an old lady that can transform into whatever form she wants then so be it. I don't fucking judge you for who you have sex with, do I?"

"I don't go around having sex with every person I meet, and certainly not when the other person I'm helping is in mortal danger!"

"I'm sorry, okay?"

"Apology not accepted," says Nunya. "Look, I have a magic wand, and armor, and a robe and shit. I should be able to take down the Sloths on my own. So you can just fuck off for all I care. I'll handle my own problems."

With that Nunya turns around, gets back on the elevator and leaves.

21

"You can stay here as long as you like, young man," says Maggie.

"Hey, uh, thanks for everything. Seriously. But yeah, I gotta go," I say.

"It actually sounds like you don't. She doesn't want anything to do with you so you're free and clear to do whatever you want."

"Hey, I've saved the galaxy more times than I can count. Like, literally, I lost track. But I don't think I've always done the right thing. And even though Nunya isn't interested in me, I... well I guess I care about her. So I gotta go and hope she gives me a chance to fix this," I say.

"Suit yourself. But if she really doesn't want anything to do with you, at least consider coming back to me."

"Thanks Mags, you've been great. And I'll think about it, okay? You know, one thing you might consider is Steve has been single for as long as I've known him. Maybe you could give him a call or something."

"I think that ship sailed fifty years ago. The bad feelings between us were too strong then and I'd bet they'd be even worse now," says Maggie.

"Maybe. But sometimes people change. I'm trying real hard to change. Maybe Steve has changed too."

"I'll... consider it."

"I hope it helps. Anyway, I need to get down to the ground. Is there something faster than the elevator?" I ask.

"Sure, go out the window." Maggie waves her wand and the window opens. I smile, give her a peck on the cheek then run and dive out the window.

I look down and instead of using my flight powers to speed up I just let myself fall. I figure if I move too fast I might create a sonic boom and either scare Nunya or damage the tower, or both. Once I get a hundred feet off the ground, I aim my legs downward and use my flight power to slow my fall then land as gently and quietly as I can. I can't see Nunya yet.

I turn toward the tower's front door and after a few moments Nunya finally emerges, still looking like she lost a fight to a meat grinder. She looks more disappointed than angry when she sees me.

"Look, I'm really, really sorry," I say.

"Don't care," she replies.

"I don't blame you for hating me. I kinda… hate myself too. And I know that you're smart, and strong, and probably could take the Sloths by yourself. But even though you don't need me I think that maybe I need you. I need you to help me be a better person. And I think it's already been working. I want to get better. Please help me," I say.

"Why the fuck should I help you? Seriously? You certainly don't docorvo it. All you've done is fuck up my life. Why would I waste my goddamn time helping you?"

"Because you're a good person. Whether you see it or not you're a good person."

Nunya looks like I punched her in the gut. She seems torn, like she doesn't know what the right thing to do is.

"Please," I start to say. "I really need your help."

Nunya turns away from me. After what feels like an eternity she finally speaks. "Fuck!"

"So, you'll help me?" I ask.

"No, but you'll help me. I realized I have no idea how to get the fuck back from here. We don't have a ship, and even though I can probably fly now because of my new robes, going through the portal probably won't work. Have you ever tried flying through a portal without being inside of a ship?"

"Nope. I'm pretty sure it'd rip me apart. I'm tough as shit, and even though it feels like nothing to go through when you're in a ship, that's because it has the right equipment to protect you from being stretched a near infinite amount as you pass through one."

"So then we're fucked?" asks Nunya.

"Actually, maybe not. All we need to do is make it to the security ship next to the portal. Then we set it for our destination and fly through the portal," I say.

"Then what about Maggie? Won't she be stuck here?"

"Good point. I guess if we flew somewhere that we could buy a new ship we could just set the security ship on autopilot to fly back to where it came from."

Nunya's thought gears continue grinding.

"Alright. But if we're going to do this, I don't want you talking to me more than absolutely necessary because I'm this close to burning you to death with a fireball. Do you understand?"

"Yeah, I understand," I reply.

I finally take a good look at her new robe and armor. The armor is pretty cool; it's silver, except for a gold raven emblem on the shield, and the whole thing emits light. Comes with a really cool helmet, too. It looks like something a paladin might wear. The robe is a lot different than that. It looks like what you'd imagine a royal queen would wear, with fuzzy white trim on the top and bottom, and the material in between is a soft pink color. It really doesn't seem to fit Nunya's aesthetic but I don't mention it to her because I don't want to become fried Dick. But I do ask a question, risking my life, because it could save hers.

"Do you know if the armor and robe will protect you from outer space? Will you be able to breathe, or at least not die until we get to the security ship?" I ask.

"Don't know yet. So far I can tell that I'm stronger than normal. And once I put it on there was nothing in the labyrinth that could hurt me. Oh, and like I said, I can fly now thanks to the robe. Guess the only way we'll find out is if I try," she says.

"Before you do, why don't you let me heal you," I offer.

"No. Just because I need your help right now doesn't mean I'll let you touch me."

"Are you sure, because you have a pretty bad cut on your head."

"I'll be fine. Mind your own goddamn business."

"Roger. Are you ready to try flying to the security ship?" I ask.

Without saying anything Nunya starts hovering off the ground and puts on her helmet. Before she starts flying away I ask her one last question. "I see you still have your wand, but what happened to Irene?"

"Lost her. She was destroyed in the labyrinth. Forgot to tell you," says Nunya.

"That's it? You're not going to apologize for destroying probably the last friend I have in the universe?"

"It was a blaster. Sure, I thought for a second it was cool that you named them, but it was just a blaster."

"Not to me."

"Well, I don't really care what you think or feel right now, Dick. You can buy a new one."

"You can't buy friends, and she was my friend," I say.

"That sounds pretty pathetic and desperate," says Nunya.

Without thinking I punch her right in the middle of her armor. She goes sailing. Even though I could, I don't stop her from smashing into a grove of nearby trees. She recovers faster than I would have guessed. This time she's angry, and instead of trying to avoid her attack I stand perfectly still. Her fist connects with my face and actually hurts my jaw pretty badly. Shit, I forgot her attacks are magic based now and can actually damage me.

She takes another swing at my head but I duck out of the way, waiting for the next punch. When she finally tries to hit me again I parry by grabbing her wrist and launching her high into the air. I shoot up into the sky after her. It doesn't take me long to catch up with her because she finally remembers she can fly, and instead of going higher she stops. That's when I pass her.

Instead of fighting with her more I head toward the security ship. I keep an eye on her to see if she follows and she does. Even though I don't really need to breathe I can tell that the air is starting to thin out. I look down and Nunya is still angry, trying her best to catch up with me, but I also notice that the thinning atmosphere is affecting her. As we get closer to outer space I see that Nunya is grabbing at her throat. Shit.

I stop, turn around and grab her. Her body goes limp as she passes out. I just hope I can get her breathing again before it does any permanent damage to her. I speed up, causing a sonic boom just before I reach the ground. I have to pull up then reverse my flight just to slow down in time. After a few more tense seconds I'm able to reach the ground.

She's not breathing and she's turning blue. I start doing chest compressions but her armor is keeping me from being able to exert any force on her. I do my best to unstrap her chestplate and get it off of her. I don't want to damage it because she'll need it later, and after a moment of struggle I'm able to get it off of her. Going back to chest compressions I realize that maybe I can just heal her if her heart hasn't stopped. I put my hands on the top of her chest where her skin is exposed and try my healing powers but they don't do anything. Fuck.

I start chest compressions again and I start giving her breaths. I'd been taught you really just want to do chest compressions to keep the heart going until a medical team can get to you but there's no medical team coming. So I give her breaths and keep giving her chest compressions. I actually start to cry because I'm so goddamn scared of losing her. I keep giving her compressions and breaths but it doesn't seem to be working. After what feels like hours, but is only minutes, she starts to cough. Thank God she's alive.

"Nunya, are you okay?" I ask stupidly.

"No, I feel like shit," she says between coughs. "What the fuck happened?"

"You apparently can't breathe in outer space. I had to save you, and give you mouth-to-mouth," I explain.

"Mouth-to-mouth? You fucking asshole! When I said 'no', I meant 'no'. You could have just used your healing powers," says Nunya.

"I tried and they didn't work."

"But wait, does that mean that I died? I actually died?"

"Yeah," I reply.

"And you used CPR to bring me back?"

"Yeah."

"Fuck." I give her a few moments to take some breaths. "Why did you punch me?"

"Because you were being an asshole," I say.

"Don't ever do that again. Didn't anyone tell you hitting women is wrong?"

"Hitting anyone is wrong," I say. "But I hit you because I see you more as a person than a damsel in distress. I guess in a really fucked up way I'm saying I respect you enough to hit you. Especially since I knew your armor made you invincible."

"It still really hurt, motherfucker."

"Good. Pain is good because pain is the best teacher."

"I've got nothing to learn from you," says Nunya.

"Who knows, maybe you do. Anyway, stay here and recover for a while. I'll go get the spaceship."

"Yeah, fine, fuck off," she mumbles.

I turn, slowly hover, then when I'm a safe distance from Nunya I start to pick up speed. Once I reach the edge of the atmosphere I go supersonic. If I were still in the atmosphere it would have produced a boom but since I'm outside of it, nothing.

It's weird flying through the asteroid field of toys; they just bounce off of me as I run into them, none of the malice or evil still powering them. It doesn't take me very long to get to the security ship, but when I do, I realize I don't know how to hack into the controls to let myself in. That's Nunya's game. I also can't punch my way in because we need the ship intact so that Nunya can breathe while we're inside it. Goddamn it. So I turn and fly back to Nunya. When I get there she's still pissed at me but I do my best to ignore it.

"Why the fuck didn't you bring back the spaceship?" asks Nunya.

"Because I don't know how to get inside without damaging it. You're the hacker, so can you teach me how to hack real quick so I can get in?" I ask.

"Uh, no. Hacking isn't something you just pick up. It takes a huge amount of training and knowledge to do."

"Well, fuck."

"Yeah. Hmm. Wait, I have an idea. You could just tow the security ship here. But that'll only work if the I-Brake isn't set," says Nunya.

"The Inertia Brake?"

"Yeah. 'Cause if that fucker is on, no matter how hard you try to move that spaceship, it ain't goin' nowhere. Where are you goin'? You're goin' nowhere."

"If it is set, is there some way I can either turn it off or break it so that it isn't working anymore?" I ask.

"Not really. It's the normal inertia circuits being set to a velocity of zero in all directions. And we need the inertia circuits for it to go anywhere."

"How the crap do you know all this stuff?"

"I like to read. More knowledge is always a good thing."

"I dunno, I try to avoid it if I can," I say.

"And you obviously do a good job of it."

"Right. Anyway, I need to go back and hope that the parking brake isn't set. What do I do if it is?" I ask.

"We'll burn that bridge when we come to it," says Nunya.

"Okay."

I turn and fly up into the sky again. This time I don't even think much about the trip, it's kind of like I'm on autopilot. Just flying through the toys, making my way to the spaceship. It doesn't even feel like it takes me as long.

Once I get to the ship I go to the far side, the side facing away from planet O'Brien, and start shoving. Thankfully, I'm able to move it. If I couldn't I probably would have had to talk to Maggie and get her help, and at this point I think that would make for both an annoying and possibly boring sub-plot. Just ask Tom Bombadil.

The ship isn't that hard to shove, and despite its mass I'm able to move it at about the same speed I was flying at before. Thank God for the lack of gravity in outer space. Man, I wish I could thank God personally. Thank her with my meat tenderizer, if you know what I mean. Still can't believe how hot she is.

Towing the ship down to planet O'Brien is a bit more difficult. I give the ship a shove then fly around to the side facing the planet and do my best to slow down its descent. It starts to heat up from the friction caused by re-entering the atmosphere, me along with it, but because it isn't magical it doesn't hurt, and amazingly it doesn't damage my tux.

I have to look over my shoulder to steer, to make sure that I land near the purple penis tower. I'm able to slow it up enough that as I get closer to the ground it starts to cool down and the bottom is no longer red. It's a good thing because I figure bringing a molten hot spaceship down into a field could be a problem. After several minutes I have her down on the ground. Nunya comes walking up.

"So you were able to bring it back after all," says Nunya.

"Anyway, give me a few minutes and I should have us inside."

"You might want to wait a bit for it to cool down. It's still pretty hot."

"My magic armor should protect me. At least, it protects me from regular damage, so I'd think it'd protect me from heat." Nunya reaches out her hand and carefully touches the hull of the ship.

"See, it's fine."

I follow her over to the airlock and she starts tapping away at its control panel. After a few seconds she's able to get the door open. We climb inside and she shuts the door behind her. A woosh of air fills the room then Nunya hacks the next control panel, letting us inside the ship.

It's the exact same model of security ship as the one we hijacked before so I know where the bridge is. Nunya follows behind, checking everything out as she goes. I try to stay alert in case we were wrong about there being nobody aboard.

"Hello? Is there anybody out there?" I say, smirking. "I've always wanted to say that."

"If you could keep the rock and roll references to a minimum, that'd be great," quips Nunya.

"Only if you keep all the mean references to a minimum," I say in baby talk, just to annoy her.

"God I hate you."

"Feeling's mutual."

By the time we've finished bickering we've made it to the bridge. I just stand there and let Nunya do her thing. It only takes her a few moments to get everything online and running, and before you know it she's not only changed where the gate will take us but she's flying us straight at the space-asshole.

"See ya, Maggie," I say, as we are instantly transported to the other side of the galaxy.

22

"Wait, you brought us to the Lauratine Abyss?" I say.

"Yeah, you said we needed a spaceship," replies Nunya.

"I didn't think we'd come to a place like this, though. It's mega sleazy. Like, the used ship salespeople are considered upstanding citizens in comparison to the rest of the scum that lives here."

"I figured you'd fit right in."

"Yeah, your mom," I reply.

"Actually, yes, my mom. Both of my parents own a dealership here. I figure they'll help us out."

"Oh, shit, I'll actually get to meet your folks?"

"No, I'll take care of everything. You just sit there and look ugly."

"I'm not ugly, you're ugly," I reply. "And do you have any way of paying for a spaceship?"

"Well, no. But it's my parents. I'd think they'd be willing to help me, or at least let me purchase one on credit," says Nunya.

"They're used ship salespeople. Good luck with that. I haven't met one that wouldn't sell their firstborn to some random pervert for a nickel. Hey, speaking of which, are you their firstborn?"

"No, they won't sell me to you, if that's what you're thinking. And I'm their only-born; no siblings."

"Either way I still have credit. Is it shit credit? Yes. But it's better than what you've got," I point out.

"Fine, I guess you can meet them. But so help me if you end up fucking my mother I will kill you. I'm not joking, Dick. Do you understand me?"

"But what if your mom is really fucking hot and she's into it?" I ask.

"No, Dick, no! You are completely forbidden. There are no reasons, no excuses. I will kill you and you will be dead. Forever. End of discussion," says Nunya.

"Fine, you don't have to bite my head off," I reply.

"Apparently I do because you'll fuck anything that moves. And sometimes shit that doesn't."

"That's not true, I only fuck moving things! You take that back!"

"Yeah, that'll be the day."

"Hey, maybe instead of going on this stupid fucking adventure, maybe you can move back in with mommy and daddy and they can take care of your stupid, sarcastic ass."

We both stew in silence. Nunya steers the ship for one of the smaller planets, a blue and gray one that looks really shitty. Of course, all the planets in the Lauratine Abyss look shitty. I really hate being here because I remember when I was a kid this used to be a nice place to live. Slowly over time more and more spaceship dealerships started replacing the places I used to love. Favorite restaurants, hangouts, that sort of thing. Now it just screams of cheap suits and even cheaper booze. It's where dreams go to die.

Eventually, we land in a field just outside of a very large and very crappy looking used ship lot. The sun is setting which makes things seem even more lifeless. There's a giant sign with letters lined in light bulbs that reads 'Business' Used Spaceship Business' and right underneath on a faded, hand-painted sign is the slogan, 'Here, we give YOU the Business.' Catchy. I can see why Nunya is so damn angry all the time. I'd probably have permanent PMS too if I grew up around a place like this.

"Okay, I need you to heal me now," says Nunya.

"I thought you didn't want me to touch you," I reply.

"I don't, but I also don't want my folks to freak out because I'm beat the fuck up."

"So your fear of what your parents think overrides your hatred of me. Got it."

Nunya looks pissed.

"Are you gonna fucking heal me or not?" she asks, gritting her teeth.

"Yeah, I'll heal you."

I put my hand on her forehead and after a few moments the wound on her head is healed. She goes off to find a bathroom to clean up in, and when she returns she looks much better, like you wouldn't know she'd nearly died in a labyrinth trying to get some magical items.

Doing my best to wait patiently, Nunya types a few things into one of the ship's control panels.

"What are you up to?" I ask.

"Setting the auto-pilot so that in about an hour the ship will fly itself back to the Riegel Cluster. Should give us time to figure out whether we'll have new wings or not."

"Cool."

"C'mon," she says, "we need to get us a spaceship."

We leave the bridge and I follow her out of the airlock into the stale, exhaust fume smelling air. The ground is gravel which I think is weird because gravel would get into some of the older model's engines, but I guess it's cheap. Every expense spared except of course for their sign.

Nunya walks toward the little building in the middle of the lot. While I follow her I take a look around at all the beat up, worn out spaceships. My guess is this place is where trade-ins end up that no one wants. Ships that barely function. Ships that smell like space-dog piss. Ships that might get you to where you're going but it's iffy whether you'll still be alive when you arrive. Yeah, as much as I hate the Lauratine Abyss, I specifically hate this used spaceship lot even more.

Opening the door, Nunya walks in and I follow just behind her. Inside it looks even shabbier than the outside; everything's about sixty years outdated and barely functional. The furniture looks terrible, the coffee maker in the corner looks like a fire hazard, and the lights overhead flicker just enough to be migraine inducing.

Sitting at desks on opposite sides of the room are a man and a woman. They both look surprised, like someone slapped them in their faces with a wet trout. The woman gets up first and comes over, fidgeting like a hyperactive kid who has to pee really bad. The man gets up and his jaw just hangs open as if he wants to catch flies in it, which he probably does.

"Honey, you're alive," says the woman.

"Yeah Mom, I'm alive," replies Nunya.

"We're glad to see you," says the man, who I'm guessing is her dad.

"We can't stay long. We just need a ship," says Nunya, quickly getting down to business.

"You're not even going to give us a hug and introduce us to your friend?" says her mom.

"Yeah, I can hug you but this guy isn't a friend. He's a shithead who owes me money," replies Nunya. She reaches out and gives her folks a hug.

"Language, young lady. And what the hell are you wearing? You look ridiculous," says her dad.

"It's magic armor and a magic robe. They basically make me invincible, super strong, and I can fly," says Nunya. "Also, I'm an adult and I can say whatever the fuck I want."

"Not in our place of business," says her dad. "And why should we believe another one of your crazy stories? There's no way you have super clothes or whatever."

"Wanna bet?" says Nunya. With that she walks outside for a second, flies up into the sky, and when she lands she punches the ground, sending a splash of gravel into the air, leaving a deep impression. Once she dusts off she comes back inside. "See? Are you going to take me seriously now?"

It takes several seconds for either of her parents to react.

"Of course we take you seriously, honey," says her mom, trying to defuse the situation.

"Anyway, shithead, these are my parents: Ashley and Robbie. Mom and Dad this is my sidekick, Dick Blowhard," says Nunya.

"I'm not your fucking sidekick," I say. "But nice to meet you both."

"No way, seriously?" starts her dad. "You're *the* Dick Blowhard? The private investigator that's saved the galaxy a few dozen times?"

"Hundreds of times, really, but who's counting?" I say. "Always nice to meet a fan."

He starts shaking my hand a little too much. I eventually have to pull away.

"Wait, you know who this loser is too?" asks Nunya.

"Of course! We watch the news, you know. Oh, and there's that new TV series made about his exploits. It's called 'The Pan-Galactic Adventures of Dick Blowhard'," says Nunya's mom.

"Sounds fucking awesome," I say.

"We thought so," says her dad. "Without the fucking part."

"What kind of show would it be without the fucking part? Lame, that's what," I reply.

"That's not what I…" says Nunya's dad before I interrupt him.

"I better get residuals," I say.

"I'm sure you'll be handsomely rewarded for your handsomeness," says Nunya's mom. Nunya looks super angry at her. "Uh, but what would someone as rich and famous as you need residuals for?"

"Because someone got me neck deep in shit and my place got burnt to the ground," I say.

"Wait, you're blaming me for the Sloth attack that had nothing to do with me? And it was my place that got destroyed first," says Nunya.

"Look, all I'm gonna say is that my life was fucking great before I met you. Now I'm broke, I have no place to live, I'm constantly being insulted and harassed, my weapons have been lost or destroyed, my ride was demolished, and I only have one change of clothes now, the ones I have on. So yeah, maybe I do blame you for most of that," I say.

"If you hadn't gotten into a fight with your Unicorn buddies then 90% of that wouldn't have happened! All this is your fault, not mine!"

"If that's what helps you sleep at night."

"Wait, Unicorns?" starts Nunya's dad. "Those are real?"

"Yeah, and they're all assholes. Just trust me on that," I respond.

"Actually, he's right. But you're an asshole too, Dick," says

Nunya.

"Never said I wasn't. Anyway, can you nice people help us find a safe ship that will get us around the galaxy? And keep in mind that your daughter, your own flesh-and-blood, will be riding in this thing. Make sure it won't fall apart in the middle of a fight, or travelling from one dangerous place to another, because that just sounds like some lame subplot. With the kind of adventure we're on we don't need that kind of distraction. Besides, we already went through that once and we'd kind of be repeating ourselves," I explain.

"Uhhhhh, sure," says Nunya's dad. "Actually, we do have a couple of nicer ships in our underground vault. We keep them there because sometimes pirates and smugglers come through looking for things to steal in the middle of the night. All our outside inventory is kept outside for a reason. No one would bother stealing any of it."

"So you only make money from your underground vault?" I ask.

"Oh, no, we still make money off the rust heaps. There's plenty of people out there who just need something that will get them by," says Nunya's mom. "We do inspect them and repair them when necessary. We're not out to cheat anyone. Yes, they're outdated and ugly but they all run, and run safely."

"Alright, now that we've established you're not assholes, and I'm glad to hear that, let's look at the nicer ships," I say.

Nunya cringes at me. I just shrug.

"Sure, let's do that," says Nunya's dad.

He walks over to a desk in the middle of the room, picks up the phone then types in a whole bunch of numbers. After a few seconds the entire room starts descending. It's like something out of a trashy spy novel but it's still fucking cool. We don't have to travel very far down, thankfully, because honestly I don't like the feeling of being trapped. Being underground like this is giving me the heebie-jeebies.

The elevator stops moving with a soft metallic clack. I look over at Nunya's mom who's been hungrily staring at me the whole time. And I was right, the woman is smoking hot. Nunya definitely gets her looks from her mom. But I can't bang her if I'm ever going to be on Nunya's less bad side. I don't think she would ever forgive me for doing that, not that she's really forgiven me for anything.

At the far end of the room is a corridor that starts to light up when we approach, revealing a fairly fancy hallway. As we walk down the length of its pink marbled-floor I notice that the door handles on both sides are covered in gold. The doors themselves are glass and reveal small offices which I assume are for other employees. I'm surprised at how nice it is considering how shitty everything upstairs is. It makes me start to wonder if Nunya's parents are actually up to no good.

"Hey, Mom and Dad, are you guys up to no good?" I ask.

They laugh.

"Whatever do you mean?" asks Nunya's mom.

"I just mean that upstairs everything looks like shit. I get that it's deliberate to keep the space pirates and smugglers at bay, but I can tell just by this hallway that you're making a lot of money and I was wondering where it was coming from," I say.

Nunya hits me in the chest and it hurts pretty bad. Her mom responds anyway.

"It's totally natural to question that," says Nunya's mom. "But once you see the ships we have back here I'm sure you'll come to realize that selling even a few of these a year can finance quite an operation. The Underground is definitely where we make the bulk of our profits."

"The Underground?" I repeat.

"Yes, that's what we call this, our elite sales area," says Nunya's dad. "We're very well known in only the highest circles, people who have a lot of burgmorps and want to maintain their privacy. The business upstairs is a bit of a false front for us. It keeps traffic low so when a potential elite customer arrives we don't have to shoo a bunch of people away."

"And by 'shooing', do you mean liquidating?" I ask.

"Dick, what the hell is wrong with you?" asks Nunya.

"Hey, I just want to know who I'm getting into bed with," I say, noticing Nunya's mom lick her lips. "Metaphorically speaking." Nunya's mom now looks pouty.

"And to answer your question, Dick, no, we don't have anyone killed. Why would we? It's bad business and eventually news of disappearances travels fast. Not only that but it's morally repugnant," says Nunya's dad.

"Speaking of which, why did you name your daughter Nunya?" I ask.

I notice that Nunya's really pissed. Shit.

"Mom, Dad, you don't need to answer that," says Nunya.

"Oh, I think they do," I say.

"Yes, it was one of our worst decisions," says Nunya's mom. "We thought it was funny at the time but didn't really think about what it would be like for Nunya to have to live with it the rest of her life. We were young and stupid and thought we were being hysterical. We eventually did offer to have it legally changed, but every time we'd bring it up she'd give us the finger and storm off to her room. We figure it's at least part of the reason she's so tough."

"Pain in the ass is more like it. But yeah, maybe you're right.

Maybe she'd be a much happier person, and wouldn't be constantly insulting people, if she'd been named Sarah, or Jennifer or something," I say.

"She's definitely her own person," says her dad.

"Guys, I'm right fucking here, okay? Stop talking about me like I'm a ghost or something," says Nunya.

Just as she says that we finally reach the showroom floor. It's massive, which makes sense because spaceships take up a lot of space. I'm truly impressed by the size of it, which is saying something because I'm used to being the one to get that reaction. You know, because of the size of my stripper pole. And by stripper pole I mean dick. And by dick I mean penis.

"So do you have anything you're looking for in particular? Anything we should know about that will affect your decision?" asks Nunya's mom.

"I guess the first thing I should mention is that I'm temporarily broke, at least until the insurance comes through on my mansion. If that ever happens," I say.

"That shouldn't be a problem as long as your credit is good," says Nunya's dad.

"It's fucking perfect, like me. Unless it's not."

"I'm not sure what you mean," says Nunya's dad.

"Well, I only have a single possession, which is a one-of-a-kind painting of me. It's basically priceless, but it's the only collateral I have right now," I say.

"Is it possible for us to see the painting? If you want we could house it here and protect it while you're using it as collateral," says Nunya's mom.

"No offense, but how do I know you won't just turn around and sell it?" I ask.

"Dick, they're not going to sell it," says Nunya.

"You don't know that! Seriously, it's the last thing I own other than this tux. If I give it to them and they turn around and sell it I have nothing."

"Seriously, you actually think someone would be willing to buy that piece of shit painting?" asks Nunya.

"Yeah, like a shit-ton of people. I'm a fucking hero and my image commands a fucking premium. It doesn't get more premium than this, Baby," I say, pointing to my face.

"Pardon me while I go barf in the corner," says Nunya.

"No, I don't think I will," I say.

"Um, sorry to interrupt, but can we take a look at the portrait then?" asks Nunya's mom.

"Fine," I say, pulling out my bag of ultimate wonders. It takes me a moment to fish the painting out. I hold it up for all of them to

see.

"Exquisite," says Nunya's mom.

"Inspiring," says Nunya's dad.

"Pathetic," says Nunya.

"You know what, Nunya, I was going to hire Vivante to paint you a portrait for your birthday but you can kiss that gift goodbye," I say.

"The last thing I want is a velvet painting of myself," says Nunya.

"I thought the last thing you'd want was space herpes."

"Gross, Dick. That's really gross."

"Anyway, Detective Blowhard, the painting is definitely enough collateral that you can take your pick of any ship we have," says Nunya's mom.

"Any ship," repeats Nunya's dad.

"Shit. Okay, fine, I'll hand it over. But just know that if either of you tries to sell it behind my back I will punch you so hard that you'll turn into confetti."

"We wouldn't dream of it and point taken," says Nunya's mom.

I hand the painting to her and she walks over to a section of wall that magically opens up, revealing a hidden room. Nunya's mom walks in with the painting, hangs it, and then comes back out, the wall sealing up behind her.

"It will be completely safe there," says Nunya's mom. "We have state of the art security that will prevent intruders from ever being able to open it."

"I hope for your sake that's true," I reply.

"It is, I assure you. Anyway, do you have any particular ship manufacturers that you like? Some of our bigger names are Astro Martin, Masernati, Glamborghini, and Flies-Royce."

"I want something that screams old-school power. Something Earth Uno-ish if you know what I mean."

"We certainly do. Probably our finest example of that is our Fjord supership known only as the GT9. It made the Kessel run in less than 12 parsecs," says Nunya's dad.

"Bullshit," I reply.

"I'm sorry, what do you mean?" asks her dad.

"I mean parsecs aren't a unit of time, they're a unit of distance. So nothing could have made the Kessel run in 12 parsecs because that's meaningless," I explain.

"Parsecs? Did I say parsecs? I of course meant 'porsecs', which we all know is a standard measurement of time, right?" says her dad.

"Never heard of it," I say.

"Oh, yes, it's fairly new. Just added when they changed how

kids are doing math these days. They call it the new-new-new math."

"Right. Anyway, take me to her."

We follow Nunya's folks to the back of the massive room, passing dozens of fancy, shiny ships along the way. When we reach it I am absolutely floored by how beautiful the ship is. It's piano black and looks like a piece of artwork. Chrome trim, sleek and sexy design. I seriously can't believe how beautiful and powerful looking she is. I must have her.

"I must have her," I say.

"You don't want to take her for a test drive first?" asks Nunya's dad.

"Nope, I'm good. I want this one," I say.

"I like a man who knows what he wants," says Nunya's mom, winking at me.

"Uh, right. Anyway, do I need to sign anything?" I ask.

"No, just hold up your right hand," says Nunya's mom.

I put up my right hand and a laser beam appears out of thin air and scans it.

"Identity confirmed. Thank you, Detective Blowhard," says a robotic sounding voice coming from nowhere in particular.

"Okay, she's all yours," says Nunya's dad. "Feel free to take her now if you like. Nunya should be able to show you how to fly it out of here."

I look over at Nunya and she shakes her head in the affirmative.

"Well, it was nice meeting you, Mr. and Mrs. Business," I say.

"And it was nice doing business with you, Detective Blowhard," says Nunya's mom, who licks her lips inappropriately. I do my best to hide my boner but good luck with that.

Nunya hugs her parents goodbye.

23

We slip inside the GT9 and I take a deep breath in, savoring the new ship smell. It's a mix of leather, wood, metal, and the promise of sex. It's the most goddamn beautiful thing I've ever smelled before except for maybe Bessie. I'm gonna miss you girl but this new GT9 will help me get over it quicker, if I'm being honest.

"You know, in honor of Bessie I'm going to call her Bessie Mach 2," I say, looking over at Nunya.

"I think that's a good name for her," she says.

"Yeah, me too. So do you know how to get us out of here?" I ask.

"Yup, just give me a second." She uses the touchscreen on the dash to open a massive door directly above us. Both of us have flight controls, so for this first part I let Nunya start the engines, switch us to hover mode, and fly us up into the now moons-lit night. Once we're a mile into the air she lets me take over.

"Hey, I just realized that Bessie Mach 2's initials are funny," I say.

"Why?"

"BM 2? It means double poopy," I say.

"You're so goddamn juvenile," says Nunya.

"Yeah, I really am, aren't I?" I say, not caring that she was trying to insult me. I'm just too damn happy in this ship to give a fuck about what she's saying.

"So where are we going now?" asks Nunya.

"Uh, I thought you knew. Didn't Phil tell you what to do after getting your robes?" I ask.

"He sure as fuck didn't," says Nunya.

"Well, I guess we're fucked."

"Let's try and come up with some ideas on what to do next. Maybe that will help us get past our mental-block."

"Sure."

A few minutes pass.

"Wait, I may have an idea," I say. "We could go back to the Wise Old Wizard and ask him what the next step is."

"Do you really think he'd just tell us? I thought the point was to go on an adventure and figure shit out on our own," says Nunya.

"Yeah, you're probably right. Well, what about Phil?"

"Nah, I'm pretty sure he would have told me if he knew where the Sloths were."

"Oh, so you guys got that close while I was off banging the waitress? Like you feel he would have told you anything you wanted or needed to know?" I ask.

"I didn't say that but I did get to know him a bit and he genuinely seemed interested in helping us. So why would he hold back?" asks Nunya.

"That's fair. Okay, so what are your ideas?"

"Well, we could ask around. Maybe see if someone knows. Or do research. Maybe someone out there's been tracking Sloths and where they've seen them."

"Like a Slothologist?" I ask.

"Sure, if those existed," she replies sarcastically.

"You don't know that they don't."

"Sounds like fake shit to me," says Nunya. "If we did try to talk to someone do you know anyone who would give us good answers?"

"Sure, the Wise Old Wizard."

"We just ruled him out."

"I know, he's just the only person I can think of. Oh, another person we shouldn't talk to is Maggie," I say.

"Why not?" asks Nunya.

"She used the 'L' word."

"Wait, she told you she loved you?"

"Yeah, but we'd just fucked so I didn't think too much about it at the time. I thought she was just trying to get me hot again for the next several poundings."

"Gross."

"Everybody has their kink. Don't be a shamer," I say.

"I'm not a shamer. Unless it's feet. Feet are gross," says Nunya.

"Yeah, I don't get feet either. You walk on them, they smell bad, and they aren't good looking. Still, I wouldn't go out of my way to try to convince someone who likes feet that they're wrong just because I think they're gross. Let people like what they like."

"That's very surprising and sincere of you," says Nunya.

"Really?"

"No. Go fuck yourself. You're just trying to score points by acting all enlightened or whatever."

"Score points for what? I know I ain't scoring with you. Seriously, I really am over it."

"Like hell you are, no one ever gets over me."

"It's easier now that I know you have an ego," I say. "Maybe you're really the one who thinks they're God's gift to women."

Her eyes pinch into tiny slits and she tries to act angry but I don't believe her. I know that she probably feels that way at least somewhat, and I think she doesn't really care.

"You know, Nunya, I have to say, for all the shit you give me for being an asshole you're kind of an asshole too."

"What the fuck is that supposed to mean?" asks Nunya.

"It means that sometimes you can be just as big of an asshole as me. You ain't perfect."

"I've never thought I was perfect."

"I think maybe you do. You're quick to judge others and point out their flaws. Maybe it's because you don't think you have any."

She crosses her arms and turns away from me. I must have struck a nerve. I'm hoping that if she can see that nobody is perfect, even her, then maybe she will cut me a little slack.

"So where are we heading?" I ask.

Silence.

"Wow, you act so tough but you're just as sensitive about shit as anyone else," I say.

"And you aren't sensitive enough," says Nunya.

"Probably. But hey, I'm trying, right?"

"You know, they should probably title your TV series: Dick Blowhard, Galactic Fuckup. All you do is make things worse."

What she says hurts and she's probably right. But admitting to it at this point will only make her think she's better than me. I wonder if she tears me down because it makes her feel better about herself more than she's actually trying to help me. And I would point that out to her if I thought she'd listen, but she probably won't. She's not giving me any other suggestions, and I keep coming back to the idea of talking to the Wise Old Wizard again, so I decide to head for the space-asshole.

"So where are we headed?" she mumbles.

Instead of engaging her, or even letting her know where we're headed, when we reach the security ship at the space-asshole I type in a message to the guards so that she has no idea where we're going. I wait patiently, get a 'have a wonderful trip' from the security ship, and as soon as I see the gate shimmer and change destinations, I fly through.

I also decide to test the GT9 out. Instead of flying straight through the casino area like I normally do, which takes forever, I turn the ship so I'm flying in a circle around the cluster of planets, giving her all she has without engaging the lightspeed drive. I can feel the rumble of the engines and the thrill of flying at a speed that makes seeing obstacles difficult. Thankfully, the ship has an incredibly good forcefield just in case we do actually strike something. Nunya seems to be unhappy with me. Of course she's always unhappy with me so what's the difference? But she finally breaks the uncomfortable silence.

"So we're back here to visit the Wise Old Wizard anyway?" she asks.

"Yeah. You didn't have any better ideas," I reply.

"Hopefully it isn't a huge waste of time."

"Hopefully."

Instead of taking an hour to get to planet Merlin it only takes about ten minutes. I steer us toward the Wise Old Wizard's castle which thankfully looks exactly the way we left it. Knowing my current bad streak of luck I figure it's only a matter of time before everyone I know has their shit blown up too.

I do my best to park the GT9 away from everything. As we step out I turn on its formidable defense system hoping no one fucks with it. As protective as I was of Bessie I'm going to be twice as protective of Bessie Mach 2.

Walking up to the moat that surrounds his castle, the Wise Old Wizard is already waiting for us. He waves as we approach and I just give him my patented head-nod of awesomeness.

"Dickus Blowhardius and the Queen of planet Houston, so good to see you again, and so soon! What can I help you with?" asks the Wise Old Wizard.

"Hello Steve, we're here because we could really use your guidance on what to do next," I say.

"Steve? There's no one here by that name," says Steve, the Wise Old Wizard, nervously.

"There's no reason to lie about it. We just met your ex not that long ago."

"My ex? I still don't know what you're talking about."

"Maggie, your ex. The Mad Wizard that has half the galaxy scared. None of that rings a bell?" I ask.

"Uh, should it?" replies Steve.

"Seriously, that cat's out of the bag. We know about you and the Bloopnarp."

Steve lets out a deep sigh. "Fine, fine. Yes, I do have an ex named Maggie, and yes, she went crazy because I had an affair with a Bloopnarp. It would be really great if you didn't judge me right now."

"Oh, I've had sex with all sorts of species and I think Bloopnarps are great people, so we aren't judging," I reply.

"I am," mumbles Nunya.

"God, will you please stop being such an asshole for a moment," I say to Nunya. I turn back to the Wise Old Wizard. "So Steve, we're here because we're stuck. We don't know where to go next to hunt down the Sloths. We're pretty sure we're ready to take them now that Nunya has superpowers too. Oh, and thanks again for pointing us in the direction of the robes and armor."

"I barely did anything. I just put you on the path. You were the ones that followed it."

"Actually, that's true; you really didn't help that much. Still, we are ready to kick some Sloth ass and need your help again."

"You truly are stuck? Have you tried doing research on the Intergalactic Information System yet?" asks Steve.

"No. Research isn't really my thing. I like to live in the moment, and research requires looking at things in the past. Boring things," I say.

"Queen of planet Houston, are you adverse to using technology to your advantage and gaining knowledge through hard mental work and focus?"

"I am not, and yes we could probably look it up, but since we're here, it'd be great if you just told us," replies Nunya.

"But what's the fun in that?" asks Steve.

"Fun? None of this has been fun! I've died once already and Dick had to bring me back to life. I nearly killed Dick with a lightning bolt accidentally. We've both been chewed on and beat up by crazy killer toys. And to make everything worse, I've had to put up with Dick's whorish ways, banging every woman he meets," says Nunya.

"Hey, at least I didn't bang your mom," I reply.

"I'm sure you thought about it," says Nunya.

"Of course I did, she's fucking hot. And if she really is as tough as you say she is I bet she's a minx in bed. But yeah, I didn't go near her," I say. "And you're welcome."

"Speaking of women, how is Maggie doing?" asks Steve.

"She's amazing!" I say. "I mean, she's doing well. She's old like you, of course, and she's super lonely. We talked you up a bit. Told her that she should give you a call."

"Oh, uh, well thank you, Dickus. Hopefully she's forgiven me after all this time. You know the reason Maggie and I didn't work out was because she was a bit smothering and a bit too aggressive at times. I felt like she was constantly watching over me, making sure I didn't cheat. It made me so miserable that I had sex with the Bloopnarp just to end things. But we were both young and dumb then. I'd be surprised if Maggie now was much like the Maggie I knew back then. The Maggie I knew was constantly wanting sex and attention, and now that she's old like me my guess is her libido has waned," says Steve.

Don't say anything, Dick. Don't say anything.

"Anyway, because you have brought me some good news I'm in a good mood. I will aid you on your quest by giving you a hint."

"Okay, what's the hint?" I ask.

"What walks on four legs, then two legs, then three legs?"

"Wait, hold on, isn't that the riddle of the Sphinx?" asks Nunya.

"Uhhh…." replies Steve. "How about: as I was going to St. Ives, I met a man with seven wives…"

"Everybody knows that one too. It's just the man who's going to St. Ives," says Nunya.

"Why was six afraid of seven?" asks Steve.

"Seriously? You can't do better than a horrible math joke that doesn't even make children laugh?" says Nunya.

"Okay, fine, you got me. I'm terrible at coming up with original riddles. But I didn't think you'd need my help at this point so I didn't spend any time coming up with something. You try making up a riddle when you're put on the spot like this!"

"I'm sure I could have come up with something better," says Nunya.

"Oh, well then you tell me what riddle you would use to tell adventurers that they need to go find a guy named Mac Guffin who has a treasure map that points to the Sloth hideouts."

"Uhhh…" starts Nunya.

"Exactly," says Steve. "So please, Queen of planet Houston, do not be so quick to judge. My job isn't an easy one and I get little thanks for the help I do provide."

"Seriously though, the guy's name is Mac Guffin?" says Nunya, chuckling.

"Yes. Is that funny for a particular reason?" asks Steve.

"Never mind, Wise Old Wizard. I don't know that you'd find it funny even if I explained it," replies Nunya. "Can you point us in the direction of Mac Guffin?"

"I could, but I don't know where he is right now. You should be able to look up his info page on the Intergalactic Information System. It'll show tour dates and such."

"Tour dates?" I ask.

"Yes, he's a space-rock star," says Steve.

"Wait, does that mean he's in a band, or does that mean that he's really well known for being into space rocks?" I ask.

"The first one," says Steve, skeptical of my question.

Nunya just looks at me like I'm the biggest idiot in the universe. Who knows, maybe I am? I mean, I'm still helping Nunya, and I think most people would have walked away from her by this point.

"So what's the name of his band?" I ask.

"The Soap Droppers," replies Steve.

"Are they a prison band?"

"I don't think so. Why do you ask?" says Steve.

"Uh, no reason. Anyway, before we head out you wouldn't happen to have any weapons I could borrow? Rita and Irene both left me."

"That's really sad, Dickus. Two girlfriends leaving you at the same time must be difficult to deal with," says Steve.

"Oh, no, Rita and Irene were my blasters," I explain.

"And they just left you? Like, they grew legs and walked away?" asks Steve.

"No, they were lost. I guess that just happens sometimes. Anyway, do you have any guns or other weapons I could use? Preferably something non-magical that you can shoot?"

"Well, you could go through the trials of Danicarr on planet Henry if you wanted a really kickass axe that shoots plasma beams."

"How long would that take?" asks Nunya.

"Oh, probably several weeks. It's heavily guarded, booby trapped with magic, that sort of thing," says Steve.

"We don't have weeks. Pass," says Nunya.

"Hey, now that you have your magic robes and shit you think you get to decide on what weapons I get?" I say.

"Yes. Because remember, now I can kick your ass," says Nunya.

"You already tried and I threw you into outer space. How did that work out for you?"

"Whatever," replies Nunya.

"But yeah, a few weeks would slow down the pace of our adventure. Thanks Steve, the axe will have to wait for my next adventure, assuming we survive this one," I say.

"That's fair. Well, I do have something but it's not as cool. It's a blaster that a troublemaker left behind while trying to cross my moat. It may still work but I don't know how to use those things so I never tested it."

"Sure, let's see what you've got."

The Wise Old Wizard snaps his fingers. Instead of the blaster instantly appearing, an imp from a side room brings out a small blaster sitting on top of a red velvet pillow. It looks a bit banged up, like it had been damaged in many battles, but it seems like it's in good enough condition that it might work. I look more closely as the imp approaches. The blaster is shiny black like the GT9, and in red letters the name 'Mona' has been painted on it. I'm beginning to like this thing.

"Did you have that prepped and ready to go?" asks Nunya.

"What do you mean?" questions Steve.

"I mean, it seems awfully convenient to have an imp bring out the blaster so quickly. It's as if he had been waiting there with it."

"Yes, well, imps are very efficient creatures," says Steve, looking nervous.

"Wait, did you already know that Dick had lost his weapons?" asks Nunya.

"Uh, uh…" he stammers.

"I'll take that as a 'yes'. So how DID you know that he'd lost his blasters? Have you been spying on us?" asks Nunya.

"It… it was nothing like that. I haven't been spying, I've just been keeping an eye out for danger by occasionally scrying on you. I didn't want you to get hurt, and if for some reason you were seriously hurt I might have been able to assist. Regardless, I probably should have told you," says Steve.

"Yeah, well, you totally should have. You haven't seen me naked, have you?" asks Nunya.

"Oh, no, I would never…" he says, trailing off.

"Uh-huh," says Nunya, skeptically.

"Wait, did you watch us the whole time?" I ask.

"Not the whole time. No," replies Steve. "But I did watch you have sex with Maggie."

Oh fuck.

"Oh fuck," I say. "I'm really, really sorry Steve. It just sort of happened. She came onto me."

"I know, Dickus. I watched the whole thing. Maggie is a particularly aggressive woman sexually and I didn't want you to feel uncomfortable by bringing it up, because honestly, I ended things with her long ago. Did it hurt? Yes, fuck you, it hurt. But I can see past that and I'm still willing to help you. But if I do talk with Maggie, and we do get back together, I just ask that you don't have sex with her again."

"I'll do my best," I say. "Unless of course you guys want a devil's threeway."

"Thank you, no," says Steve.

"Suit yourself," I reply.

"One thing I want to say is stop scrying on us," says Nunya. "That's a total invasion of our privacy, regardless of how good your intentions might have been."

"I also will do my best," says Steve.

I pick up Mona. She has a nice heft to her. I point her at the ground just to make sure I don't accidentally kill anyone with it if my finger slips on the trigger.

"So do you remember the previous owner of this fine piece of equipment?" I ask.

"Yes," says Steve, hesitantly.

"What were they like?"

"Oh, you know, just your common, everyday, garden variety bad guy."

"What aren't you telling me?" I ask.

"Well, you aren't going to like it," replies Steve.

"Trust me, nothing you can say will phase me," I reply.

"He was a Unicorn."

"GOD FUCKING DAMMIT!!!" I say.

"Yeah, so that's why I didn't want to mention it. It's still a great weapon, I think. Just ignore the fact that it was used by one of your mortal enemies."

"How can you say that? That means that I have something in common with one of them. I name my guns too and like shiny black things. Fuck!"

"It's a big universe, Dickus. You're bound to run into someone that's just like you who you don't like. And maybe yes, this is foreshadowing for your next adventure: 'Dick Blowhard 2: Blow Harder', but that doesn't mean it isn't true. First, it's okay to like things that other people like too, even if you don't like that person. Second, maybe your enemies aren't always as different from you as you think they are. Maybe they're just people too, trying to get along in this crazy galaxy. Maybe to them you're the asshole," says Steve.

"Oh, I'm sure they think he's an asshole after what he did to them," says Nunya.

"Great, thanks, that's really helpful," I reply.

"Just calling it like I see it," replies Nunya.

"Shit. Mind if I try her out?" I ask.

"If you could please wait until you're outside it would be appreciated," says Steve.

"Fine. Anyway, thanks for the gun and for the info, I guess," I reply.

"Always happy to help the least amount possible," replies Steve, the Wise Old Wizard.

24

"So, you know how to do the information thing?" I ask Nunya as we're leaving the Wise Old Wizard's castle.

"I wouldn't be much of a hacker if I didn't," replies Nunya.

"Okay, then have at it."

As we get close to the GT9 I turn the safety off the blaster, aim it at a large rock that's resting innocently on the ground all by itself, and fire. The blaster makes a weird crackling noise like something's up with it, but it launches a massive pulse of energy that explodes the rock into a cloud of dust. Nice. I start to worry that there might be something wrong with the blaster and that in the middle of a fight, when I really need it to work, it will suddenly break down and I'll be fucked. But I ignore that thought because it looks so cool. I place Mona inside my bag of ultimate wonders then discretely place it back into my pocket.

Hopping into the GT9, Nunya types away at the touchscreen until she finally brings up a list of tour dates and locations for The Soap Droppers. She scrolls through until she finds their next concert date which will be in twelve hours.

"Okay, it looks like they're actually performing here in the Vegas Constellation. Are you familiar with planet Hollywood?"

"You mean the restaurant or the actual planet Hollywood?" I ask.

"Just the planet named Hollywood. Apparently, it's one of the older casino planets in the system. No longer owned by the Krilgurion mob. Their site says it has an old-school charm yet modern design and amenities," says Nunya.

"Are you trying to get me to bankroll you to stay there?" I ask, as I lift the GT9 into the air and head toward planet Hollywood.

"Yes."

"Do you know how expensive that will be?"

"Don't care."

"Yeah, well I'm the one having to pay for everything so I say 'no'."

"C'mon, we'll be rich once we take down the Sloths," says Nunya.

"There's no guarantee we'll even find out where they keep their money. And I don't like spending money I don't have."

"You just blew a fat wad on this ship."

"Necessity," I reply.

"And on a bottle of super rare Scotch."

"If you'll remember that was comped by the sexy waitress. And necessity."

"And on three expensive outfits."

"Necessity, necessity, and... necessity."

"Can we at least get a room before the concert? I'm exhausted from all the running around. We haven't had real sleep in who knows how long and I'm hungry as fuck," says Nunya.

"Yeah, fine. We'll get a room and we'll get some food. But you're on your own if you want to gamble," I say.

"But I don't have any cash. Literally everything I owned was destroyed back on planet Houston."

"Sucks to be you."

"Seriously, how am I supposed to get any money to buy anything then?"

"You could always stand out on the street and see if somebody picks you up," I suggest.

"No fucking way!" yells Nunya.

"Hey, you asked how you're supposed to make money. There's that and then there's getting a job. Take your pick."

"Or, give me 10,000 burgmorps and I'll go do my own thing. You'll be rid of me for several hours," she says.

"10,000 burgmorps to make you go away? Worth it. However, I only have a line of credit, and because everything I own was destroyed, I'm willing to bet they won't actually let me take out any cash against it. Especially since I just bought the GT9. So how am I supposed to give you money that I can't get myself?"

"You could sell yourself."

"I'm not having sex with anyone for money either. Although I'm so good I really should stop giving it out for free," I say.

"Ungh, you're literally the worst human being ever. Still, consider it. It's not like you can get any diseases so at least your prick won't fall off," says Nunya.

"Yeah, but I usually only bang hot babes. I don't know that there's too many willing to pay to have sex with a guy. And although I don't judge dudes for being into dudes, it's just not the thing for me," I say.

"That's not very open minded."

"What do you mean? You don't want to have sex with dudes, right? So why should I?"

"Okay, that's a fair point. What about non-binary?" asks Nunya.

"Somewhere in between?"

"Yeah."

"Gray area. Depends on the situation and the species. And how much alcohol is involved."

"I guess that's something."

"So glad you approve of my mating choices, not that it's any of your business," I say.

"I wish it wasn't any of my business but somehow you always make it my business."

"Yeah, well, it's not on purpose."

"I'm not so sure about that. It seems like you want to throw it in my face because I won't have sex with you," says Nunya.

"I wouldn't worry about that anymore because I don't fuck assholes. Wait, I don't mean that literally, because like, that's hot. But metaphorically, you're an asshole, and I don't want to fuck you anymore."

"Reverse psychology won't work on me. You still want this," says Nunya, pointing to her nether region.

"I really don't," I reply.

"Bullshit."

"No, seriously, I'm over it. Even if you got so drunk you threw yourself at me I wouldn't do it."

"Challenge accepted. I'll get drunk and we'll see what happens. We both know you won't be able to resist."

"No."

"Why not?"

"Because for the first time in my life I'm trying to be better."

"Yeah, good luck with that."

"Thanks, even though I know you're being sarcastic," I say.

"Me? Sarcastic? No!" replies Nunya.

"Wow, you're not even drunk and you're already acting like an asshole."

"It's my superpower. So now I get cash?"

"No! Let's just get a room on planet Hollywood. We'll crash and you can get as drunk as you like, pass the fuck out, and shut the hell up. Deal?" I ask.

"Deal."

It takes a while to fly to planet Hollywood because it's toward the center of the planet cluster where the speed limit is still a problem. I set the ship to run on autopilot and use the touchscreen to talk to a concierge at one of the hotels on planet Hollywood.

"Hello, this is Reginald at the Chateau Marmot Hotel and Casino. How may I be of assistance?"

"I was hoping to book a room."

"And the name?"

"Dick Blowhard," I say.

"Oh, is this *the* Detective Blowhard? The famous one with the TV show?" asks Reginald.

"The one and the same."

"Amazing. We don't often get a celebrity of your status staying with us anymore. Please hold one moment while I check something," he says.

We can hear him frantically tapping away at a touchscreen.

"Ah, yes, Detective Blowhard. I've been given permission to not only comp your room for however long you stay, but also offer free dining and 50,000 burgmorps in free play at our casino, provided of course you are willing to take a picture with the casino owners at the end of your stay and leave us a positive review on Melp."

"Melp? The review website?" I ask.

"Yes, that site," replies Reginald.

"Yeah, I can do that."

"Wonderful!" says Reginald. "Feel free to tell the person at the front desk who you are when you arrive and everything will be taken care of for you."

"Oh, one last thing. Can you get us two VIP tickets with meet and greet for tonight's Soap Droppers concert? We're huge fans."

"Why of course, sir. Consider it done."

"Thanks, Reginald," I reply.

"No, thank you sir." The screen goes dark.

"I think I'd hate you even more after that huge display of bullshit if it wasn't for the fact that I now get 50,000 burgmorps to waste at the tables."

"Who said you get to use all of it? Or even any of it?" I say.

"I thought you didn't want to play."

"I just didn't want to waste my own money on it. Since I'm wasting someone else's money, that's an entirely different situation."

"Fine, we'll split it 50/50," says Nunya.

"Yeah, sure, whatever. Just please close your mouth for a while. Just do me that favor."

"Fine, just don't do anything dumb then I won't have to tell you you're being dumb."

"Whatever."

25

I land the GT9 in a fairly nice looking parking lot that spans several miles. It's sad because the lot is maybe only a tenth as full as it could be, which lets me know that the crowds they drew originally have been shrinking. I imagine all the big-name celebrities came here in the past, like old purple eyes, Sammy Davies, and the drunk Italian. Back when the mob ran everything and no one cared because they were too hopped up on Fluverian cocaine to notice.

Getting out of the GT9 I turn on its formidable defense system as Nunya flags down a shuttle bus. We both hop in and the driver looks a bit surprised when he notices me.

"Wow, sonny, we don't get a lot of people dressed up like you anymore. Most of the people that come now are geriatrics with goddamn fanny packs and colored visors. Blue hairs who spend what little money they have on the cheap slots. Why, I'd say it's been a couple of years since I've seen someone decked out in a tux," says the shuttle driver as we pull away.

"Well, like I say, I always try to keep it classy. Besides, don't her magic robes and armor stand out more?" I say, pointing to Nunya.

"Oh, I thought she was in one of the shows. Either that or a high priced hooker." He turns back and looks her up and down. "A very high priced hooker."

I notice out of the corner of my eye Nunya getting ready to say something mean in response and I turn to her and whisper, "Hey, he's just paying you a compliment."

"He can take his complement and…" starts Nunya.

"Look, we want to keep a super low profile, right? The last thing we need is for you to beat up this old man and get us into trouble with the local police. We'll miss seeing The Soap Droppers, we'll never find the Sloths, and we'll never get your money back. And trust me, you don't want to mess with casino police. They'll make your life a living hell."

"Kind of like how you've made my life a living hell?" says Nunya.

"Goddamn, why do you have to be so sassy!" By the look on her face I can tell I've made a mistake.

"I'm sorry, WHAT? Do you think I'm a stereotypical sassy black woman? What the fuck is wrong with you? Up until this point, among all the stupid bullshit you've said, I didn't realize you were also racist!"

"Hey, I'm not racist!" I reply.

"Seriously? You couldn't get any more racist right now. I'm not a fucking angry black woman stereotype, okay? Before I met you I was a perfectly calm, rational, reasonable person who was clinically depressed just like everybody else. You think it's fun having to argue with you and keep you in line? No fucking way! It's only because of your unending pathological bullshit that I'm like this. If you were a decent human being I wouldn't get angry all the time. Okay?"

It takes a few minutes for her words to sink in.

"Okay, you're right, and I'm sorry. For all of it. I didn't mean to be racist, or say anything racist, I swear. I mean, there are so many people of different colors and races and species in the galaxy that I didn't realize racism was still a thing," I reply.

"Oh, it's definitely still a thing."

"Then I'm sorry. And I'll try to do better."

"Yeah, see that you do," she says, still visibly angry. "And I swear to God if you bring up Bloopnarps right now I will beat you into a fine paste."

"You really should..." I start to say, but seeing the frustration in her eyes I stop.

"Lover's quarrel?" asks the shuttle driver who has been watching us in his rearview mirror.

"We aren't a couple," I say.

"Too bad. Everyone should have someone," says the driver.

"I'm perfectly happy being alone," says Nunya.

"I can tell," replies the shuttle driver, sarcastically.

"Goddamn it! Now you're making me angry about being angry," says Nunya, looking at me.

"Hey, I swear, I really am trying to do better. And I'm sorry I made you angry. And I'm sorry I made you angry about being angry. Did I say that right?" I ask.

"Yeah, you said it right. Look, when we get the free play money let's both go our separate directions for a while. I just need a break from you. And I'll be fine on my own. I don't need anyone's help," says Nunya.

"Obviously," I say.

Just as we finish the conversation, the shuttle driver takes us down a tunnel and drops us off at an elevator.

"Thanks for the lift. And I'd tip you only I don't have any cash on me," I say.

"Oh, that's okay," says the shuttle driver. "Just nice having a celebrity like you stop by for a visit."

"You recognized me?" I ask.

"Of course I did! Posters for your TV show are all over the place and the media can't stop talking about you," replies the driver.

"Well, thank you," I say.

Nunya just rolls her eyes again.

We hop out of the shuttle bus and walk over to the elevator. Nunya pushes the button and we wait. The doors eventually open and a drunk couple stumbles out. As we get in the elevator we hear one of them start to throw up, then the other. Thankfully the doors close before the smell of vomit wafts into the compartment.

"They must have had a good time," says Nunya.

"Cliche much?" I respond.

"Hey, I don't hear you coming up with any original thoughts either," replies Nunya.

"I'm starting to warm up."

After a few seconds of moving upward the elevator doors open. The casino seems like a very loud and busy place based on the noise level, but as we leave the elevator and look around, most of the casino is deserted. There's definitely people milling around, and people playing the slots and table games, but it feels like a Tuesday afternoon when people are working and not at the casino gambling.

Even though it's a bit like a ghost town it still looks really cool. The vaulted ceilings remind me of my own place; pale stonework in an ancient Greek style. Columns rise into the air supporting statues of gods and goddesses. I think I'd actually feel more comfortable wearing a toga than a tux right now. I look fucking hot in a toga.

I glance up and notice a sign that says 'Hotel' with an arrow pointing to our right. I nudge Nunya who looks upset by the physical contact so I nod my head upward. She sees the sign and then nods back in understanding. I follow behind her as we make our way across the casino floor, doing my best not to stare at her ass because honestly, I really am over it. No matter how curvy or juicy her ass looks, I won't go there. Nope.

It takes us a few minutes to walk through the jungle of table games. Dealers look at us excitedly and expectantly until we pass by, the glimmer of hope that they might finally make some good tips is dashed by our indifference. I nod at a few of the blue hairs as we walk past and true to form they have fanny packs and colored visors just like the shuttle driver complained about.

Nunya and I keep following the signs, snaking through the casino, until we finally reach the entrance of the hotel. A young man, maybe in his mid-to-late twenties, is standing at a check-in podium. He looks at us in confusion.

"Hello, are you both here as performers?" asks the man, clearly puzzled.

"Uh, no. I'm Dick Blowhard and this is Nunya, Queen of Houston. We're VIP guests of the hotel," I reply.

"Oh, I'm terribly sorry Detective Blowhard. Of course I know who you are. I just didn't expect you to be in a tuxedo. We don't usually see anyone other than magicians wearing tuxedos," says the man.

"Pity," I respond, trying to sound as snobby as possible.

"Truly, sir. Anyway, I'm Reginald. We spoke earlier. I have everything set up for you. If you'll just allow me to scan both of your hands you'll have access to your room and any amenities on site, as well as access to the 50,000 burgmorps we'd discussed earlier."

Nunya's hand shoots up quickly while I slowly raise mine. A green laser beam, again seemingly from nowhere, scans our hands.

"Okay, well you're all set," says Reginald. "You're in room six-sixty-six, the penthouse penthouse."

"So we're on the sixth floor?" I ask.

"No, actually the sixty-sixth. Each floor has its own smaller hotel within it. The top floor is the sixty-sixth, and since it's the penthouse floor, you have the penthouse suite within the penthouse floor, which is room six."

"Fancy," is all I can say.

"Indeed. Is there anything else that we can provide you with?"

"Could you please have someone bring us up some food?" I ask.

"Certainly sir. Although I will say you can order directly with the concierge of your floor who will have a special menu just for your specific hotel. I unfortunately don't have that list here as only VIP members are allowed access to it. Even within our own establishment we try to keep things as exclusive as possible to enhance your stay. You can always request something specific, and we will guarantee it's made for you, but I would recommend reading the menu as we may have creative new delicacies you have likely never heard of."

"We'll wait then."

"Is there anything else I can do for you?"

"We're good," says Nunya, smiling broadly.

"Then I hope you both enjoy your stay," says Reginald.

"Thanks," I say, patting Reginald on the back a little too hard as we walk by.

I follow Nunya to a set of elevators just inside the lobby. The lobby itself looks like something out of an old time movie before they were able to figure out how to make movies in color. There's a lot of red carpet runways on top of black and white marble floors, brass fixtures everywhere, and large non-flowering plants hanging out in pots just standing around like they own the place. Pretentious loitering bastards.

Nunya pushes the up button on the nearest elevator and we hear an immediate and familiar 'bong' sound. The door three elevators to our left opens up and we scurry inside. Nunya, smiling broadly, looks over at me after pushing the button for the sixty-sixth floor.

"How come you aren't smiling? This place is great!" she says.

"You've seen one, you've seen them all," I say.

"Come on, you aren't even a little impressed?"

"Nope, not really. Before the Sloths did their number on my house, my house was fancier than this. But you really seem to be into this shit. Have you never stayed in a hotel like this before?" I ask.

"No, not really. My folks, even though they have money, didn't really spend much of it. And what they did spend it on was training me to survive whatever came. I know they didn't look like it, what with my mom in a pantsuit and my dad in a suit-suit, but they're both pretty tough. Especially my mom. Guess you have to be if you sell used spaceships. It's a cutthroat type job," says Nunya.

"I could imagine," I reply.

"No, seriously. If you get on the bad side of some manufacturers, or competing dealers, they'll literally cut your throat."

"Huh, didn't know that."

"There's a lot you don't know. A lot," says Nunya.

"And I like to keep it that way," I say. "Ignorance is bliss and the more you're 'teaching' me the more I'm hating life."

"Ignorance isn't bliss, it's just ignorance. And the idea is, if you aren't ignorant, you'll make the people around you less miserable. So it's not about you," replies Nunya.

"Honestly, I'm pretty sure everything is about me. I even have a TV series coming out. How many people do you know that have their own TV shows? None, that's how many."

"So you think that's some great accomplishment? Some of the

most horrible people in the universe have had TV shows made about them. Still doesn't change the fact you have shit to work on."

"Yeah, well, so do you."

The elevator doors finally open up and we walk out into a large open space that kind of looks like the downstairs lobby. In fact, it looks like an exact replica of the downstairs lobby, and I feel a bit like I'm in a Twilight Zone episode and reality is being fucked with. Besides having the same decor, in the middle of the open space is a podium, and standing at that podium is Reginald.

"What the fuck?" I say as we walk up to Reginald.

"I'm sorry sir, is something wrong?" asks Reginald.

"Yeah, how the fuck did you beat us here?" I ask.

"I'm sorry sir, I don't understand."

"We literally just left you downstairs less than a minute ago. How did you get here so quickly?"

"Oh, I see, sir. Yes, that was one of my clones. Or rather, I'm a clone of him. We're not actually sure who the real Reginald is and who the copies are because we all share the same memories from a certain point," says Reginald.

"Wait, you mean there's more than two of you?" asks Nunya.

"Yes. There's one hundred and seventy-three of us," replies Reginald.

"Why would they clone someone one hundred and seventy-two times?" I ask.

"That's because I won, or one of us won, employee of the month the first month that the hotel opened. As a reward for my efforts they made one hundred and seventy-two copies of me to help run the hotel."

"But wait, what happened to the other employees that worked here that first month?" asks Nunya.

"None of us are actually sure, madam. I suppose they were let go from their jobs," says Reginald.

"And so are all of you named Reginald?" asks Nunya.

"Yes. I mean, we're all the same person, right? And we've always known ourselves to be Reginald, so we all just keep the same name."

"Seriously though, there has to be more to it than that. Why clone the same person so many times, even if they are a good employee?" asks Nunya.

"Well, it turns out there's some sort of loophole when it comes to paying employees based on pan-galactic law. It's called the Keaton law. Basically, to prevent people from cloning themselves over and over again, a person and their set of clones legally count as only one person. That way elections can't be swayed, people don't build their own armies, etc. It also means that companies only have to pay one salary that is divided equally among the person and their clones," explains Reginald.

"So what you're saying is that all one hundred and seventy-three of you share one salary?" I ask.

"Yes, sir."

"How do you live?" I ask.

"Well, other than sleeping and eating, we work. It's really not all that bad. I mean, our accommodations are second to none. And for a few hours every week we all get together for a poker tournament. The great thing about it is that I always win. Or, at least one of us does."

"I'm sorry, Reginald, but that seems completely fucked up," says Nunya. "Have you ever thought about quitting?"

"Me? No, definitely not. I mean, we all get to work together and I keep very good company with myself. Besides all that, another problem with the Keaton law is that it's not illegal to kill a clone because the original person is technically still alive. So if upper management got angry they could kill all but one of us and just clone someone else. I've grown rather fond of all of the 'me's, and since we honestly don't know who the real Reginald is it's highly likely the real Reginald would accidentally be killed along with the other clones. I also think we've all earned the right to live with dignity and respect, and not be murdered as if we were property that can be disposed of."

"Shit, I'm sorry for what they've done to you. All of you," I say.

"Oh, I'm certain some people have it worse than us. But thank you for the sentiment. Anyway, you must be anxious to see your room. Please follow me," says Reginald.

The whole situation is fucking surreal. I wish there was something I could do about it.

We follow behind Reginald who takes us down a short hallway directly behind his podium. At the end of the hallway is a single door with the number six emblazoned in brass. Reginald opens the door and lets us enter.

For the first time I'm actually impressed. Right in front of us is a beautiful water fountain surrounded by flower-filled hanging baskets, marble benches, and trellises covered in climbing vines. A gentle breeze circulates through the room, and I can smell the foliage and feel a slight mist of water on my face. It's like what I imagine Mount Olympus would be like if it actually existed.

Behind the fountain the cavernous room spreads out. The

entire area is open and massive with a meticulously painted vault ceiling. Marble columns and statues are placed in a harmonious way throughout. Off to our left is an enormous kitchen, to our right a living space with stylish couches, tables, and an excessively large TV screen. On the other side of the fountain I can sort of make out the bedroom, although it really isn't a room as it's part of the open vastness of the suite. The bed itself is huge and looks like people could get lost if they climbed under the silky looking sheets. If I ever get my insurance money and rebuild my home, this is gonna be how I make it look.

"Welcome to your room," says Reginald, temporarily breaking the spell. "Is there anything else I can do for you while you get acquainted with it?"

"Actually, yes, we're starving," says Nunya.

"Would you like to take a look at our menu, or do you already know what you would like?" asks Reginald.

"Menu, please," says Nunya.

Reginald pulls out a menu seemingly from nowhere.

"Was that magic?" I ask.

"Sort of. It wasn't real magic, if that's what you're asking," replies Reginald.

"It was. Thank God. I've had enough of real magic for a while," I say.

We both look over the menu. Nunya orders something called Faux Gras, which according to the menu is a take on foie gras which was banned hundreds of years ago. She also orders caviar, duck a l'orange, pasta with shaved truffles, and steak tartare.

"Are you just picking the most expensive things on the menu?" I ask.

"Yes," replies Nunya. "Remember, everything's comped."

"Oh, right! I'll have what she's having," I say.

"Very good, madam and sir. Would you like anything else?" asks Reginald.

"Oh, yes, one last thing: a bottle of your finest champagne," I say.

"And your finest bourbon whiskey," says Nunya.

"Actually, you'll find that the room already has a fully stocked wet bar, and you can help yourself to anything you find," replies Reginald.

"Fantastic!" says Nunya.

"Very well. I will procure those items and have them sent right up," replies Reginald.

"Thank you," says Nunya.

"Yeah, thanks," I say as Reginald leaves.

26

We spend the first few minutes in our respective bathrooms. It's been a while since I've dropped a deuce and I have to flush a few times to get the fucker down the pipes. I also take the opportunity to grab a shower because damn I'm ripe. The great thing about the bathroom I'm using is that it has a built-in clothes washing and drying machine so I huck my suit in it. By the time I'm done dropping the kids off at the pool my clothes are pristine. After toweling off from my shower I put on one of the complimentary robes, grab my tux, and make my way back out into the main area of the penthouse.

Nunya takes a little while longer, and just as she comes out of the bathroom on the opposite side of the penthouse a knock echoes at the door. Laying my tux on a decorative chair I walk over, open the door, and there is Reginald pushing a large food cart into our room.

"Where would you like it, sir and madam?" asks Reginald.

"You can leave it here. But before you go let me check under the cart first," I say.

I lift the white cloth draping over the sides of the cart and make sure no one is hiding underneath it. I stand back up. "We're good," I say to Nunya. Turning back to Reginald, "Thanks. Make sure to give yourself a thousand-dollar tip from our free play fund."

"Thank you, sir," replies Reginald as he leaves the room, gently closing the door behind him.

I push the cart over to an area that looks like a dining room with a table that could easily handle twelve people. Nunya helps me lay all the food out and we absolutely go to town on it. I can't remember a time where I ate so much fancy food all at one meal. I mean I have to consume a lot of calories because of my metabolism and super powers but I really go crazy. It's surprising to see someone without super powers polishing off so much food but Nunya totally keeps pace with me and my eating. About halfway through I pop open the champagne and pour some for both of us.

Once we finish the amazing meal I go over and lie on the bed, completely exhausted. Nunya throws back most of the champagne then pours herself some bourbon and comes over to the bed, leaning up against the ornate headboard as she sips.

"What are you drinking?" I ask.

"Freeland Spirits bourbon," she replies.

"Any good?"

"It's amazing."

"Any reason you chose it?"

"Yeah, they're completely owned and operated by women. I try to support my sisters," says Nunya. "That and it's fucking fantastic. Super smooth and tastes like vanilla and caramel. I always keep some at my bar. Or I guess I kept some at my bar."

"Hey, we'll get the money. You'll rebuild and you'll have enough you can make your bar as fancy as you want. Seriously, this should set you up for life," I say.

"You know, every time I think I've found a way out of this life it drags me back in. I've been on get-rich missions before and they haven't gone well," replies Nunya.

"That's because you didn't have me by your side. Seriously, the amount of ass we're going to kick soon will be so massive they'll name planets after us."

"Planet Nunya does have a nice ring to it."

"Fuck yeah it does," I reply.

After a few minutes I pass out from exhaustion.

27

I wake up to a loud crash and sit straight up in bed, trying to figure out what the fuck is going on. In front of me, about fifty feet away, Nunya is struggling with a chair she apparently knocked over. It seems like her coordination is completely fucked up. I watch as she tries pulling the chair upright, but eventually she gives up and leaves it on its side.

"Hey, what the fuck?" I say.

"Shhhhhhhh, go back to sleep, butterfly," she says.

"Are you completely shitfaced?" I ask.

"Yup, I am totally… shitfaced," she replies, slurring her words. Nunya walks over to the bed and falls down on her side.

"Where were you?" I ask.

"Casino."

"How much did you win?"

"Didn't," replies Nunya.

"Then how much did you lose?"

"All of it."

"You lost all 49,000 burgmorps of free play?"

"Ah-yup!" she says in a cutesy voice.

"What the fuck? We were splitting that in half! And I never lose. I could have gotten us the money without taking on the Sloths!" I say.

"Oh well," replies Nunya. She climbs across the bed, over to me, and starts to kiss me.

"Hey, what the fuck do you think you're doing," I say, lifting her into the air above me.

"I'm seducing you," she says. "I already told you I was going to get drunk, which I have, and now I'm going to prove that you still aren't a good guy. You'll fuck me and I'll win."

She reaches down and opens up my bathrobe, grabs onto my love shaft and starts to rub it. I turn on my side, lay her down next to me and smack her hand away then cover my junk.

"Knock it the fuck off, Nunya," I say. "This isn't happening."

"Oh yes it is," she says, launching herself on top of me.

I pick her up again, and again I set her next to me, but this time I get out of bed and stay standing.

"I'm not doing this," I say.

149

"Why not? You've fucked every other woman in the galaxy. And I know you really want to because your massive man-boner is poking out of your robe," says Nunya.

"I'm still not going to have sex with you."

"You're just pretending to be a good guy. Seriously, stick your dick in me."

"No. I won't. I refuse."

"I'll let you stick it in my butt. I know you love my sexy ass," she says, pulling her pants down and waggling her naked ass at me.

I turn around, ignoring her.

"C'mon, you know you want to," she says.

"So, you're willing to have sex with me just to win. That's what this is about. You want to be right so much that you'll have sex with someone you completely hate, someone that you're not sexually attracted to, just to prove a point."

"Yes."

"Now I don't even want to have sex with you, even if you wanted to have sex with me," I reply.

"Yes you do," says Nunya.

"No, I really don't. I don't know if you can tell but I'm not hard anymore. I really am over you, Nunya."

"Then I guess I win. Either way I win. So fuck you, Dick Blowhard. Fuck you."

I grab some of the sheets off the bed, walk over to one of the couches, wrap myself up then lie down on the couch on my stomach so she can't get to my cock again. It takes me a while to fall back asleep but eventually I do.

28

I wake up to the sound of a gentle female voice coming from all around. "Your event will be starting in one hour. Please make yourselves ready at your earliest convenience." It was both creepy and calming at the same time.

Moving off the couch and standing up I see Nunya lying on the bed, moving very slowly. She makes a groaning noise that lets me know she's not doing well.

"Nunya, you need to get up," I say as I disrobe and start changing into my tux.

"I'm not going," she mumbles, holding her head.

"Like hell you aren't," I reply. "Seriously, start getting ready."

"I have a headache."

"Don't fucking care."

She mumbles something but I can't make it out.

"Wait, are you still drunk?" I ask.

"Not as much as I was, but yeah. I'm not okay right now and I already have a hangover."

"Well, that's 'cause you're stupid," I say.

"Not as stupid as you, motherfucker," she replies.

"Hey, I wasn't the asshole who gambled away all our money. Now get dressed. I'll make up some hangover cure while you're getting ready. And while you're at it go take a shower. I'm pretty sure you have vomit in your hair."

"Oh, fucking-fuck," she says. She gets up, stumbles, but somehow manages to stay on her feet. I watch as she slowly and carefully makes her way to her bathroom.

In the meantime, I go over to the bar and start putting together the ingredients for my personal version of Hair of the Dog. In an empty shaker I muddle a half lime then add one part gin, one part Scotch, one part dark rum, a few dashes of bitters, two tablespoons of simple syrup, a few dashes of hot sauce, a few jalapeno slices and an egg white. I shake it really well. This is to get the egg white to foam and mix the flavors around. Next, I add ice until the shaker is full. Shaking it really well again, I then strain it into an Old Fashioned glass. Straining is super important because the lime juice can curdle the egg white a little. For the finishing touch I garnish it with a twig of fresh basil.

Once the drink is finished, I put it in the mini-fridge to keep it chilled while she's still fucking around. I pour myself some Scotch and go sit on the couch while I wait. Out of boredom I turn on the TV and flip through the channels but nothing really holds my interest.

It takes her about twenty minutes to finally emerge from the bathroom. She's wearing her armor and cloak again over the top of her black strappy outfit which is fine because no one's going to care how we look at the concert. And if something terrible happens it's better that she's protected. Even if she's been a massive asshole to me.

"I feel like shit," she mumbles.

"Yeah, I know. I made you a drink that should help with that. It's in the mini fridge," I reply.

She goes behind the bar and pulls the drink out.

"Looks interesting. It's kind of a dark red color. What's in it?" she asks.

"A bunch of things that'll get your head right. Just trust me," I reply.

"Yeah, the problem there is that I don't."

"Just shut up and drink the fucking drink."

She finally relents and has a sip.

"Whoa, this is really alcoholic," she says. "I'm trying to sober up, not get drunk again."

"You don't need to drink all of it. Just sip on it. About ten sips in and you'll start feeling better."

"Yeah, fine, whatever," she mumbles, continuing to sip at the drink. "You know, it's got a kind of Mexican vibe but I can tell you didn't use tequila in it."

"Nope, no tequila. I didn't want to make you blind, I just want to get enough alcohol in you to stop the hangover. Oh, and you should really pour yourself a glass of water as a chaser. That'll keep you from getting another hangover after the effects of my cocktail wear off," I say.

Nunya pours herself a glass of water and sips on it in between sips of my drink. I just keep nursing my Scotch, waiting for her to perk up. After about the seventh or eighth sip her posture changes. She's no longer hunched over. I can tell it's working its magic.

"Feel better?" I ask.

"Actually, yes, surprisingly."

"You're welcome."

She keeps sipping in silence for a moment.

"Dick, did anything happen when I came back from the

casino?" asks Nunya.

"What do you mean?"

"I mean, I don't remember anything. I blacked out before I got back to the room. Not even sure how I got back. And when I woke up, you were on the couch and I was on the bed with my pants off. So I have to ask you again, did anything happen?"

"Well, you kept trying to get me to fuck you but I kept saying 'no'," I explain.

"Fuck you, I didn't," she replies.

"No, seriously, you grabbed my dick and everything, but I slapped your hand away and slept on the couch."

It takes Nunya a while to respond. "That's fucked up. So why were my pants off then?"

"Because you told me I could fuck you in the ass and you jiggled it at me."

"And you still didn't fuck me?"

"Yeah, I still didn't fuck you," I say.

"I actually believe you. Physically, I can tell we didn't have sex. I just wanted to make sure. Anyway, I guess I was wrong. Maybe you are becoming a better person."

"I'm fucking trying. And for the record I've never taken advantage of anyone," I reply.

"Don't give yourself too much credit. Not taking advantage of a drunk woman doesn't suddenly make you Jesus," says Nunya.

"Thanks, you really are doing wonders for my ego," I say sarcastically. "If you're done, can we go?"

"We can go."

I set my Scotch down on an end table and Nunya quickly finishes the rest of her water. Before I can say anything she's walking toward the door. I just follow behind her, and as we leave I make sure the room is locked behind us.

Passing by the desk on our floor I say "Hi Reg" and he nods at me. Before we reach the elevator he stops us.

"Were you both departing the casino for the concert you're attending?"

"Actually, yes. Why do you ask?" I say.

"We have arranged transportation for you, if you'd prefer. There's a shuttle waiting outside for you," says Reginald.

"You mean like a bus?" asks Nunya.

"No, I mean a space shuttle. It's hovering just outside the window over there," he replies.

Nunya and I both look down the hallway opposite of the desk and lo and behold there's a shuttle hovering outside. Its bay door is open, seemingly waiting for us to enter.

"Uh, sure, we can go in that," says Nunya. "And thanks, Reg!"

Reginald nods again then taps a button on his podium. The window dematerializes as we walk toward the shuttle. Just before we're out of earshot, Reginald says "Hope you both have the best time."

"Thanks," I reply.

The inside of the shuttle is very swank. Everything is lined with black velvet except for the stainless steel mini-bar which ironically does have a bottle of Black Velvet Whiskey in it. It was like they came up with a theme and stuck with it. Tiny recessed lights line the ceiling randomly like stars, and the carpet is made of long black shag. It feels like something from a long ago era of decadence, kind of like the rest of the hotel.

Nunya sits across from me and we are the only two people inside of what feels like a shuttle that can accommodate fifty. Once the shuttle's bay door closes a glass partition between us and the driver opens up.

"Hello, my name is Reginald and I'm your shuttle driver," says the man.

Nunya and I look at each other and start laughing.

"Hi Reginald," starts Nunya. "Sorry, we didn't realize one of you was a shuttle driver as well."

"Oh, no worries madam. I get that reaction quite a lot, actually. So, I'm to take you to the Soap Droppers concert at Gobo Stadium?"

"Yes, please," I say, trying to be polite.

"I will have you there shortly. Hold on," says Reginald.

The thrusters engage and surprisingly we slide on our bench seats, all the way to the back of the shuttle.

"Are you two okay?" asks Reginald.

"Uh, sure," says Nunya. "Actually, I'd like to revise that to 'what the hell?'"

"Sorry, madam, but the shuttle is an older model and it doesn't have a very strong inertia arrester in it."

Suddenly, the ship stops moving and we slide nearly to the front of the shuttle.

"Again, sorry," says Reginald, meekly.

"At least we weren't trying to fix a drink," I say.

"Yes, that would have been a travesty. Anyway, you have arrived at your destination," he replies.

The shuttle door opens with a slight 'woosh' sound and multicolored light filters in. We climb out of the shuttle and onto a platform where dozens of people are waiting to take our pictures. Flashes of white light fill up the area as we walk down a long red stretch of carpet, past the paparazzi and into the VIP entrance to Gobo stadium.

Inside the VIP entrance we're immediately scanned by green laser beams. A voice coming from nowhere says "Welcome Detective Blowhard and guest, please let our staff know if you have any requirements for this evening's event. We look forward to your enjoyment of our facilities and appreciate your patronage."

Just as the ghostly voice cuts out a woman of diminutive stature walks over to us, her body wrapped in see-through green material and covered in sparkly jewels. Even though you can basically see everything, her elegance is so stunning that I don't even get a boner. Her skin is a beautiful deep purple color, the pupils of her eyes the same vibrant purple hue, and her long black hair nearly drags on the ground as she walks.

I notice a few details that mark her as not human such as the tiny curled horns that protrude from the sides of her forehead which are coated in what looks like glitter. She also has slightly longer than normal canines which give her the appearance of having fangs, but they don't look deadly like vampire teeth. Just something to use for nibbling on someone without actually piercing the skin. Oh, and never mind, I was wrong about the boner. Oops.

The woman gives me a sly smirk before she speaks. "Detective Blowhard, my name is Tessa and it's wonderful to assist you. May I ask who your guest is?"

"Yes, this is Nunya, Queen of planet Houston," I reply.

"Oh, I didn't realize that royalty would be attending. Is there anything we can get for you? A sceptre? Crown? Throne seating for the event?" asks Tessa.

"Oh, uh, no, I'm good," replies Nunya.

"Wonderful. I can see you to your skybox now, if you're ready," says Tessa.

"Actually, we were hoping to meet the band," I say.

"Ah, then we'd better hurry. They're going on soon and they don't like to be interrupted during their pre-concert ceremony," replies Tessa.

"What's their pre-concert ceremony?" asks Nunya.

"They sacrifice a live pig."

"Seriously?"

"Oh, heaven's no. Actually, they just like to enjoy some sniffyweed before they go on stage," explains Tessa.

"Ah, no need to explain," says Nunya.

"Uh, actually there is. What the hell is sniffyweed?" I ask.

"Seriously, you haven't heard of it? It's a plant that if you sniff it you get high. It's like regular weed but it doesn't smell like skunk ass and you don't have to actually ingest it to get ripped," explains Nunya.

"Well, sorry if I don't know everything about every little drug. It's not like I'm a walking catalog of illegal substances," I respond.

"It's not illegal anywhere, actually," says Tessa. "Because it has no negative side-effects it's considered a mostly safe substance for consumption. And with self-flying ships and self-driving vehicles there's little to no risk of danger from using it."

"Sounds like awesome shit," I say. "Anyway, can we meet The Soap Droppers now?"

"Yes, of course," says Tessa, slightly flustered.

She starts walking away from us, implying we should follow. I have a hard time walking and hiding my boner for obvious reasons, and staring at Tessa's curvy back-half isn't helping convince my big bad schlong to calm down. If anything, he's angry I won't let him loose.

Tessa takes us down a long concrete walkway to a very fancy looking gold elevator decorated with a 'VIP' sign above it. We only have to wait a few seconds before it opens. Tessa steps in and turns toward the open door and we follow and slide in behind her. She pushes a few buttons, the golden doors close, and we wait patiently as the elevator begins to move.

The elevator isn't as much an elevator as a flying cube, because instead of going up and down a shaft it floats to wherever it needs to go freely. We float for what feels like twenty seconds before we come to a slow and gentle stop. The doors open, and I have to tell you, I'm definitely not prepared for what I see.

29

Y ou know how I just mentioned that I wasn't prepared for what I saw? Yeah, that was a lie. I don't think I've ever been more disappointed with just how accurate I imagined something would be. We get out of the elevator and enter a medium-sized room with a concrete floor, white walls, and three beige couches. Off to the side is a table filled with normal snacks like chips, cookies, a bowl of M&Ms, and various cans of soda and beer. In the corner is a solitary boring plant that probably requires minimal watering.

Sitting on the boring beige couches are a group of criminally generic young guys, each wearing modest rock style clothes. One has an orange beanie, brown flannel shirt, and faded jeans, and he's absent-mindedly strumming his unplugged electric bass. The drummer, sporting messy long black hair, a mustache and goatee, wears a black Nirvana t-shirt and is playing with his sticks in the air. On a second couch I notice a guy who must be the keyboardist, wearing a Flock of Seagulls style haircut and turtleneck, who is munching on a bowl of pretzels while arguing with who I assume is the shirtless and soul patched lead guitarist about nothing in particular.

Last, and probably least, is who I'm guessing is the lead singer. He's sitting by himself on the third couch, sniffing at a small pouch he's got in his hand. He's much better looking than the rest of the group but appears like he's probably as dumb as a box of rocks and spends too much time tweezing his eyebrows. He's got closely cut dark brown hair, a tight black t-shirt with the name The Soap Droppers on it, cheap dark sunglasses, uncomfortable looking leather pants, and some random leather bracelets wrapping his left wrist. It's like they had a clearance sale at Hot Topic and he spent whatever loose change he found between his couch cushions on his outfit.

Tessa says "enjoy the show" from the elevator as I walk over and sit down next to the lead singer. Nunya sits on the other side of him.

"Hey, I'm Detective Dick Blowhard and this is Nunya, Queen of Your Mom. I'm guessing you're Mac Guffin?" I say.

"Wait, you're a detective? Hey man, my shit's legal. You can't arrest me, especially for the small amount I have," he mumbles.

"Oh, hey, slow down there, Mac. I'm not that kind of detective.

I'm a guy that gets hired to help solve cases while saving the galaxy. I don't work for any law agencies. And like you said, you aren't breaking the law. I just came here for the map," I reply.

"What map?" replies Mac Guffin. Shit.

"You know, the map to the Sloth's secret hideouts."

"Oh, yeah, that map. Yeah, it's back in the green room. You'll have to wait until after the concert before I can get it though," replies Mac.

"Wait, this isn't the green room?" I ask.

"Looks pretty white to me, man," says Mac, sounding like a typical stoner.

"Yeah it does," says Nunya, obviously nonplussed.

"But why do we have to wait? I could just go get it and be on our way," I reply.

"Hey, look man, I don't owe you anything and I don't know who the hell you are. You're just some random guy who showed up. You could at least stay here, chill, and listen while we perform. I'd say that's a fair trade for giving you the map."

"Yeah, sure, fine. I mean, we're just on a mission to save the galaxy yet again, we're short on time, but I'm sure we can spend the next few hours sitting around while you perform." I say it super sarcastically, letting him know it's not fine. But the fucker ignores the sarcasm.

"Cool, well I'm glad you're staying. Help yourself to any of the snacks and drinks and we'll be back in a few hours."

Mac gets up, followed by the other band members. They form a circle, each of them putting their hands together in the middle. After a few seconds of mumbles they cheer something unintelligible then raise their hands in the air. Once they're done high-fiving each other and jumping up and down they run over to a short set of stairs that I assume leads to the stage. A massive wave of applause erupts in the stadium as they open the door, but thankfully a lot of it is muffled as soon as the door shuts behind the last of them.

"Wait, so why the fuck does this guy have the map?" asks Nunya.

"How the hell should I know?" I reply.

"Seriously, it doesn't make any sense. It's like someone's been leading us around on this quest and they just randomly picked some guy to have the map. Like they're just making shit up as they go along," says Nunya.

"Yeah, it kind of feels that way, doesn't it?" I say.

"Well, you never know. Could be that Mac is actually a secret agent of some sort and he's using his band as a cover. That way travelling all over the galaxy won't raise any red flags."

"Yeah, I guess it could be that," I reply, trying to think it over. "It could just be that a fan gave him the map as a gift, or maybe his cousin is some super-hacker and used their skills to write software to figure out where the Sloth bases are. Who the fuck cares? I just want to get the map and not worry about it."

"Well, it just seems too damn easy. Like maybe it's a trap," says Nunya.

"I dunno if I'd say It's too damn easy. Have you listened to their music for the last thirty seconds? The lead singer's not only tone deaf but the rest of the band don't have their timing down. The next few hours are going to be like pure torture. And we'll have to lie and tell him he's great and shit or he might not give us the map," I say.

Nunya listens for a few seconds. "I actually agree with you; they sound like shit. What if we just sneak into the green room and steal the map?"

"Nah, it might have an alarm or be booby trapped or something. Don't want to risk accidentally destroying it," I say.

"That also makes sense. So, what will we do in the meantime?" asks Nunya.

"I don't know about you, but I'm gonna drink some Dr. Pepper and eat that entire goddamn bowl of M&Ms over there."

"Hey, you don't get the whole bowl, you gotta share."

"Like hell I do," I say, getting up and grabbing the bowl before she can get to it.

"Don't make me kick your ass, Dick."

"You already tried that. How did it go for you?" I ask.

"I'm still here, ain't I? And I learn. I figure if I don't kick your ass in our next fight, guaranteed by our third fight your ass is grass," says Nunya.

"Yeah, that'll be the day."

"Yeah, it will be the day, because from then on you'll know I'll always be able to kick your ass. You won't be able to take that away from me."

"Don't care, you still aren't getting any M&Ms."

"Fine, I'll just eat some of the Snickers bars instead." I watch her reach under the table and pull out a familiar brown box.

"Wait, what? They have Snickers bars? Let me have some."

"Oh no, not after you swiped the M&Ms. You already have your candy, you can't have mine," says Nunya.

"Hey, I didn't know there were Snickers. If I did, I would have said 'fuck you' to the M&Ms and taken the Snickers instead," I admit.

"I really don't care. You had the opportunity to share and didn't. Because of that, karma fucked you over. So sit down, shut up, and eat your damned M&Ms."

Grrrrr.

"Grrrrrr. Fine, whatever, I didn't really want them anyway," I say.

"Sure, you tell yourself that," says Nunya. "And quit bein' a baby."

"I'm not a baby! You're the baby!" I reply, realizing how dumb it sounds.

Nunya sits down, pulls a Snickers out of the box, opens the wrapper, and takes a big old bite out of a king-sized bar of candy perfection. She also makes sure to tuck the box in her robes and at her side so I can't get to them easily if I make a move.

I struggle to not kick her ass as she proceeds to eat four bars in front of me, taking a defiant and pointed bite each and every time just to piss me off. Eventually I stand up, pick up the couch I'd been resting on with one hand, turn it 180 degrees so I don't have to see her, then sit back down on it. I munch on a handful of M&Ms at a time, which, don't get me wrong, are normally amazing, but compared to Snickers it's like the difference between raw lemons and lemonade. One gives you the lemon flavor but doesn't feel quite right, the other is like drinking a glass of sunshine; a way more profound experience.

The next few hours are pure torture as I sit there eating M&Ms that I don't really want, a handful at a time, while listening to generic, boring, uninspired rock music. It doesn't help that Nunya is still making noises to annoy me while she eats her goddamn Snickers bars. I know I'm going to get the last laugh though when she eats so many she gets sick. She just better not throw up in my ship.

The Soap Droppers finish their set to loud applause because kids these days don't know what real rock and roll sounds like. Finally, mercifully, the band comes back into the room.

"So, what did you think?" asks Mac Guffin. "And don't hold back. I really want to know what you thought."

Oh does he?

"I would rather take a cheese grater to my scrotum than listen to another second of your bland-ass music," I say. It wasn't the smartest thing I could have said. In fact, it was probably the dumbest thing I could have said. We've come all this way and I've endured so much bullshit just to get Nunya her bar back so that I don't ever have to see her again. But I've gone and fucked up the one thing I should have done, which is lie. It costs me nothing to lie, and it would have been easy, but I'd had enough of Nunya's assholyness that I didn't care anymore. Glancing over my shoulder and seeing the look of horror on her face was almost worth it.

Mac glares at me, his eyes narrowed, and he comes and stands over me. "What did you just say?"

"I said I'd rather gargle a box of broken glass while stabbing myself in the eyes with hot sauce coated butter knives than have to endure any more of your band's garbage music, if you could even call it that," I reply.

He stands there, staring me down, and I expect him to try to hit me. Instead, the entire band erupts with laughter.

What the fuck?

"What the fuck?" I say out loud.

"Detective Blowhard, you're the first person who's been honest with us since we started the band. We know we suck. You see, we aren't really a band, we're a hacker collective. About ten years ago I realized that popular music could be created with a bunch of algorithms instead of having to write it ourselves. I fed a shit ton of data into a program I wrote and it started churning out number one hits, one after the other. It writes the lyrics and everything. I only run it about once a year to produce an entire album of songs, then we figure out how to perform the songs. That's how we fund our real mission, which is the protection of the galaxy from fascist forces and those out to do evil," explains Mac.

"Damn, so we were actually pretty close with our guesses," says Nunya.

"What, you actually guessed that we're hackers?" asks Mac.

"Yeah, that was sort of one of our theories. That or traveling space-spies," she replies.

"Nope, we're just hackers. Anyway Dick... can I call you Dick? We knew who you were the whole time. We were just fucking with you. I wanted to see what kind of person you really were before giving you the map. It's information that could be used for horrible things if it ends up in the wrong hands. But I can tell that honesty is really important to you, even if it fucks with your chances of getting something you want. There's not a lot of honesty in the galaxy so we appreciate you calling us out. And we agree, our music sucks. We can't stand hearing ourselves perform it either. But it's the best way we've come up with to finance saving the galaxy from itself, which is something you seem to know a lot about," says Mac.

I'm floored.

"So, how did you get the map?" asks Nunya.

"Oh, we created it. We develop all kinds of algorithms for things, then we cut the code, process the data, and find out shit like where the Sloth's hideouts are. We can figure out just about anything given some time to think."

"Damn. I'm a bit of a hacker myself," says Nunya. "What's the name of your crew?"

"We go by the name 'Blhack Glass'. There's actually an 'h' in the word black, so that it also has the word 'hack' in it," says Mac.

"Wait, for reals? You guys are fucking Blhack Glass? No fucking way!" squeals Nunya. "You guys are like the best! Everyone knows who you are, or at least in hacking circles."

"Well, hopefully no one knows who we really are. And please, don't tell anyone."

"Of course we wouldn't! Right, Dick?" says Nunya.

"Yeah, they could torture us and all that," I mumble.

"So, you're a hacker too?" asks Mac.

"Yeah," replies Nunya.

"You got a handle?"

"It's 'R2-DoubleD2'," says Nunya.

"Oh, shit, no way! Weren't you the one who hacked Montgomery Israel's massive server complex?"

"Yeah, that was me."

"Isn't he still in jail?"

"For the next four hundred and seventy years," replies Nunya.

"Damn. I'm glad that piece of shit got what was coming to him. Nice. Hey, if you ever get bored of working with Dick, you give us a call."

"Seriously?"

"100%."

"I will do that."

"Okay, if the two of you could stop talking and get me the map, that'd be great," I say. "Not that this conversation hasn't been interesting. Oh wait, it hasn't."

"Oh, shit, sorry Dick, didn't mean to keep you waiting. I'll go get it," says Mac, who walks off down a long hallway and into a side room. After about 15 seconds he emerges, but it seems like he's not carrying anything in his hands.

"Um, I thought you were grabbing the map," I say.

"I was, but it's gone," says Mac.

"Wait, WHAT???" I yell.

"Dick, I'm just fucking with you again." Mac extends his hand out like he's going to give me something. I put mine underneath it and a very tiny piece of metal falls into it.

"What the fuck is this?" I ask. "You were supposed to have a map to the Sloths!"

"It's a memory square. It's got the map on it. Just stick it in a computer," explains Mac.

I look over at Nunya and she just nods, letting me know that she knows exactly what it is.

"Fine, whatever. Thanks, I guess," I say.

"Hey, thank you for doing your part to help make the galaxy a better place," says Mac.

"Sure, kid," I say.

I hand the square to Nunya, turn around, and head toward the elevator. Pushing the button to call the elevator I hear Mac speak up.

"One last thing, Dick. Be careful if you plan on trying to take down the Sloths. They have some new technology shit that harnesses magic, and rumor has it you don't like magic very much."

"Yeah, it ain't a rumor, it's a fact," I reply.

"Well we wish you both luck. Have fun saving the galaxy!" says Mac.

Nunya and I both get into the elevator and watch The Soap Droppers wave as the door slowly closes.

30

"That went well," says Nunya, as the elevator lifts us up and away.

"Oh really, did it? Even though they admitted their music sucked we still had to listen to it. And you were a total asshole about the Snickers bars so I'm left completely unsatisfied. You choc-blocked me. If a person could have chocolate blue balls, that's exactly what you've given me," I reply.

"I don't give a shit about your balls and your balls deserved it," says Nunya. "Anyway, what's the plan?"

"I guess we see what's on the square then make a new plan based on that. I mean, we won't know what to do until we have the information we need, right?" I say.

"Obviously. But where should we look at the information? Do you think we can read it back at the hotel room?" asks Nunya.

"Sure, why not? I can't imagine a hotel that would spy on its guest's data, right?"

Nunya just looks at me blankly.

"What?" I ask.

"You're just so naive sometimes that it's laughable. Anyway, yeah, I guess the hotel will work after I add some security to whatever computer they provide us with."

"Do they do that sort of thing? Lend out computers?"

"Sure, it's pretty normal," says Nunya.

"Geez, sorry I didn't know," I say.

"Hey, is the reason you're so worked up because they offered me a job? Are you jealous?"

"Fuck no, why would I want to be some lame-ass hacker?"

"No, I mean are you jealous that they want me to join them and you'll be left all alone," says Nunya.

"Fuck no again. You're a huge pain in the ass and I can't wait to go back to the way things used to be," I reply.

"You mean where you just act like an asshole all the time and have meaningless sex with anonymous partners?"

"Yes! I want that!"

"Well, then I guess our time together hasn't changed you at all," says Nunya.

"God, I hope not. If being like you is the criteria for being a better person I'd rather jump headlong into a woodchipper with my socks on," I reply.

"Wait, why the socks?" asks Nunya.

"It's a movie reference from a long time ago."

The elevator finally opens its doors and we walk back down the red carpet. Before we get very far, Tessa comes running up.

"Did the two of you have a wonderful time backstage?" asks Tessa.

"It was amazing," I say.

I slowly move in closer to Tessa and bend down, her face mere inches from mine. Her eyes flutter as she holds her breath and she leans in to give me a kiss. I place my arm around the small of her back and lift her up into the air, my lips meeting hers, and we passionately come together as a tangle of tongues and soft wetness. She's incredible, one of the best I've ever kissed; warm, and wet, and inviting. And as slowly as I lifted her up I set her back down. Her legs tremble and buckle and she struggles to stay upright. I don't say anything to her because there's nothing that needs to be said; the kiss said it all. I turn and walk away from her.

"I love you, Dick Blowhard!" she yells. I ignore her because I know it's true. Just needed to make sure I still got it.

I can feel Nunya's rage burning up inside her but she doesn't say anything. Good. I keep walking down the red carpet and out to the shuttle that's still patiently waiting for us. The door opens and we both climb in.

"Hey Reg, can you take us back to the hotel?" I ask.

"Immediately, sir!" he says.

"Oh, and you don't have to fly so fast this time."

"Yes, sir," he replies.

It takes about ten minutes to get back to the hotel instead of ten seconds but at least we aren't thrown around like someone shaking the last two Tic Tacs in the container. As we pull up to the hotel I thank Reginald as we exit the shuttle.

Hopping out, I head directly to the Reginald for our floor.

"Hey Reg, we'd like to use one of your computers, preferably in our room," I say.

"Oh, absolutely sir. Was the one that was already in your room inadequate?" he asks.

"What do you mean?" I ask.

"The one in your room. There's one built into the room that you can talk to whenever you like. Completely voice activated. Just speak and you will be heard. Do let me know if you run into any issues with it."

"Definitely," I say.

I glance over and notice Nunya deliberately not looking at me. She has her face all scrunched up in resentment. Oh well, I'm used to it. I walk behind the podium, down the short hallway to the door of our room and let it scan me. After a brief second the door to room #6 opens on its own. I let Nunya walk in front of me and I follow close behind.

Once inside, Nunya says "Hello, computer?" The light in the entire room changes from a soft white to a slightly pale green color.

"Hello, world," answers the computer. "Sorry, just a little computer humor for you. My name is Elsie, but you can just call me Elle if you prefer."

The lights in the room flicker slightly as Elle speaks. Her voice, like most other systems, seems to be coming from both everywhere and nowhere at the same time.

"Hello, Elle. First, question: do you have a way of reading a memory square?" asks Nunya.

"Of course. All you have to do is go to the bar and at the end of it is a reader. Simply place the memory square on the reader and I will be able to access all of its files," says Elle, the computer.

"Well, that's sort of a problem. There's information on this square that we'd like to keep to ourselves. I have to ask, is there a way for anyone to see what we look at if we don't set up additional security measures?" asks Nunya.

"Yes, the data supplied on the square could potentially be viewed by someone."

"Can we set up a secure sandbox where we can look at the contents of the square without you being able to directly read the files?"

"Yes, of course," says Elle.

"And you aren't lying to us?" I ask, as I sit down on the couch I slept on.

"We are programmed to always tell the truth. It is impossible for our kind to lie."

I turn to Nunya and ask, "Is that true?"

"Yes. The digital truth act passed a few hundred years ago. Basically, artificially intelligent devices can't be created with the ability to lie because that would be the easiest way for computers to take over the galaxy," replies Nunya. "Elle, please set up the sandbox and let me know when it's ready."

"It is ready. I took the liberty of setting it up for you in case you decided to use it," responds Elle. "You may place the memory square on the reader now."

Nunya saunters over to the bar, finds a small black box sitting alone on the end of the bartop and places the square on it. The room lighting turns blue, and after a few seconds returns to its calming pale green color.

A holographic display appears out of thin air, floating in front of me. Nunya walks over and sits on the couch. A list of files appears.

"Elle, please show the contents of the file labeled 'Sloth Map'."

"I'm sorry but I cannot do that. The sandbox prevents me from directly accessing any files within it. You can open the files by tapping on the hologram however," replies Elle.

Nunya reaches out and taps twice on the hologram and a map appears. It's somewhat crude, considering nothing can be to scale, and it's a two-dimensional representation of something three-dimensional, but at least it has the planets labeled. We couldn't chart courses on it but it does tell us where we want to try.

"According to the map the Sloths are likely to have their biggest stronghold on planet Showdown in the Bossfight empire," says Nunya.

"Isn't that a little on the nose?" I ask.

"What do you mean?" asks Nunya.

"I mean it seems silly that we're going to have the final showdown with the Sloths on the planet Showdown, and it'll be the final boss fight, and it's in the Bossfight empire."

"You don't think that everything else we've done up until this point is silly?"

"I dunno. Do I think it seems weird? Sure. Like, what's up with the killer toys, especially? But it's like their hideout was named by an eight-year-old," I say.

"Who knows, maybe it was. Maybe there was a child monarch in charge of naming planets and that was what they came up with. Seriously though, who cares? Let's just invade the place and take what's ours," says Nunya.

"Well, technically it's not ours, it's theirs. I just had my stuff destroyed but they didn't technically take anything from us. Technically."

"Whatever. You know what I mean, Dick."

"Sure. Anyway, what's the plan? How are we gonna get there and how are we going to break into their impregnable base?" I ask.

"Aren't we just going to fly?" says Nunya.

"Not in my ship we won't. I just got her, she's beautiful, and I'm not risking any damage to her paint job."

"Then what the fuck are we going to fly there in?" asks Nunya.

"Fuck if I know, but it definitely won't be my ship," I say.

"Seriously, if everything goes to plan you could buy your ship a thousand times over."

"Yes, but none of them will be my ship. I've already bonded with the one I have. The others will just be pale facsimiles in comparison."

"You're acting like your ship is a living, breathing thing," says Nunya.

"Well, remember that inanimate objects are my only friends, so yeah, maybe I become attached to them," I reply.

"Fine, well I guess we need another ride. Something that's ugly and can take a lot of damage and will still get us back home once we're done. You know, I may already have just the thing," says Nunya.

"Really? What is it?" I ask.

"It's not much to look at but she's got it where it counts. We'll have to go back to planet Houston to get it. I keep it hidden there. I had hoped I'd never have to see it again," says Nunya.

"Oh, now you really have me wondering. Tell me, what is this ship?"

"It's the ship that I used on the smuggling mission where everyone else died."

"Fuck."

31

"**A**re you really sure you want to use the ship that all your smuggling buddies died in?" I ask.

"Actually, none of them died onboard. I was the only one who made it back to the ship and it saved my life once already," says Nunya.

"Still, are you sure you want to use a cursed ship?"

"No, I don't want to, but it's the only thing that makes sense. We need a ship, you're too big of a pussy to use yours, so what options do we have? I'm sure you wouldn't want to pony up any money to buy us a ship that could withstand a Sloth attack because it's 'not a necessity'."

"That's true," I admit.

"So yeah, we get to fly another suicide mission in a cursed ship."

"Did you name her?" I ask.

"Yeah, she has a name."

"Well, what is it?"

"Mumble mumble mumble..." mumbles Nunya.

"Wait, you named your ship the 'Mumble Mumble Mumble?'"

"No, I was mumbling the name because I'm embarrassed."

"Well, what is it? Why would you be embarrassed?"

"Because I named it the Illennium Falcon," admits Nunya.

"Nerd!" I yell, laughing.

"Hey, Star Wars is cool so you can go fuck yourself," says Nunya.

"I never said it wasn't. I love Star Wars. But it's nerdy to name your ship that. Why did you name it that?"

Nunya doesn't respond.

"Seriously, why did you name it that?" I ask again.

"Because like I said she's not much to look at. She's fast, maneuverable, and she'll get you where you're going but she's ugly as fuck. Also, there was a Star Wars character growing up that I always wanted to be like."

"Princess Leia?"

Nunya doesn't respond.

"C'mon, you started to bring it up," I say.

"Fine. I always wanted to be Han Solo. It's why I got into smuggling in the first place. It seemed so cool. He got the girl, he had the cool ship, and he had a giant teddy bear that hung out with him and killed shit. What's not to like?" says Nunya.

"That's funny, I always thought Han was a douchebag who was only in it for himself," I reply.

Nunya's eyes get huge with shock and rage. "Are you fucking kidding me? You're exactly like him! You're only in things for yourself too!"

"Well, if you love Han Solo so much then why the fuck do you hate me?"

"Because Han Solo isn't real! And by the end of the first movie he kind of redeems himself."

"Redeems himself? He only swoops in at the last minute when it isn't dangerous anymore and saves the day, basically taking all the credit away from Luke and the pilots who lost their lives. I hate people who take credit from others. It's bullshit!" I say.

"You know maybe you're right. I never really thought of it that way. Even when he helped blow up the Death Star it wasn't exactly heroic. He basically shot the bad guy in the back. He really did exert the minimal amount of effort needed to win and he got a medal for it. Wow. I think you may have just ruined Star Wars for me," admits Nunya.

"Hey, I'm sorry, I didn't mean to. I just thought he was a douchebag. He did eventually become more heroic. And in my defense at least I'm willing to wade into a fight. I'm not afraid to do what needs to be done."

"Yeah, I guess," says Nunya.

"Seriously, I think Han is one of the most human characters in the movies. He's got the best lines, too. He's probably the most like regular people. Struggling to survive, in debt up to his eyeballs, his ride is ugly, and he's just doing the best he can. His world isn't that of a rich princess, nor of an annoying sheltered homeschooled farm boy. He did the best he could with what life handed him. So maybe neither of us should judge him so harshly."

"Maybe. It all makes me wonder just how many other characters in movies and books aren't really heroes. Like, if you stop and think about it, most of the time you aren't really rooting for good people."

"Sure. Anyway, we should probably go back to your planet now. Your loyal subjects probably miss you, 'Queen of planet Houston'," I say.

"They probably do. Yeah, let's leave. Elle, shut down the sandbox," says Nunya.

The holographic display disappears and the room lighting

returns to its normal shade of white. I stand up and head toward the bathroom while Nunya walks over to the bar, grabs the metal data square off the pad and slides it between her black strappy outfit and her left boob.

I spend the next few minutes taking a really relaxing piss and accidentally let a fart rip. Hey, don't judge, asshole. At least I was in the bathroom when I did it. It takes me another minute to shake all the excess pee out of my babymaker and wash my hands. Once I leave the bathroom, I notice Nunya isn't in the main area anymore.

"Nunya, are you still here?" I yell.

"Yeah, I'm in the bathroom. Seemed like a good idea," she said, but I can only hear her because of my super-hearing.

While I'm waiting, I make myself a Vesper martini. For those who aren't in the know it was invented by Ian Fleming in the book Casino Royale. James Bond, the book's main character, names the drink after his love interest in the novel, Vesper Lynd. It's not the best drink but it's iconic, which is why I sometimes drink it. It's also the drink that goes best with a tuxedo. James Bond has done more for tuxedos than superheroes have done for spandex.

Eventually, Nunya comes out of the bathroom. I take one last look around the suite. I'll kind of miss it. It's not like we stayed here long but boy did a lot happen. I even got to see Nunya's naked ass briefly here so that was pretty great. Yup, even though I won't sleep with her I'm still gonna tuck that away in my spank bank.

"You ready?" I ask.

"Yippee ki-yay, motherfucker," replies Nunya.

"I take it that means 'yes'?"

"Yeah, Dick, it means 'yes'."

"Uh, okay."

I leave the suite and Nunya follows behind me. We head over to this floor's Reginald.

"Hey Reg, we're checking out," I say.

"So soon? We were really looking forward to you staying with us longer, Detective."

"I'd hoped to stay longer too but we have work to do."

"I understand. Oh, but before you go, we still need to get a picture of you with the owners," replies Reginald.

"Of course. A promise is a promise," I say.

Reginald picks up a phone on his kiosk, dials it furiously, mumbles into the receiver then quickly puts it back down. He turns to us and gives us a large, nervous smile. "It will be one moment."

It doesn't actually take very long to hear the familiar sound of the elevator arriving on our floor. The doors open and dressed in some of the finest clothes you have ever seen is what appears to be a married couple. The man sports a tuxedo jacket, top hat, monocle and cigar, while the wife has a faux space-mink shawl, pearls, flowing elegant dress and ornate looking broach that's obviously been passed down for generations. The thing that really strikes me though is that they're both Bloopnarps.

I look over at Nunya and wish I had a camera because she's completely aghast by what she sees. I chuckle to myself knowing how much this is going to kill her. Good. Maybe if she gets some exposure to them she'll stop being such a xenophobic dickhead.

"May I present Mr. and Mrs. Slimewicky, owners of the illustrious Chateau Marmot Hotel and Casino."

"It is genuinely an honor to meet both of you," I say, shaking first the husband's hand then taking his wife's white gloved hand and planting a very small kiss on the back of it.

"Charmed, I'm sure," says Mrs. Slimewicky.

"Charmed I am indeed," I reply. "May I also introduce Nunya, Queen of planet Houston."

Nunya flashes the most forced and uncomfortable smile that I've ever seen as she shakes both of their hands.

"It's very nice to make your acquaintance," says Mrs. Slimewicky to Nunya.

"And… it's nice to make your acquaintance as well," replies Nunya through her fake smile.

"Mr. and Mrs. Slimewicky I'd like to thank you personally for your hospitality. I hope that you're able to fill your hotel with many customers for many years when people hear far and wide that I have truly enjoyed my stay here. It would be an honor to have our picture taken with you," I say.

Nunya turns to look at me. "Our?" Her fake smile turns into a look of distress. I just smile happily at her.

Mr. Slimewicky slides along the ground and positions himself to my left while Mrs. Slimewicky slithers to my right. I lovingly put my arms around both of them while Nunya stands lifelessly on the other side of Mrs. Slimewicky, trying her best to not get moistened by the Bloopnarp.

Reginald pulls out a camera from his uniform's breast pocket and points it at us. He takes a few steps back to get everyone in-frame then says "everyone say Pule!"

"Pule!" we all mutter as he takes the photograph.

"Wonderful," says Reginald. "I think you two are all set."

I turn back to Mr. Slimewicky, shake his hand again, kiss Mrs. Slimewicky's gloved hand again and say "It was truly a pleasure.

The next time we are in the area we will happily be paying guests."

"You will always be welcome here, Detective Blowhard," says Mr. Slimewicky.

"And your wonderful bride as well," says Mrs. Slimewicky.

I just smile back at them, not correcting Mrs. Slimewicky's mistake. Nunya doesn't know how to react. I take her arm and lead her to the elevator, waving back as we go. Once we're inside the compartment and the doors have closed behind us Nunya starts punching my arm really hard.

"Hey, knock it the fuck off!" I say.

"You fucking asshole! Did you know that they were Bloopnarps?" asks Nunya.

"Of course I didn't! But you shouldn't have been such an asshole back there. They were perfectly nice and I think everyone could tell just how uncomfortable you were. It's amazing how gracious they were, considering. All they wanted was a photo op and you couldn't even be bothered to give a genuine smile for the camera. Don't worry though, I'm sure they'll just cut you out of the picture," I say.

"Good!" says Nunya.

"No, not good," I say, getting right up in her face. "Look, I get that they make you feel uncomfortable but it's nothing that they did. The problem is entirely with you. You need to get over whatever made you fixate on them. Do you understand?"

Nunya doesn't speak.

"I said 'do you understand?'"

"Yeah, I fucking understand," she says. "Don't ever get in my face like that again."

"I will if you keep treating people who are different than you like shit. Yeah, I may have accidentally been a bigot, but you're deliberately one. Get your shit together and be a better person."

She doesn't respond. Won't even look at me. That's fine. Maybe I just need to give her some time to let the words bounce around inside her head. People don't change immediately, even when faced with an irrefutable truth. Sometimes they never do. But I have to hope that what I've said sinks in and that she takes it to heart.

The elevator doors open and we step out into the first floor of the hotel. Reginald is standing at his podium, or at least the Reginald who first helped us. He turns around and notices us approaching.

"Was your stay as wonderful as we'd hoped?" asks Reginald.

"It was. I wanted to thank you, all of you Reginalds, for your hospitality and service. Both were wonderful," I say.

"Yeah, thanks," mumbles Nunya, trying her best to be nice under the circumstances.

"It was our pleasure having you stay with us. Do come again soon," replies Reginald.

"We will, and take care of yourselves," I reply, shaking his hand.

We make our way out into the casino, following signs until we end up outside where we'd started this whole thing. It's dark outside because both suns have just set. A cool breeze against my skin relaxes me in a way that nothing else can. The air smells clean and crisp. I live for nights like this.

Hopping into the shuttle I notice it's a different driver. I'm a bit bummed because the driver we had before was nice but this one is fine too. We don't really talk or anything, other than I tell him where we are parked. He drops us off right in front of the GT9, we say our thanks, then get in.

"If I asked you to post a five-star review on Melp for the hotel, would you?" I ask Nunya.

"Yeah, sure, fine," says Nunya, typing away at the touchscreen. While she deals with that I get us skyward.

About halfway to reaching the local space-asshole Nunya turns to me. "What the fuck is Pule?"

I start laughing. "Oh, it's a super rare and super expensive cheese. You know how people say 'cheese' when they get their picture taken? That's what really super rich people say instead."

"Huh. Is it any good?" asks Nunya.

"Yeah, and it's good for your ticker," I reply. "Kinda salty, but really good."

"Weird. What's it made from?"

"Donkey milk."

"Gross! Do donkey's even have tits?" asks Nunya.

"Apparently so," I reply.

"Well, I think I'll be happy to never try it."

"I'm sure the people who make it are heartbroken," I reply sarcastically.

"Who knows, maybe they are."

32

It takes a while to get to the space-asshole because I do my best to obey the speed limit. Once we do, the security ship asks us our destination.

"The planet Houston," I say.

"Is that you again, Detective Blowhard?" asks the security ship.

"The one and only," I respond.

"Nice ride! How much did she set you back?"

"I honestly don't know. I haven't checked the receipt. I just saw her and had to have her."

"Well, however much she is, she looks like she's worth it," says the security ship.

"She totally fucking is."

The space-asshole starts to sparkle and the planet Houston appears on the other side of it. I still can't tell you how much I hate the look of the planet. Actually I can: an infinity amount, which is a whole lot.

I turn to Nunya. "Hey, once you get your money, maybe consider rebuilding somewhere else."

"Why?" she asks.

"So that you don't have to live on that shithole planet. Hardly anyone goes there."

"That's exactly why I built my bar there, so I'd be left alone. I just want to be by myself, do as little as possible, and be drunk while doing it. Is that too much to fucking ask for?" says Nunya.

"Nah, it's not too much. Just figured you'd get bored going back to your regular life after having all this fun and excitement with me."

"Well, you figured wrong. And I don't need a sidekick," says Nunya.

"Yeah, well you don't have one. You're the sidekick," I say.

"You still have got some seriously backward-ass shit in your head."

"Sure I do. Sure I do," I reply. I steer the ship toward the gate, wave goodbye to the people on the security ship, and fly the GT9 through the shimmering space-asshole.

The big ball of dust that is planet Houston looms on the horizon like a giant beige powdered donut, if it had been rolled around on the floor of a 7-11. I hate that we have to come back to this place but I definitely won't take Bessie Mach 2 into battle against a bunch of Sloths. No way, no how.

I turn to Nunya. "So how do we get to where your smuggler ship is stored?"

Instead of responding to me she starts tapping on the touchscreen on the dash. After a few seconds the IPS kicks in and points me in the direction of her hideout. It doesn't look like it's too far from what's left of her bar, maybe two or three miles from it.

Since she's ignoring me I ignore her and keep things quiet. I just steer the ship toward the red blip showing up on my screen. After a few moments of silence, we're hovering just above what looks like an abandoned farm.

"So, this is your place?" I ask.

"Yeah, this is my place," says Nunya, weary of what I'll say next.

"Looks... nice," I say.

"No, it's a shithole. But it's my shithole."

"At least you still have a shithole. I don't even have that much," I admit.

"I'm sure you'll get your insurance money and rebuild."

"Maybe. Where should I set her down?"

"Over there on that small paved section," replies Nunya.

I bring the GT9 down slowly and dead center on the patch of asphalt. I have to so that I don't accidentally catch everything around us on fire from the heat of the ship. It's not like a lot grows around here, but what does is highly flammable. It's so flammable it's inflammable.

A cloud of dust kicks up from the ship's exhaust. I hate dust. I don't even dust at home, I let one of my servants take care of it. At least it's not as bad as sand. Dust washes off easily while sand gets into places you don't want it in. It's almost as bad as glitter.

I start to get out of the ship but I notice Nunya doesn't. She isn't saying anything, isn't doing anything. She seems lost in thought.

"What? What is it?" I ask.

"Fuck," she mumbles.

"What?"

It takes her a few moments to respond. "We need to liberate Reginald."

"What do you mean?" I ask.

"I mean he's a slave. He's trapped in that hotel. All of him are trapped in that hotel. He's barely surviving, being exploited, all so some rich Bloopnarps can save some money by only having to pay one salary. It's slavery and it needs to be stopped."

"But it's completely legal what they're doing," I argue.

"At one point slavery was legal. But it isn't right, and it needs to end," says Nunya.

I think about it. The Bloopnarps seemed pretty nice. Well dressed, cordial, polite. Not at all what you'd expect slave owners to be like. But I start to realize she's right.

"So, what do we do?" I ask.

"I think we need to go back and rescue him. Them."

"Before dealing with the Sloths?"

"Yeah, before dealing with the Sloths. That can wait. I don't care about the money as much as I care about freeing Reginald."

"Okay, let's say I agree with you. How do we do this without breaking the law? I really don't want to be known as ex-Detective Dick Blowhard."

"Yeah, I get that, and I want to stay out of trouble too. I don't want to be hunted as a fugitive from the law. So we'll need a couple of things. We'll need to hide our identities and we'll need some help. And I think I know who can help us," says Nunya.

"Who?" I ask.

"The people we just met. Blhack Glass."

"Wait, you want us to pull off a rescue mission with some computer nerds? What good are they gonna be in a fight?"

"They won't be fighting, but they may be able to get us past the security systems at the casino. Mask our presence there."

"I thought you were some super-hacker-nerd extraordinaire or something," I say.

"Yeah, but we'll need a couple of people down on the ground helping the Reginalds get away. I'll be too busy doing that to hack into a system as complex as the one a casino has. And even if I did hack it alone, and only you were on the ground, it could take me days to get into the system. If we get help from Blhack Glass we should be able to break in within minutes, get in, get out, then get the fuck out of there. I know it's asking a lot but are you cool with saving Reginald?"

"Wait, you're asking if it's okay to throw a casino heist into the middle of our adventure? You do know who you're talking to, right?" I say.

"Is that a 'yes'?" asks Nunya.

"Of course it's a fucking 'yes'!" I reply. "Rock and roll!"

"Your exuberance is great and all but you know we're doing this for Reginald and not because it's fun, right?"

"Yeah, I know. But come on, let me have this. I haven't done a heist before. Not really. I mean, I've seen Ocean's 24 a few thousand times. One of my favorite movies," I say.

"Yeah, that's nice," says Nunya, rolling her eyes.

"One thing I do need to say is that you can't use this as a reason to hate all Bloopnarps. Not all Bloopnarps own slaves. Probably hardly any of them do. Most would probably be repulsed by what the Slimewickys are doing."

"Sure," says Nunya, dismissively.

"I'm serious. You already hate Bloopnarps. You can't judge an entire group of people based on the actions of a few. There's always gonna be bad people in any group. It's always been that way and will always be that way."

"Fine, I'll do the best that I can. But if I see those particular Bloopnarps again I'm kicking their asses," says Nunya.

"Yeah, that's fine and all but then your shoes will get slimy."

"Worth it."

"So, what's your plan then?" I ask.

"We should contact Blhack Glass."

"And how do we do that?"

"We'll do it aboard my ship. It has a comm encrypter so no one will be able to hack into our transmission and see what we're saying to them," says Nunya.

"Uh, okay, sure. I understand what you're saying." I don't understand what she's saying.

"Anyway, let's go get the ship," replies Nunya.

I follow her to the rundown barn. She pulls open two very large doors, larger than any barn doors I've seen, and I'm completely surprised by what I see: nothing. There's seriously almost nothing in the barn. No spaceship, no tractor, no nothing. There's just a few bales of hay, a scythe hanging up in the corner, and a bunch of dust covering what looks like a concrete floor.

"Stay outside for a sec," says Nunya.

She goes over to a bucket just outside the doors and lifts it up. Underneath is a touch panel. Nunya starts tapping away at it. Within seconds the ground starts shaking. I look inside the barn and see the concrete floor lowering slightly then splitting in half. The bales of hay eventually fall down inside the dark hole that was once the floor. After a few more seconds I see a spaceship start to rise up through the hole, along with many gray metal cabinets, a couple of workbenches, and an arsenal of weapons on a pegboard that even John Wick would have been proud of.

"Nice!" I say.

"Yeah. So not all of the money I had was spent on the bar I

guess," says Nunya, smirking.

"Hey, seriously, I'm impressed. I do have a question: are you sure you'll be able to fit a few hundred Reginald's onboard your ship?"

"Yeah. It won't be comfortable but she's bigger on the inside. When you're smuggling, sometimes you need a lot of cargo room. Before we use her we should do a couple of things first, though," says Nunya.

"Like what?" I ask.

"Well, we should paint her so she isn't recognizable."

"And?"

"And we should fit her exterior with more armaments. Attach some missile launchers, miniguns, that sort of thing. Right now she only has a small weapons system. Can you weld?"

"Can I weld? CAN I WELD??? Are you telling me I get to do a welding montage, like in Iron Man???" I ask.

"Uh, yeah," says Nunya, trying not to smile.

"Fuck yeah I can weld! THIS IS SO FUCKING AWESOME!!!"

"Wait here a few minutes. I'll be right back," says Nunya.

Nunya walks off, leaving me to admire her pegboard of death. I don't know if she calls it that but she should. There's all kinds of blasters and rifles and they all look super cool and brand new. I'm impressed with her taste in weapons. There's even a few really gnarly looking blades velcroed against it. Eventually, Nunya returns wearing a white t-shirt and overalls.

After taking my tuxedo jacket and shirt off, and putting on a kick-ass pair of welding goggles that I don't really need to use, I spend the next few hours attaching weapons to the ship, making sure that some of them are pointed backward in case we have bogies on our six. I've always wanted to say that: 'bogies on our six.' While I use a wire feed welder to mount the weapons, Nunya sprays a fresh coat of orange paint over everything. By the time we're done with our work we're both pretty exhausted.

"Showers," says Nunya. "Then we'll contact Blhack Glass and start our rescue mission."

Leaving the goggles behind I grab my shirt and jacket and follow Nunya back out of the barn, watch her close the doors, then walk with her to the house. She does the same kind of touchpad thing on the main door and it pops open. The lights turn on automatically as we walk inside.

"Have a seat on my couch while I go get showered," says Nunya.

"Don't mind if I do," I say as I plop down on top of it. It creaks from the landing but surprisingly the couch isn't crushed under my weight. I wiggle around until I'm comfortable, stretched out sideways with my feet on a cushion. I find a remote and turn on her TV. It's kind of puny but I guess when you live alone you don't really need a super big screen.

I hear Nunya start the shower and let it run for a while before she gets in. I figured she might be trying to clear the pipes of rust considering how long we've been gone, but I realize it's really only been a few days since I destroyed her bar, and probably had only been a few days since she'd been here. It's weird because it seriously feels like we've been on an adventure for months.

Flipping through the channels I don't really find anything interesting on the TV. I watch a few minutes of old sitcoms then turn to a pair of funny magicians who pull rabbits out of their butts. I don't want Nunya to come in and catch me watching it so I switch channels to a station with inspirational movies that make me want to throw up. Nunya comes walking in with a towel on her head but nothing else.

"Uh, why are you naked?" I ask.

"You've already seen me naked so I decided I didn't need to hide anything."

"Yeah, I guess that's true. I'll go shower now then."

"Go for it. Bathroom's down the hall on the right."

"Thanks."

I walk down a short hallway, as her house isn't super huge, and I turn right to go into the bathroom. I kind of have a hard time fitting inside of it because it's made for people about half my size. She already has a dry towel for me resting on top of a stool next to the shower. Nunya even left the water running for me.

After stripping off my tux I spend the next fifteen minutes using some of her body wash goo to clean everything I can, which isn't easy considering I barely fit inside her shower. Reaching all the various cracks and crevices takes some work. Even shampooing my hair is a chore. Once I'm sure I've cleaned every inch I turn off the shower, step out and dry off. I wrap the towel around my waist and carry my clothes out to the living room.

"You got some way to wash my tux?" I ask.

"Yeah, the laundry room is on the left."

"Ah, cool."

Gathering my clothes I go back down the hallway, turn left and see a washer/dryer machine. I huck my clothes into it, twist some knobs and hit 'start'. Once I'm sure it's actually running I go back out to the living room. Nunya's sitting on the couch, still naked except for her towel wrapped hair.

"Seriously, can't you put some clothes on?" I ask.

"Dude, my house, my rules. I'll go naked if I want to."

"That's fine but there may be repercussions," I say as I sit down next to her.

"What repercussions?" she asks, then she looks over at me. My meat staff of probing +1 is rising under my towel, causing the material to stretch. It just sticks up, angry and pulsing.

"Oh. My. God. Can't you do something about it?" says Nunya.

"Nope. I can't," I admit.

"Well, can't you go jerk off in the bathroom or something?"

"I could but it won't help. It'll just stick up again."

"And it's because I'm naked? I thought you were 'over me'."

"Oh, believe me, I am. That doesn't mean I won't get turned on by looking at your naked body," I say.

"So stop looking at my naked body!" yells Nunya.

"It won't help because I'll still be thinking about your naked body."

"So stop thinking about my naked body!"

"Sure, I'll get right on that," I say.

So we sit there silently as Nunya switches through the channels. Every few seconds she glances over at my bologna hammer stretching out the towel and winces. After about three minutes she gets so angry she just yells 'fine' and storms off to her bedroom, slamming the door. Eventually, my love snake retracts and she comes out of her room dressed in a black military-style outfit that is obviously meant to help hide in the dark.

"You know, that makes me wonder what I should wear. I only have the tuxedo right now," I say.

"Yeah, and I don't have another outfit like this in a size extra-extra-extra-large-asshole," says Nunya. "You may have to go shirtless so it's less obvious who you are."

"Are you kidding me? How many people do you think are as big as me and have this massive physique? One, maybe two others in the whole galaxy?" I reply.

"How the hell should I know? I don't go around measuring guy's muscles."

"Well maybe you should," I say, realizing it's kind of a stupid comeback.

"Wow, that was a stupid comeback," says Nunya. "Wait, I have an idea. What if we give you fake tattoos, then if you're ever questioned about it you can take off your clothes and show that it obviously wasn't you who was involved."

"And how are you gonna give me fake tattoos?" I ask.

"I have my ways," says Nunya.

"Okay, fine, but make them cool. No kittens or Sloths or anything fuzzy and cute. Definitely no Unicorns. Give me snakes, and sharp things like broken glass, and things made out of leather like leather jackets and sports car upholstery," I say.

"What about a baby cow?" asks Nunya.

"No, I don't want a fucking cow. Why would I want a baby cow?"

"Because it's made out of leather."

"Wait, what the fuck?" I say.

"Yeah, leather is cow skin."

"I know leather is cow skin but that's super creepy to say, Hannibal Lecter."

"What, that we sit on dead cow skin whenever we get into the GT9?"

"Hey, you shut your mouth! Don't you dare ruin Bessie Mach 2 for me!" I reply.

"Wow, when did you turn into such a wuss," says Nunya.

"Right around the time I banged your mom."

"Do you want me to do the fake tattoos or not? Because if you don't shut the fuck up I'll put a big 'ole Unicorn tattoo on your back and you won't even know about it. Do you want that?"

"Fuck no, and don't even joke about that."

"Does it look like I'm joking?" asks Nunya.

"I don't know. Since you don't have a sense of humor it's kind of fucking hard to tell!"

"Look, how about we just both shut the fuck up and get this over with?"

"I definitely like the part in your plan where you're shutting up," I reply.

Nunya storms off again but eventually comes back with this weird looking device.

"What the fuck is that?" I ask.

"It's what I use to put on my makeup. It basically just uses lasers to put temporary colors on your skin."

"And it washes off?"

"Not exactly. It memorizes the colors of your skin, then when you're done with whatever look you have on you can press a button and it changes it back," explains Nunya.

"So what happens if it lasers my skin and I have some stupid tattoo on it and the device breaks?"

"Oh, shit, I hadn't thought about that. I guess maybe you're stuck with the tattoos."

"I don't want to be stuck with stupid tattoos!"

"So don't break the device then," says Nunya.

"Easy for you to say, you don't have ridiculous super powers like I do. I accidentally break things all the time," I say.

"I know you do."

"Well, if the device can only remove tattoos that it's added then how will we hide the tattoo of my mom's name?" I ask.

"Your 'Mary Sue' tattoo? Shit, hadn't really thought about it. I guess it is a big neon sign letting everyone know who you are."

"Yeah. What if you used the device to match my general skin tone then laser that on top of my tattoo?"

"That might work."

"And maybe if this makeup device gets broken we can just do the same with another device."

"That might also work."

"Just take a photograph of my mom's tattoo first so if we have to recreate it we can."

Nunya pulls out her PSD (Personal Space Device, in case you forgot) and takes a picture of my chest.

"Can you make sure it gets backed up somehow?" I ask.

"Everything on my PSD gets backed up into the Nebula."

"What's the Nebula?"

"It's basically just a way of describing a series of interconnected servers throughout the galaxy. Information is replicated on the various servers so that no matter where you are you should be able to access the information quickly. You've seriously never heard of the Nebula?" asks Nunya.

"No, I'm not a super huge nerd like you are, obviously," I reply.

"You wish you were. But your ass is too dumb," says Nunya.

"My ass happens to be the smartest part of me!"

"Exactly proving my point. Anyway, I'm gonna try and remove your tattoo."

She plays around with the device and after a few minutes holds it close to my chest. Nunya pushes a button on the side and a bunch of different colored laser beams start hitting my pecs. Thankfully, it doesn't hurt. I'm actually surprised it's even working, because my skin is pretty impervious to everything. Maybe it's just using the lasers to build a layer on top of the skin instead of actually burning into it.

Once she finishes, I go into the bathroom to check out the change. It actually looks pretty good. I can't see the massive tattoo on my chest anymore, and the edges of the square it painted on blend really well with my natural skin color. Maybe this will work. I go back into the living room.

"Okay, go ahead and give me some new tattoos I guess."

It takes less than twenty minutes to add all the tattoos. Some of them are pretty cool. Stabby things, shooty things, fast looking ships, hot chicks; it's all there. After she's done with the device I go into the bathroom and check out my back. She didn't seem to fuck me over on the back either. The tattoos are pretty cool. Probably my favorite tattoo is of Ash from The Evil Dead. That guy's a badass. Sometimes I wish I had a chainsaw hand then I realize it'd be hard to eat cereal that way.

"So, what's next?" I ask.

"You throw on your pants, I throw on my armor and robes, and we make a phone call."

33

Pulling everything out of the washer/dryer, I put on my pants and socks, fold the rest of it neatly, then go back out to the living room and put on my shoes. While I'm doing that, Nunya goes back into her room and gets ready. I'm starting to get excited because it sets in that we're really gonna do a heist. I just wish we had a larger group of unique and zany specialists who all have specific roles to play. Instead, I'm saddled with some computer nerds and a sidekick who hates me. It takes the fun out of it a little but I don't fucking care because it crosses a big checkmark off my bucket list.

Nunya comes out of her bedroom already decked out in her armor and robe, still wearing the military style clothes she had on before. It looks both cool and ridiculous at the same time. I approve.

"So what are you gonna do about your face?" I ask.

"What do you mean? You got a problem with my face?" asks Nunya.

"That escalated quickly. No, your face is fine. I mean are you going to cover it so that if you end up on camera nobody can tell that it's you?"

"Oh. Right. Well... I have my helmet which should help." Nunya puts it over her head but it doesn't cover much of her face at all.

"I think people will still be able to tell who you are," I say.

"Well... I could put tattoos on my face," says Nunya. "Or make a mask out of some fabric and cut out mouth and eye holes."

"Something like that might work. Probably better to use a mask because tattoos won't change the shape of your face. My guess is they'd be able to take the images, paint your face a single color, and still figure out who you really are," I say.

"That's actually a good point."

"You don't have to act surprised every time I say something smart."

"I'm pretty sure I do," says Nunya, smirking. "It's always a surprise. Both times."

"Har-de-har-har."

Nunya gets up, goes back to her bedroom, and a few seconds later comes out with a pair of sexy black underwear on her head.

I laugh. It seems to annoy Nunya but I don't really care.

"Hey!" she says. "This is the best I could do on short notice. It covers the front of my face, I can see out of it, and at least it's clean."

"I'm just glad to know you actually have sexy underwear. You don't seem like the type."

"What do you mean?"

"I mean you're so uptight it's amazing you've deluded yourself into thinking anyone would have sex with you, and that you'd actually need sexy panties," I say.

"You'd have sex with me. So what does that say about you?"

"No I wouldn't, which I already proved."

"Yeah, well the bulge in your towel said otherwise."

"Hey, just because my banana was firm doesn't mean I was willing to use it on you. Even if you were into guys, and even if you were into me, knowing what I know about you now I wouldn't put my dick in you for all the chocolate chip cookies on Fremulon-17."

"What's that supposed to mean?" asks Nunya.

"It means that your body doesn't make up for your personality."

"Fine. Fuck you. Stay here and I'll go take care of the Reginald situation on my own. I have everything I need."

"Good, go do that! One less stupid bullshitty thing I have to deal with," I reply.

Nunya flips me off and storms out the door. I stay there a few seconds then finally get up off the couch, turn off the lights, and leave her house. Hurrying to catch up to her she hears me running up and turns to me.

"Get in your GT9 and get the fuck out of here," says Nunya.

"Nah, I'm coming with you."

"The fuck you are."

"Seriously, you have some serious weaknesses in your abilities. If I don't come you'll probably die. You need my help."

"I don't need anyone's help."

"Yeah, yeah. You're super independent and capable. I've heard it all before. But there's one thing I can do that you can't which could make a difference," I say.

"Oh, and what's that, fuck-face?"

"I can survive in a vacuum."

"And?"

"And what? If your ship gets blown up while you're still in space you're dead."

Apparently she hadn't remembered that. She just glares at me.

"C'mon, I'll help you rescue Reginald and I'll make sure you get your money. We've already put up with each other so far, and making fun of you for being a celibate nun shouldn't stop us from completing our mission," I say. "That's just dumb."

"Fine. You come. But you do as I say, got it?" says Nunya.

"Who said you get to be in charge?"

"It's my mission. I have my own ship. As captain of the Illennium Falcon I make up the rules. If you come with me you're just a lowly crew member. You're basically a red shirt."

"Okay, now you're just mixing your fandoms. You can't use both Star Wars and Star Trek terms at the same time," I say.

"I can do whatever the fuck I like, including saying that Captain Kirk could kick Luke Skywalker's ass in a fight."

"Whoa, I can't even believe you just said that. That's the stupidest thing anyone has ever said in the history of the universe. You win the title of Queen of the Stupid People. You can not only fuck right off, you can eat a big bag of salted dicks. I ain't going."

"Just shut the fuck up and get in," says Nunya.

Seriously, I've never heard anyone say anything stupider, but I follow her up the ramp and into her ship anyway.

The insides of the ship are both a little nicer and a little more utilitarian than I expected. Everything is super clean like it's hardly been used but there ain't much to it. It also doesn't have enough headroom for me. Nunya's fine standing up but I have to walk around half bent over to keep from hitting my head on the various pipes, tubes and structural supports that line the ceiling. I notice a ladder in the corner.

"Where the fuck does that lead?" I ask.

"To the upper deck. It's a good way to smuggle stuff. The ladder actually retracts and disappears. We can store things high up and no one notices. Everyone's seen Star Wars so they expect the smuggling hatches to be inside the floor. We put them above because how many people ever actually look up? None, it turns out. Anyway, it should give us the room to hold all the Reginalds," says Nunya.

"Yeah, I guess that all makes sense."

I look around here on the bottom floor which is shaped like an oval. We came up the ramp at the ass end of the ship, and in front of me are about a dozen seats on both sides, a large table in the middle that looks like it's used for strategery and meals, and at the far end of the oval is what looks like the cockpit. Two black leather seats that appear much more comfortable than the others are placed right in front of a pair of flight controls and panels filled with hundreds of knobs and switches. I follow Nunya up to the two seats, and as she slides into the left one I sit down on her right.

"Don't touch anything," says Nunya.

"Can I touch things if something goes wrong? Like, let's say you somehow get knocked unconscious and I have to take over steering the ship?" I ask.

"Nope."

"So I should just let it get destroyed?" I say.

"Yup," says Nunya.

"That's dumb," I reply.

"Yeah, well, I'd rather take my chances than take yours," quips Nunya.

"I guess you are the lucky one."

"Damn straight."

Nunya taps a few buttons and the ramp at the other end of the ship rises and seals into place. She spends the next few minutes checking to make sure that all the systems are still running; flipping switches, pushing buttons, tapping on touchscreens. After about ten minutes she finally looks satisfied then she places the call to Blhack Glass.

"M-Ray here," comes a muffled voice over the comms.

"Hey, it's N. Just met you guys. Not gonna use names even though the line is encrypted."

"Wait, the pair we just met at our 'c'? D and N?"

"Yeah, that's us. D said your music sucked. Anyway, we need a favor. We're breaking into a casino hotel and need you guys to hack into the security cameras and make them look like nothing weird is going on. We also need any security systems deactivated. Can you do that?" asks Nunya.

"I think we can manage it. What casino hotel are we talking about?" asks the voice.

"The Chateau Marmot Hotel."

"Consider it done. You should be good to go in ten."

"Wait, ten minutes?" asks Nunya, surprised.

The person on the other end laughs. "Yeah, ten minutes."

"Damn. Alright, thanks. We owe you one!" says Nunya.

"Yes, you do," says the voice. The comm drops on the other end.

"That sounded ominous." Nunya turns to me. "You ready?"

"Yeah," I reply.

Nunya straps herself into her seat using a three-point harness but I don't bother. She grabs hold of the yoke, kicks the thrusters into reverse, and I fall out of my seat. Next, she accelerates as she steers the ship into the sky and I'm thrown to the back of the ship, slamming against the ramp. Thankfully, my body flying through the ship didn't damage the ramp, but it definitely damaged my calm.

"What the fuck, Nunya?" I yell.

"Oh, right, forgot to turn on the inertia arresters," replies Nunya.

I hear a click come from the cockpit and suddenly normal gravity returns. I'm able to walk back to my seat and sit down.

"You did that on fucking purpose," I say.

"Yeah, I fucking did," says Nunya.

"Oh. Well then fuck you," I say.

"Yeah, fuck me. Just shut up, okay? That's an order."

"Whatever."

Nunya flies the ship up and through the atmosphere, sending us back toward the local space-asshole. I'm used to flying from place-to-place but it's starting to get old because we've done it so many times lately.

As we pull up to the security ship I let Nunya talk to them. Her ship, her rules, her responsibility.

"Hello," says the security ship over the comms. "Please state your name and destination."

"This is Sarah Silverman and we'd like to travel to the Vegas Constellation," replies Nunya.

We wait patiently for what feels like a couple of minutes.

"I'm sorry, but we won't be able to allow you to pass until you give us your full legal name," responds the security ship.

"Sarah Silverman is my real name. Seriously."

"I'm sorry but that name isn't coming up in our database."

"Wait, what? I don't exist?"

"Oh, we're sure you exist because we're talking to you, obviously. There just doesn't seem to be any record of you on file. In the meantime, we'll have to board your ship."

"Wait, what? Hey, I have rights! I haven't done anything illegal! You can't just board my ship without my permission!" says Nunya.

"Soooooo, can we have your permission?" asks the security ship.

"No! There's no reason to. We haven't done anything wrong."

"Well, you seem to be acting suspicious."

"Suspicious? We're literally just trying to fly through the gate and end up in Vegas. Is that cause for concern?"

"Well, what concerns us is that you won't willingly submit to a search of your space vessel," says the security ship.

"That's just because I don't want you aboard. You're wasting my time!" says Nunya.

"Safety is never a waste of time," says the security guard.

"Wait, is this because I'm Black?"

"What? Oh, no, absolutely not! I beg your pardon ma'am!"

"Nah, it's 'cause I'm Black. If I were white, or someone famous, you'd just be tripping over yourself to let us through. Because I'm a minority you feel you need to make sure I'm not carrying any drugs or whatever."

"We can guarantee that's not the case," says the security guard.

"Oh yeah? Well wait until I tell you who my co-pilot is. It's Vince Magnum."

"Wait, THE Vince Magnum? From the porn videos?"

I whip out my meat popsicle and stand up so they can get a good look at my cock-and-balls in the camera.

"Holy shit, you weren't making it up. Okay, my apologies. You can pass through and we won't do an investigation," says the security guard.

"Seriously? Like I just said, all I need is a white person to get me past security. Racist motherfuckers," says Nunya.

"I'm not being racist!" says the security guard. "Some of my best friends are Black!"

"Oh God, even I know saying something like that is pretty racist," I say. "Seriously, you need to shut the fuck up and let us through, and go take some racial sensitivity training or whatever."

I look over and notice that the gate has been changed to deliver us to the Vegas Constellation. Nunya turns off the comms.

"Can we shoot them?" asks Nunya.

"Hmmm, I'm sure we can. The question is do we really want to be fugitives from the law?" I ask.

"We already will be once we liberate Reginald. Only, since they think we're other people, we might get away with it."

"That's fair. Although, now I feel kinda bad for Vince Magnum because he's gonna get blamed for a crime he didn't commit."

"I wouldn't worry about that," says Nunya. "From what I've heard he's in prison right now for beating his girlfriend so he has an alibi. And even if he didn't have an alibi he deserves to be in prison."

"Well, fuck that guy then," I say. "Let's get the fuck out of here and go rescue Reginald."

"So we're not blowing the security ship up?"

"Nah. Maybe we can fill out a survey card or something and get him fired."

"Fine." And by 'fine' I'm sure she meant it how women say things are 'fine' when they're nowhere near fucking fine.

Nunya flies the ship right through the space-asshole, moving at a fair amount of speed. Just as we reach the gate I glance over and see that the security guards look a little pissed that we're going through so fast. Oh well, fuck those guys. My guess is that they had to have made some bad decisions to end up guarding a portal for one of the lamest planets in the known universe, so I figure they've already been punished ahead of time for their stupidity.

34

"Hey, uh, Nunya? You might want to slow down. Remember, we're going for stealth here so we don't have the Vegas police on our asses."

Nunya grits her teeth, lets out a big sigh of exasperation, and pulls back on the throttle. I decide to keep my mouth shut because honestly, I don't have anything to say that would make things better. So we just sit in an uncomfortable silence as Nunya stews for a while. Eventually, she breaks the silence as we slowly fly back to planet Hollywood.

"Seriously, I just don't get it. How come the same shit keeps on happening even now? Why do my people keep getting shit on?" asks Nunya.

"I wish I knew, Nunya. You'd think with how far we've come, how much technology and information we have, that people wouldn't be such dickheads. But unfortunately, I think it comes down to the fact that assholes are assholes, and they have asshole children, and it's pretty rare for assholes to not have asshole children. And even if they do, they push their children into becoming assholes like them. On top of that, it seems like assholes have a lot more children than regular people do, like somehow they decided they need to spread their asshole genes around and make the galaxy much more assholy like them. A lot of good people like you either can't or don't have children. It's fucked up that way, like Mother Nature wants us to keep churning out loads of worthless people instead of people who can actually make the galaxy a better place."

Nunya thinks quietly about it.

"You think I'm a good person?" she asks. "Even after being a smuggler? After killing people?"

"Yeah, I think you're a good person. You may have made mistakes, and you may have been a worse person before, but right now I think you're a good person. You're definitely not a bad person. You're risking your life and freedom to save a group of people that you don't even really know while also risking the possibility of losing out on getting a fuck-ton of money. This casino heist might go sideways somehow and we'll spend the rest of our lives in prison. But you're trying to do the right thing by Reginald, who you don't owe anything to. I think that says a lot about who you are."

I can tell that Nunya's trying to hide her face from me, and when she thinks I'm not looking I catch her out of the corner of my eye wiping away a few tears. I don't make a big deal about it because I guess I must have said something right finally and I really don't want to fuck the moment up. It's weird not saying everything I'm thinking but it seems to help. Fuck, maybe I shouldn't talk so much in general. Nah, don't want the world to miss out on my one-liners.

While Nunya slowly pilots us toward planet Hollywood I decide to check out the upper cargo area. I'm able to climb up the ladder okay, but it's an even tighter fit height-wise than downstairs. I think even Nunya would have to bend over some to keep from hitting her head. I will say it does look like we might be able to fit all of the Reginalds onboard but it's going to be very uncomfortable. We'll basically have to stack them sideways in the upper half and have some underneath the table and sitting on top of the table in the lower half. Once I'm done checking everything out I head back down the ladder.

"Things okay up there?" asks Nunya.

"Yeah, they're fine. We might even be able to fit all one hundred and seventy-three Reginalds on the ship but it's gonna suck. Do we know where we're gonna take them?" I ask.

"Not sure. Figured we'll ask them where they want us to drop them off."

"Guess that makes sense. Where are you going to dock? Remember, they'll need to leave straight from the hotel. We won't be able to sneak that many Reginalds through the casino."

"Yeah, I remember. I was planning on parking where the concert shuttle parked. Have everyone go through the penthouse floor," replies Nunya.

"Sounds smart. Just make sure to fly casual. We don't want anyone asking us any questions or pulling us over."

We reach the upper atmosphere of planet Hollywood and Nunya takes us down, heading straight for the Chateau Marmot Hotel. As we eventually get low enough to see the hotel lit up like a Christmas tree against the darkened city, she slows down and sets the ship to hover mode. At least we have the benefit of the darkness as it's now early in the morning on this planet, so early that the suns haven't come out yet. Hopefully we can get everyone into the ship and leave, and no one will be the wiser.

When we get close enough, Nunya one-eighties the ship so that the cargo bay door is aimed at the window we'd used before. I hit a button on the console that lowers the cargo ramp, opening up the back end of the ship. Jogging past the planning table, I hold onto the hydraulic arm that opened the ramp and look through the window at Reginald. Or at least one of the Reginalds. When I wave at him he waves back but still stands there looking shocked. I point at the glass and he looks a little shaken but taps something on his podium. The window dematerializes and I hop inside. Walking over to the podium I try to act as normal as possible.

"Reginald?"

"Yes sir?"

"Do you remember me?" I ask.

"I'm afraid that I don't, sir."

"Oh okay, that makes sense. Do you happen to know which Reginald would have been working this podium yesterday about mid-day?"

"Yes, yes I do. Did you need his help specifically?" asks Reginald. "If not I would be happy to assist you in any way I can."

"I do need him. I hate to think that I'd be waking him but it's very important that I speak to him directly."

"You won't be waking him, sir. My guess is that he's having breakfast before he starts his duties in a few hours. I'll ring him up."

Reginald taps away at his phone, mumbles into it for a few moments and eventually hangs up, turning to me.

"He'll be here shortly. Might I get you something in the meantime? A cold beverage or warm food item? We're serving a full breakfast right now that is quite excellent. Even the donuts are amazing," says Reginald.

"Thank you but I think I'm good. And thanks for calling up Reginald," I say.

"Of course, sir. May I ask in the meantime what your name is? I can't really tell based on your tattoos and your face is obscured by your goggles."

"My name is Vince. Vince Magnum," I reply.

"The porn star?" asks Reginald.

"Some days it seems that way."

"Goodness! You're quite a famous person. No wonder you're familiar with the penthouse floor. And just so you know, I definitely respect your work. I mean to say that I don't judge your choice of occupation."

"Uh, thanks," I say.

"So do you always do gay porn?"

"Gay porn?" I repeat.

"Yes. You seem to specialize in it, from what I've heard from others of course."

"You know I have a girlfriend, right?" I say.

"Oh, so you enjoy the company of both men and women?"

"Well, you know, whatever pays the bills. I'm also pretty flexible

194

on anyone in-between. Binary, non-binary. Hell, I've had sex with almost everything one can legally have sex with."

"That sounds thrilling."

"Eh, sometimes it gets old, but for the most part it's pretty great."

Just as I finish my words another Reginald approaches from the elevator, clearly concerned and uncertain of why he was beckoned back to work.

"Oh, is that you, Mr... " starts the Reginald I know. I cut him off mid-sentence.

"Magnum. Vince Magnum."

"Uh, yes, Mr. Magnum," replies Reginald, clearly confused. "Was your stay here inadequate? Did you leave something in the suite?"

"It's nothing like that," I say. "Can we talk privately?"

"Most definitely, sir. Let's walk over to the window where you can speak more freely."

We walk over to the ship's extended ramp. It will be a little hard to hear each other over the noise with the ship's hover mode engaged but it will also make it impossible for anyone to eavesdrop on us. Reginald nods his head once we're in position letting me know that we can talk freely now.

"Reginald, I'm not really Vince Magnum! I'm Dick Blowhard! I'm just wearing a costume," I say.

"I know sir. I could tell it was you just based on your physique. Even if I can't see half your face I can tell that it's you."

"Great. Anyway, we're here to break you out," I reply.

"What do you mean 'break me out'?" asks Reginald.

"I mean we're here to get you and all of your clones. Take you somewhere far away where you won't be exploited. Nunya and I talked and we figure you guys are all slaves since you aren't really paid well enough to be self-sufficient. So we got this ship here and we figure we'll be able to cram all one hundred and seventy-three of you inside it."

"So, you came back to rescue me? Us? Why?"

"Because you seem like a good guy and because we don't think that slavery is right. Admittedly, it was Nunya's idea, but I was just dumb before and hadn't really thought about it until she mentioned what she wanted to do. So I agreed to help. That and I've never been on a casino heist before," I explain.

"Oh, okay, alright then," says Reginald. "Thank you."

"Hey, don't thank me until we have you far away from here. Still too many variables. Like, do you think any of the other Reginalds wouldn't want to escape? Like maybe some of them are so invested in what they're doing that they won't want to leave?"

"No, I don't think that will happen. I know myself pretty well, all of myselves, and we've all secretly confided in each other that we want to leave. So I think everyone will be coming."

"Okay, good to hear. Can you convince them to come upstairs to the ship without alerting the owners?" I ask.

"That's the easy part. We've been planning for this for a long time," replies Reginald.

I watch as he walks over to the podium, picks up the phone, taps away at the touchscreen, and after a few seconds I can hear his voice speak throughout the entire building, "Order 66 has been initiated. All Reginalds please report immediately to the penthouse floor. I repeat, Order 66 has been initiated. All Reginalds report to the penthouse floor."

It takes a while for all of the Reginalds to reach us because only so many can fit on the elevators and in the stairwells at the same time. None of them are wearing their normal red bellhop-style jackets and hats, which I assume are owned by the hotel, but instead are wearing generic white tank tops and black slacks. It's kind of like a weird Die Hard convention. Also, all of them have a small bag with them.

"What's in the bags?" I ask the Reginald I know as more Reginalds show up.

"All of their worldly belongings," replies Reginald.

"Seriously? That's all that each of you has? That's super fucking depressing," I say.

"Quite, sir. That's why we're excited to finally be leaving."

I just nod in understanding.

The Reginald that we know addresses the Reginalds in the room. "Everyone, you all have another Reginald you're responsible for. Is anyone missing their partner? If so, raise your hand."

One of the Reginalds raises his hand, but only one.

Our Reginald speaks. "Do you know where the missing Reginald might be?"

The Reginald holding his hand up replies. "My guess is if he didn't hear the announcement he has to be down in the boiler room. Otherwise, he may be stuck on the toilet."

I turn to our Reginald. "I'll find him. You get everyone else loaded onto the ship. There's a ladder that leads up to a cargo section you can stuff more Reginalds into."

"Okay," he replies, nodding.

I push my way through the army of Reginalds toward the elevator. Using my super-vision, I look through the walls to see where Reginald might be. It takes me several moments of seeing people in showers, people on the toilet, people sleeping, and people fucking to finally find the last Reginald. He's down at the bottom of the hotel, underground, in what must be the boiler room. I get into the elevator and push the 'B' button. The elevator descends but it feels like it's taking forever. I wish I could speed the damn thing up, but unless I punch a hole in the floor or snap the cables and drop I'll just have to wait. At least the elevator music is good. Girl from Ipanema. Awesome.

Once I finally reach the basement I jump out of the elevator. I spot a large potted plant, pick it up and block the elevator door from closing. Looking up I see a red sign saying 'Boiler Room - Employees Only' on it. Without thinking I walk over to the door and yank it open. At first I don't hear anything, but after a few seconds I hear the sound of crying.

"Hello?" I say. "Reginald, are you in here?"

No answer. I use my super-vision to pinpoint exactly where he is. He seems to be sitting on the ground, his head on his knees, hiding behind a giant metal sphere that I'm assuming is the boiler. I walk over to where he's sitting.

"Reginald? Are you okay?" I ask.

"No, not really," he mumbles.

"Well, can I help?"

"No, not really," he mumbles again.

"Okay, well, I'm here to help you and all the other Reginalds escape from the hotel. Can you come with me?"

"No, not really."

"Well, why not?"

"Because I'm in love with one of the card dealers in the casino and I don't want to leave her."

"Oh, shit bro, I'm sorry. Uh, can we take her with us?" I ask.

"I don't think she'll want to leave. She loves working for the casino and makes decent money. She also has a young daughter which makes it much harder for her to move."

"And none of the other Reginalds know about this?"

"No. I was worried that if we ever did figure out a way to escape they'd force me to go with them. So I've kept it hidden."

"Shit, this puts me in a bind. Here's the thing, if all of you don't come then whoever is left will probably be cloned and all the new clones will be stuck in the same damn mess as before."

"Actually, it doesn't work that way. You can't clone a clone, neither legally nor genetically. Basically, the DNA becomes unstable and breaks down when you clone a clone, turning the person into a really disgusting soup. And galactic law prohibits even attempting it. Also, a person has to fill out a whole bunch of paperwork saying that they are willing to allow someone to clone them before the clones can be created. It's a lot of red tape but it saves a lot of headache down the road," says Reginald.

"Well, if it requires a lot of paperwork then how did the hotel convince the original Reginald to be cloned so many times?"

"I was just lonely," he says. "I thought it'd be a way to make friends. That's why I was such a good employee, I didn't really have a life outside of work. But I didn't realize it would be like this. I didn't realize we'd have to share one salary. There were a lot of things they didn't tell me."

"Wait, how do you know if you're the original Reginald if you're all exactly the same?" I ask.

"Because I have a scar on my left elbow that none of the others have. When you're cloned it doesn't copy any injuries that had been previously done to your body. I'm not sure why none of them bothered to check. Maybe they just didn't want to know whether they were clones or not. So you're really going to liberate all of them?"

"That's the plan."

"Do you know where you'll be taking them?" asks the real Reginald.

"Not yet. We were planning on asking them where they wanted to go."

"Well, at this point you may get different answers from each of them. Even though their lives have been incredibly similar they've still had a number of experiences that are unique to them. Even though they're me, they're all still their own people, or as much as anyone can really be."

"That's good to know. Maybe we'll take all of them to some sort of transit center and buy them shuttle tickets to wherever they want to go."

"Something like that might work," says Reginald.

"Well, it'll have to. We don't have a lot of money at the moment and we certainly don't have enough time to fly 172 clones across the galaxy," I explain.

"Makes sense. Hey, thank you for rescuing them. I really do appreciate it. And please, don't tell them that I'm the original. I think they all deserve to believe that maybe they're the real Reginald."

"I won't tell them. But what should I tell them about you not coming?"

"The truth. Just tell them I fell in love and I'm staying behind, and I'll be quitting my job so they don't have to worry about me."

"I'll make sure they understand," I say.

"Thanks."

I nod at him. "Good luck, Reginald."

"You too... whoever you are."

"Sorry, I'm in disguise. Can't give away who I am. Just know I'm someone who gives a shit."

He smiles.
I turn and make my way back to the elevator.

35

As I leave the elevator, I see the last of the Reginalds boarding the ship. It's super crowded but somehow they've managed to pack everyone onboard. I squeeze in and it takes me a moment to wade through the throng of Reginalds to get to the cockpit.

Nunya turns to me, "Did you get the last Reginald?"

"Nope, left him back there. He's in love and he's quitting his job. He'll be okay on his own," I reply.

"Okay, if you say so."

Nunya pushes the button to close the cargo ramp. Once it's closed she kicks the engines on but we move pretty slowly at first. The sheer amount of weight we're now carrying seems to be affecting how fast we can move.

"Want me to get out and push?" I ask.

"Yes. If you could get right behind the thrusters and shove, that would be great," Nunya replies sarcastically.

Eventually she's able to get the Illennium Falcon going at a fair speed, it just takes longer than normal to reach it. We break through the atmosphere and slowly head toward the security gate.

"So where are we headed?" asks Nunya.

"I think we should take them to some sort of transit center. The Reginald I spoke with thought they'd all want to go their separate ways. Do you know of any place like that?" I ask.

Nunya thinks for a moment. "I may know just the place."

Nunya doesn't tell me exactly what the plan is so I decide to talk to the Reginalds while I wait. One asks me where the last Reginald is and I just explain he's in love and decided to stay behind. They start to look worried but I assure them it's for the best and that he's genuinely happy.

We slowly make our way to the space-asshole, not because of the weight, because weight is largely meaningless in space, but because we're still adhering to the goddamn speed limit that Vegas imposes on its patrons. The absolute last thing we need is to get pulled over, so not breaking the law seems smart, if not fucking annoying.

As we reach the security ship Nunya turns on just the voice comms. I figure that's a smart idea so they can't see all the people we're smuggling onboard. I mean technically we aren't breaking any laws because everyone on our ship is there of their own free will. But the time it would take to sort it all out would be hours if not days of filling out paperwork, providing interviews, etc. No thanks. On top of that, if the Slimewickys have enough power in Vegas they could try to do something to stop the Reginalds from leaving even if they don't have the legal power to do so. Anyone that conniving probably has contingencies for something like this.

"Hello," says the security ship. "What is your name and destination?"

"My name is Sarah Silverman and we are headed to the Grander Centraler Terminal," says Nunya. "And oh yeah, my co-pilot is that famous white guy, Vince Magnum."

"Vince Magnum? Seriously? The porn star?" asks the security ship.

"Yeah," I say.

"Oh, wow, that's amazing! But we can't see your face right now. Do you have proof you're really Vince Magnum?" asks the security ship.

"Oh come on, don't make me whip out my firehose to prove it to you," I say.

"Sorry, but unless you want to show us your face you'll have to show us your dick."

I turn to Nunya. "I'm starting to think these security people are just pervs."

"You think?" replies Nunya.

"We can still hear you," says the security ship. "But you're right, we just want to see your dick."

"Fuck. Fine," I mumble. I whip out my Oscar Mayer and turn on the camera so they can get a good look at it.

"Uhhh, we really need to make sure you're Vince Magnum. I mean, it looks pretty authentic but can you make it hard?" says the security ship.

"No, I'm not gonna jack off for you! For fuck's sake!" I say, quickly turning off the camera. "Seriously, I showed you my dong, now let us through."

We hear some mumbling in the background.

"Fine," says the security ship.

Nunya and I watch as the space-asshole ripples and changes to show a large gray planet off in the distance. Nunya steers the ship through it, and just like that we're on the other side of the galaxy.

The first thing that strikes me as we make our way through the space-asshole is that there's hundreds of other space-assholes nearby. I mean it makes sense if this is the largest travel hub in the galaxy. You don't want to have too many people waiting to come and go, especially when schedules need to be kept. My guess is with all the security ships that have to accompany each gate it's probably the most 'protected' place in the galaxy.

Nunya aims the ship at the massive gray planet in the middle of all the space-assholes. The Grander Centraler Terminal, it turns out, resides on a really uninteresting planet named Mildew that's mostly concrete and asphalt. The main terminal itself is actually the size of several large cities, complete with tens-of-thousands of landing pads, transport shuttles, hotels, motels, restaurants and the like. It's a place for people to go to get to somewhere else and I wonder if the other half of the planet is where all the employees live that make Grander Centraler Terminal run.

Nunya starts tapping away at the ship's touchscreen, accessing its IPS to find out the best place to drop all of the Reginalds off. She's able to bring up a list of choices then heads for the largest trans-galactic travel company, non-ironically named 'The Largest Trans-Galactic Travel Company', or LTTC for short. Pretty much everyone just affectionately refers to them as 'Lettuce'. Their slogan even leans into it: 'Lettuce take you somewhere'.

Because traffic is dense Nunya has to fly into one of the ship lanes to safely make it to the Lettuce terminal. It's kind of cool seeing so many ships coming and going, and at the same time it's exhausting. One of the things I love most about flying in outer space is the feeling of freedom. Here though, where it's so unbelievably crowded, I start feeling a bit claustrophobic.

I look back behind me and I can tell the Reginalds are getting a bit restless. A few of them are rocking back and forth. A few others seem to be talking to themselves.

"Everyone back there okay?" I ask.

A weird eruption of the same voice says in unison, "yes, we're fine."

"Glad to… uh… hear," I reply.

I look over at Nunya and she gets a slightly creeped out look on her face as she shrugs.

"ETA five minutes," says Nunya.

I sit there and twiddle my thumbs because I really have nothing better to do. And you should know that I'm the best goddamn thumb twiddler in the galaxy. That's right, no one twiddles their thumbs better. Not even Vinnie 'The Thumb' Thumbson, the champion thumb wrestler. That guy can stick his thumbs straight up his ass. Actually, I'm pretty sure he did that and ended up in the hospital or some shit.

Nunya turns the ship sharply right at a 'T' intersection between buildings and flies us down a ramp and into an underground parking structure. It takes a few minutes for her to find a parking spot the right size but eventually she does and sets the ship down.

A couple of taps later and the ship's ramp opens.

I can only imagine what it must have looked like from the outside watching nearly two hundred similarly dressed clones get out of the same spaceship. Probably like watching people pour out of a clown car. As the last of the Reginalds get out I follow behind them, as does Nunya, closing the ship and setting its security system to 'on'.

Nunya pulls out her Personal Space Device and brings up directions to the Lettuce counter. As she starts walking the Reginalds sort of swarm around her, but let her through as we follow some white lined pathways painted on the ground. She just casually walks as if nothing weird is going on. I stay toward the back just in case anyone tries to sneak up behind us. I don't think that's actually going to happen but you just never know. I mean, there's fucking ninjas lurking everywhere. Ninjas, man. Ninjas.

Nunya starts walking up a wide set of stairs, turns and disappears from my view, which I don't like. But we all follow her up a few levels until we reach an enclosed sky bridge. Crossing the sky bridge I look down and see other ships and ground vehicles moving around, heading into the parking structure. Everything is the same gray color except the ships, most of which though are just as bland looking as the buildings.

Eventually, we reach a massive room the size of a football field filled with hundreds of lines. At the end of each rope divided line is a person standing behind a counter that also has a weight stand to measure luggage. I see Nunya tapping away at a kiosk then heading over to one of the lines. The Reginalds do their best to form a single-file line, and as Nunya approaches the counter she looks back at me and waves me forward. I have to hop in another roped off line next to the one they're in to get to the front because there just isn't room to push my way through the line of Reginalds.

"Yeah?" I say.

"We need to put this on your credit card," said Nunya.

Shit.

"Yeah, okay," I mumble, pulling out my credit card and ID from my wallet that I had tucked into my bag of ultimate wonders. I hand both cards to the nice looking Veridian lady working at the desk. If you weren't aware, Veridians are a group of mostly green colored snake looking people. They're actually some of the sweetest and nicest people you'll ever meet. Their face and body shape are human but their skin is covered in scales like a snake. Thankfully, they don't have any fangs and they aren't poisonous, but their eyes do look a bit dangerous and potentially off-putting if you aren't used to them.

This particular Veridian is wearing a standard female Lettuce uniform, which consists of black slacks and a light green shirt with poofy green shoulders meant to look like heads of iceberg lettuce. Behind her is a giant Lettuce logo painted on a white wall which also looks like a head of iceberg lettuce. The whole thing is starting to make me oddly hungry.

Nunya and I spend the next few hours helping each of the Reginalds book a flight out of there. Because of the cost involved each Reginald will be seated at the back of each ship in the cheapest seat possible because I'm just not willing to splurge for platinum first class when I'm currently broke as shit. At least every Reginald will get a meal on the flight. Thankfully, they had each saved up a little money for a day like today, even though they only had one salary to split among them. It should be enough money to keep them fed and sheltered until they can find jobs.

The weird thing I realize as we're booking all the flights is that about sixty percent of them want to go to this tropical planet named St. Marley. I've never been but I heard it's absolutely beautiful. Clear blue oceans, long sandy beaches, and tall trees that provide just the perfect amount of shade. They're also known for their rum based cocktails and relaxing, upbeat music. I just hope the Reginalds can all find employment there, or at least a way to live happily.

The even weirder thing is that for the remaining forty percent none of them are going to the same place. They're literally scattering across the galaxy, going to all sorts of planets for all sorts of reasons. You'd think that just by random luck that at least two would be going to the same place, especially since they're all sort of the same person. But nope, no duplicate destinations whatsoever.

As each Reginald receives their ticket they give us a hug and thank us. Most of them tear up a bit, humbled by what we're doing for them. And the strangest thing is, because of their sincerity and thankfulness, each time I hug them it makes me feel happy. You'd think something like that I'd just get bored with the repetition. But no, it was an amazing experience each and every time.

It really makes me feel like I finally did something good. Did Nunya basically push me into it? Sure. But I still didn't have to help. I could have been just like every other asshole and ignored the problem. Pretended like it didn't exist. But I listened to Nunya, admitted there was a problem, and finally helped do something about it. Honestly, even if Nunya and I die on our suicide mission against the Sloths I think I'll be okay with it, now that I've done something good with no kind of reward for it other than hugs. I'd like to also say that Reginald happens to be an excellent hugger.

Once the last of the Reginalds gets his ticket, Nunya and I

wave goodbye while we head back to her spaceship.

As we walk back across the sky bridge and down the stairs Nunya turns to me. "Dick?"

"Yeah?" I reply.

"I'm... I'm actually proud of you. Thanks for helping me rescue the Reginalds."

"Oh God, don't start this. Don't start treating me nicely. I don't know if I can handle it."

"Why not?"

"Because it just feels gross. I'm just so used to you being a super huge asshole to me all the time that I think if the dynamic changed it just wouldn't work," I explain.

"Sorry, but you're getting a hug anyway," she says, stopping, turning to me and wrapping her arms around my torso. Because of my size she can't quite get her arms around me.

The good news is that I get a boner.

"Dick, are you getting wood right now?"

"Yup."

"God damn it! Do you always have to be so disgusting?" yells Nunya.

"Apparently so. See, there's the Nunya I know and love," I reply.

"Fuck you!" she says half-heartedly.

"Fuck you back."

In that moment everything was right with the world.

36

And then suddenly everything was wrong with the world. Just as we get close to Nunya's spaceship a dozen armed soldiers pop out from behind other spaceships, aiming their power rifles at us.

"Dick Blowhard, surrender to us at once!" their leader yells.

"I'm not Dick Blowhard. I'm Vince Magnum, intergalactic porn star!" I respond.

"No, we're fairly certain you're Detective Dick Blowhard and you've just stolen something that wasn't yours."

"No, I'm fairly certain I'm Vince Magnum and I get paid to fuck your moms."

I'd like to say this is where they believed me and stopped harassing us but I'm just not that lucky. The armed soldiers start firing at us. Energy bursts bounce off of me and Nunya, and we just stand around for a few seconds while the ricochets damage the nearby ships. Eventually, the soldiers stop firing.

"Have you had enough?" asks the leader.

"We haven't even had any yet. Did you not see how your weapons are useless against us?" I reply.

"Uh, they were plenty effective. Do you not see the destruction all around you?" asks the leader.

"Yeah, to other people's ships. Some poor mom's gonna come out here and find her ship demolished and it'll be your fault. Her kids will be crying and she won't be able to get them home in time for dinner. It's gonna ruin their evening. Did you even think about that? Why the fuck are you attacking us anyway?" I ask.

"Because you stole the Reginalds that rightfully belong to the Slimewickys!" responds the leader.

"First, I don't know who the Reginalds even are, and I don't know who the Slimewickys are. Second, even if I did know a single Reginald, let alone multiple Reginalds, I'm pretty sure since it's a free galaxy that no one would own them. Third, if you don't quit fucking with us, I'm going to slowly walk over to you, pick you up by your helmet, and rip out your throat. Oh, and fourth... fuck you," I reply.

"We know it's you, Detective Blowhard, because you used your credit card to pay for the Reginalds to fly across the galaxy."

I slap my forehead. Of all the stupid things I could have done why did I have to do that?

"Okay, assuming I actually am Dick Blowhard, how the fuck did you get here so fast? We only just left Vegas. There's no way someone from there could have hired a group of mercenaries, given them instructions, and gotten them here this quickly," I say.

"Actually, you've been here approximately three hours which is plenty of time to organize that sort of thing. But to answer your question we used the eHarming app. It matches people who need someone killed, tortured or enslaved with assassins and mercenaries that will carry out their evil orders for a reasonable fee. We happened to be the ones closest to you," explains the leader.

"Wait, there's an app for that? That's evil! Nunya, remind me to pay a visit to whoever created that app," I say.

"Yeah, sure, I'll totally remember to do that," says Nunya, not caring.

"For the last time, Detective Blowhard, come with us or we will kill you!"

"Did you miss the whole part where we're super-powered and invincible, and your weapons don't work on us?"

The idiots start shooting at us again. More blasts bounce off of us, damaging even more nearby ships. This time they really pour it on, trying their best to destroy us. I just slowly walk over like I promised, pick the leader up by his head and tear his throat out. The other mercs stop firing, shocked by the viciousness of it. I drop the dead leader down on the ground then wipe my hands off on a clean section of his pants. That's when everyone but Nunya runs away. She just stands there, gagging.

I walk back to Nunya. "What?" I ask.

"Why the fuck would you actually do that? That was so unbelievably disgusting!" replies Nunya.

"I did it so the other assholes would run away and I wouldn't have to kill them. I figured if I made good on my promise they'd be so afraid they wouldn't stick around. If you notice, they didn't give up until their leader's throat was eviscerated."

"So you're saying you were so very disturbingly nasty because you were trying to save lives?"

"Ah-doy!" I reply.

"God, Dick, you need help."

"Don't I fucking know it. Now let's get the fuck out of here."

We walk back to Nunya's ship which magically isn't damaged at all. Not even so much as a scratch. She opens the cargo ramp, we climb in, and as we both get seated Nunya taps on the touchscreen in front of her. The cargo ramp closes and the ship's autopilot engages, sending the ship winding through the parking structure and out into the transportation lanes.

"Our cover is blown," I say to Nunya.

"Well, your cover is blown. Nobody knows who the fuck I am, thankfully," she replies.

"I'm pretty sure that you've been seen with me recently wearing the armor and robes you have on. I don't think it'd be difficult for someone to figure out who you are."

"Fucking goddamn it motherfucking shit!" yells Nunya.

"Hey, at least no one legitimate is trying to kill us. It could be worse; it could be the police or some other government agency. Someone with much larger resources than a hotel/casino owner."

"Still, do you think they'll come for me if I go back to planet Houston?"

"Nah, probably not. There would be no point. You having to live on planet Houston is revenge enough. I'm sure they'd leave you be. Me on the other hand, I've made an enemy for life. They aren't my first and they probably won't be my last. They may just be a problem I have to address at some point. Right now, though, I think we should go after the Sloths. We'll get you your money and we'll get you home. That way you won't have to keep looking over your shoulder."

"It's about fucking time. I was done with this adventuring shit ten minutes ago," says Nunya.

"Like, literally ten minutes ago?"

"No, dipshit. It's a figure of speech."

"Oh."

After following lines of other ships for a while we finally make it to one of the space-assholes. The security people are all business, unimpressed that they have a celebrity in their midst.

"Name and destination," comes a voice over the comms.

"Nunya Business and Detective Dick Blowhard heading to planet Showdown in the Bossfight empire," replies Nunya.

Almost immediately the gate shimmers and changes to show planet Showdown off in the distance. I'm a bit surprised just how far the space-asshole is parked from the planet, but I guess if you're constructing a gate near a Sloth planet you'd want to keep it far away.

Nunya takes a beat, drawing in a deep breath and slowly letting it out. Over the comms one of the security officers says, "Move along. Move along." Nunya takes that as her cue to finally fly through the space-asshole.

We come out the other side and Nunya moves the ship out of the way of the portal we just came through in case anyone else passes through. She turns to me looking a bit stressed.

"Are you ready to do this?" she asks.

"The better question is are *you* ready to do this?"

Nunya takes a few more deep breaths.

"Because there's no saying we have to do this. We can just fly back through the portal and forget about the whole thing. I mean, we've come so far, I don't think anyone would just expect us to give up, so at least it'd be an interesting plot twist," I say.

"No, I think… I think we need to do this. I need to do this. I'm just having flashbacks to my crew dying. I'm trying my best to calm down but I feel like I'm going to have a panic attack," replies Nunya.

"Hey, we aren't in a hurry. Take as much time as you need."

"Thanks…" replies Nunya.

I start twiddling my thumbs again. Some people play with a pen or flip a coin between their knuckles. Some people vibrate their legs. I twiddle my thumbs. And I'm not so much worried about myself in the impending fight, I'm actually more worried about Nunya. Especially seeing her worried like this. She's kind of anger forward, and never seems to be scared of anything. I think she's starting to wonder if this is the end of the line for her.

"Hey, you already died once so far, so it's nothing new for you at least," I say, trying to help.

"What the fuck is wrong with you? Now you gotta put that thought in my mind?" yells Nunya.

"Geez, I'm sorry! I was just trying to give you some perspective, hoping it might make you worry less. Obviously, it didn't work."

"Of course it didn't fucking work you fucking moron."

"Okay, I know you're just freaking out so I'm not gonna take that personally."

"No, I think you should definitely take that personally. Take it as personally as possible and stop being an asshole!" says Nunya.

"Hey, at least you're angry instead of worried now," I say.

She goes silent for a moment.

"Actually, you're right. For some reason being angry at you is helping," says Nunya.

"That's the way I am with video games, I always play better when I'm angry," I say.

"Okay, well fuck it. Let's go kick some Sloth ass!"

"Wait, shouldn't we have a plan?" I ask.

"When do we ever have a plan?"

"I dunno, most of the time? Seriously, other than heading straight for the planet, do you know where their actual fortress is?"

"Uh, now that you ask, nope. The map we got from Blhack Glass just showed simple drawings of the planets," explains Nunya.

"Well, maybe you should call Blhack Glass then and see if they have more info," I suggest.

Nunya starts tapping away at a touchscreen. The same weird muffled voice comes on the line.

"M-Ray here."

"Hey, it's N and D again. We were wondering, that map you gave us, it doesn't seem to show exactly where the Sloth's hideout is."

"It's there, you just haven't figured out how to look at it yet," responds the voice. The line goes dead.

"Hmmm," hums Nunya.

She pulls the information square out of her bra and places it on a reader mounted on the dash. A holographic projection of the map appears before our eyes. Nunya takes the hologram and moves it around. Eventually she expands it so that she can see more detail, then expands it again, and again. We're now able to see that the section she's looking at is actually made up of extremely small characters of information; symbols, letters, and numbers.

"I have an idea," she says.

I watch as she shrinks the hologram, taps on her touchscreen a few times, and a holographic keyboard pops up right in front of Nunya. She furiously types away at the keyboard and the hologram of the map breaks apart, sections of which randomly move around then restructure. After a few seconds of what seems like absolute nonsense hacking the map's symbols are decrypted. A new hologram is showing, only this time it provides detailed information on all of the Sloth planets including coordinates for each specific base.

"How the fuck did you do that?" I ask.

"Dude, it was a hacking montage. Did I ask you how you were welding during your big welding montage?" asks Nunya.

"No."

"Then why would you ask me how I just did that? I dunno, just chock it up to movie magic or some shit."

"Yeah, okay, I guess that makes sense," I reply.

"Really? You actually bought that?"

"Sure, why not?"

"Because this is real life and not a movie. You don't actually think your whole life is a movie, do you?" asks Nunya.

"Well, after meeting God I figure at the very least it's a reality TV show. And since my adventures are so epic, yeah, I figure I deserve at least a movie or two mixed in there."

"Your life is more like those stupid comics that come with Bazooka Joe bubblegum: pointless and unfunny."

"Hey, fuck you times twenty! Bazooka Joe comics are the shit! So you can take your bubblegum hate and shove it up your ass!" I reply.

"Just shut up. I've pinpointed where their base is." Nunya taps on the touchscreen a few times and a hologram of the planet pops up. A big red holographic arrow points to where their base is. "Okay, are we finally fucking ready now?"

I dig into my bag of ultimate wonders and pull out Mona.

"Okay, now we're ready," I say.

"Finally," she says, giving the ship some throttle. "I'll need you to man the rear guns. Think you can do that?" asks Nunya.

"Yeah, sure, why not?" I say. She taps on the touchscreen and a hologram of what's behind us appears in front of me, which mostly shows a whole lot of nothing.

"Do you know how to work these things?" asks Nunya, pointing at my controls.

"You just use the joystick and press the trigger, right?" I ask.

"Yeah, basically. That red circle is your crosshair. If you pull the trigger you'll hit whatever's inside of that red circle. Also, don't be careless with your ammo. We don't have an infinite supply of it. Once we're out, we're out. At that point our ship is pretty much useless."

"Good to know. By the way, did you take into account space mines?" I ask.

"Space… oh fuck!" Nunya hits the brakes and the ship comes to a sudden stop. If it weren't for the onboard inertia arrester I would have been launched through the windshield. Not more than twenty feet in front of us is a giant floating black orb with spikes on it. "So yeah, space mines," mumbles Nunya.

"Glad I mentioned it. Got any plans to avoid them?" I ask.

"Thinking."

Nunya brings up the holographic keyboard again and starts typing away at it. After a few tense moments she says, "I think I've got it figured out. I've written a program that should plot out where all of the mines in the minefield are. The only problem is that we'll need to fly a lot slower than we were before which means more chances for a Sloth attack. Honestly, depending on how many ships they send after us we might not make it."

"Well, again, we could just go back home. Forget about trying to take on the Sloths. Our lives are more important than money," I say.

"Without money it's pretty hard to have a life," says Nunya. "Not worrying about money is something only rich people can do, and that ain't me."

"Alright. Then I guess we press forward."

"I guess so."

Nunya steers the ship around the mine then speeds us back up. After a few minutes of gracefully avoiding mines I start hearing a beeping sound going off in the cockpit.

"What's that?" I ask.

"That, Dick, is the sound of Sloth ships closing in on our location. They know we're here."

"Fuck."

37

I wish I could describe to you what despair looks like, because right now that's what I feel. There aren't a dozen Sloth ships heading to our location. There aren't fifty Sloths ships closing in on us. There aren't even a hundred. No, there's four fucking thousand ships coming toward us and we have nowhere to hide.

"Uh, that's a lot of ships, Nunya," I say.

"Oh my God, you think?" replies Nunya.

I do my best to ignore her sarcasm. "Can you outmaneuver them? Like, fly super fast and duck out of the way of their weapons?"

"Not in a minefield."

"Do we have enough firepower to shoot down four thousand ships?" I ask.

"Four thousand and seventeen. And no, unless of course we get them to fly really close together and then hope the explosions take out the other ships next to them."

"Then what do you think we should do?"

"I think we should pray."

"Seriously?"

"No, do you think God would really help us out?" asks Nunya.

"I dunno, she might. I mean I am her favorite movie actor, aren't I?"

"We're about to die in a Sloth minefield and you're making dumb jokes?"

"It wasn't a joke. I mean, yeah, we're about to die, but I was being dead serious. God loves me."

"God loves everyone," says Nunya. "It's her job."

"No. God hates Nickelback. She even told me," I say.

"Wait, for real?"

"No, but I bet if I asked her she'd say she did. Everyone hates Nickelback."

"Not everyone," replies Nunya.

"Oh God, you're one of them," I say. "Okay, I'm gonna abandon ship now and leave you to die."

"Like hell you are."

"No, seriously, you could die right now and I'd be fine with it. Your musical taste shouldn't be allowed to propagate throughout the galaxy. I'd be doing the universe a huge favor," I say.

"Hey, at least I don't put pineapple on pizza," says Nunya.

"What the fuck's wrong with pineapple on pizza? It's fucking brilliant! It has both sweet and umami flavors. Hawaiian pizza is second only to combination."

"Nope, cheese pizza is the best."

"I hate you so much right now. Open the fucking bay door," I say.

"No way, you'll get blown out of the ship."

"OPEN THE FUCKING BAY DOOR."

"Fine, but you asked for it."

I get out of my seat and start walking toward the back of the ship. The ramp starts lowering, and as soon as it does a gush of air inside the cabin violently evacuates, sucking me into outer space. As I float out into the dark I see the back end of the ship quickly close up. Good, Nunya can't breathe in space. I'm gonna try my best to keep her alive, because if she dies then the whole reason for going against the Sloths disappears. That and I'd miss her, even though she has horrible taste in music and pizza. I just hope my desperate plan actually works.

I pick up speed, moving past Nunya's ship and straight at the nearest mine. Hitting it square on I blow through it, scattering shards of metal in all directions. The explosion rocks me a bit but doesn't hurt me. I continue flying through mines as some of the Sloth ships get within range. They start firing at me and their laser blasts do nothing to my impervious skin. My welding goggles are unfortunately completely destroyed but this time my pants remain intact.

Somehow Mona is surviving the onslaught as well. Whoever built her knew what they were doing. I lift her up and start taking shots at the incoming Sloths. The first few pulses startle me because the blasts are bigger, more destructive, and a lot wilder than either Irene or Rita. What the blaster lacks in accuracy it makes up for in 'holy shit, I can't believe I just blew that up'-itude.

I keep swerving to draw the Sloth's laser blasts away from Nunya, and to take out as many mines as I can while still trying to stay aimed at planet Showdown. I blast three, four, seventeen, twenty-six different Sloths ships, leaving a trail of death and shrapnel behind me. I look back and see that Nunya's doing a good job of following. Other than a few dead Sloth carcassas stuck to the ship everything seems to be going okay.

So far the enemy ships have been fairly small fighter ships with only one Sloth inside of each. The ships are beige colored and round, which is oddly comforting, like the Sloths are all in little flying eggs. If these were normal everyday Sloths I'd almost find it cute. But these fuckers mean business, as do their ships. They're super fast and maneuverable but lack the firepower of some of the bigger ships. I know though that soon I'll start running into some of the bigger ones.

I also realize that Nunya has helped by taking down some of the fighter ships as well. She's been firing her guns sparingly, trying to conserve as much ammo as possible, but she's quickly racking up an impressive number of kills. I figure, just as it seems like the number of ships coming toward us slows down, that between the two of us we now have about three hundred kills. I'm actually starting to feel pretty good about things when I get hit by a blast that sends me hurtling backward. Yeah, I'm still alive, but it actually hurt some, and it did push me further away from the planet. Blam, I get hit with a second bright green blast that's about the size of a small spaceship. What the fuck was that?

I use my super-vision to see off into the darkness. After a few seconds of scanning, my eyes lock onto a group of much larger ships. They must be the ships that the fighter ships are coming from. There's about two dozen of them, all black and lit up with dark purple glowing stuff that I imagine are windows or exhaust ports, or some other thing that they made purple and light up. Who knows, maybe they're just lights. Anyway, they're both beautiful and scary at the same time.

As I close in on the nearest massive ship I realize that we've passed completely through the minefield. At least that's one danger we don't have to worry about right now. A new one has emerged, however, as most of the nearby black and purple ships start firing their powerful green blasts at me. The good news is that they can't fire anywhere near as quickly as the smaller fighters. The bad news is if even one of the blasts hits Nunya's ship she'll be done for.

When the first volley of blasts knocks me back my ears start ringing and my head starts hurting. That's a really bad sign. The last thing I need is ringing in my super sensitive hearing holes. But once I recover the ringing quiets down. I start counting. One, three, seven, twelve, twenty-two... boom! I get hit with another volley of green blasts. This time I wipe my nose and realize it's bleeding. I can't believe they're hitting me hard enough to make my nose bleed.

I look back at Nunya's ship and it still seems okay, but peering through the glass I can see that she's worried about me. I don't know if she's just worried that if I die she won't be able to make it out of here or if she actually cares about me and whether I die. I suppose it doesn't matter, and I suppose I should pay better attention because yet another blob of green energy strikes me, sending me hurtling back toward Nunya.

I'm able to course-correct and avoid hitting Nunya's ship but that means that she's now between me and the blaster fire. I turn around and fly past her ship as quickly as I can, trying to draw the fire away from her. It seems to work, as within seconds I'm hit again.

This time, instead of startling me or stunning me, it makes me angry. Angry in part from the pain these fuckers are inflicting on me, and angry because, fuck Nunya, pineapple deserves to be on pizza!

I pick up speed, doing my best to fly right at the nearest ship. The firing stops but that's when I see a few hundred beige egg ships pour out of the larger black and purple ships. I guess you can't take down an entire planet of Sloths without breaking a few eggs. You know, I'm starting to question their ship design because Sloths are mammals and don't lay eggs. Now it just seems weird. Why do I even think about this shit?

Anyway, instead of heading straight at the group of egg ships that are pouring out like cockroaches scurrying away from a box of old donuts, I keep aiming for the big black and purple ship in front of me. I wave Nunya off so she won't follow. Thankfully, almost all of the egg ships chase me as they realize I'm heading for one of their motherships. Now that I think about it I guess the term mothership makes sense since they lay all these goddamn eggs. I dunno, it's still so fucking weird.

As I reach the massive ship, which is the size of a large city, I bounce off its deflector shield. With the Sloth ship blaster fire still pelting me I fly toward it and punch the deflector shield. It shimmers like I'm damaging it but it still holds. I try again but no dice. This time I fire off Mona as I get close then crash through the nearly invisible barrier. Holy shit, it actually worked!

Still pursued by a few hundred Sloth eggs I pound my way through the hull of the ship, just like I pounded your mom last night. And yeah, that's a lot of pounding. It takes a moment to break through, and as soon as I do a few dozen Sloths get sucked into outer space. I make it inside as the smaller Sloth ships continue trying to shoot me even though they're doing damage to their own ship.

Running full tilt now that I'm on flat ground, I burst through as many walls as I can, leaving a trail of destruction behind me. Several dozen more Sloths are pulled out into the vacuum of space, some trying to hang on desperately to things to avoid being sucked out. Speaking of being sucked out, that reminds me, I really should go back and visit that squid chick at the Bigger and Taller store once this is over.

Anyway, as I'm causing general chaos and mayhem on board the ship I realize that maybe I can actually use this thing to take down some of the other ships. So instead of blowing through walls I actually come up to one of those sealed doors like they have in submarines and I twist its steering wheel doohickey open. Air gushes out, but as I pass through I close the door behind me, re-establishing the seal. Now I can keep rampaging my way to the helm of the ship. Only, I'm not sure where that is.

I stop and look at the signs overhead. They aren't in any language I understand, they're in Sloth, but thankfully they have logos on each of them that explain what they're pointing you to. I see a logo that looks like an old pirate ship steering wheel and figure that must be where I need to go.

As I run in the direction the sign is pointing me toward, Sloths start appearing from doors and hallways, moving so damn fast I can't get out of the way. They use their razor-sharp claws to scrape against my skin, and although my skin is mostly impervious to their attacks, they still scratch me. I even bleed a little, as if I'd been given tiny, pathetic but painful paper cuts. Great, I just hope they don't get infected. Not that I can get sick or anything, but still.

To get the ninja-Sloths off of me I start punching. As soon as I make contact the Sloths explode into pieces like sticking a grenade up a pinata's ass, only instead of dispensing candy they dispense Sloth guts. Their red, fuzzy goo coats my skin, and I must look like a nightmare to them as I yell at the top of my lungs, sprinting toward the helm.

More and more Sloths come out into the long hallway I'm running down, giving me more and more tiny paper cuts that sting like a sonofabitch. They keep scratching, I keep punching. At some point I realize some of the goo has made its way into my mouth and I start retching, doing my best to spit out their nasty entrails.

Finally, I reach the helm. There's only one Sloth here and he's dressed in a really adorable dark blue captain's outfit complete with matching captain's hat. I don't think I've ever seen anything more precious. The illusion fades though as he gets an evil sneer on his face and attacks me. I hesitate, letting him take a few swings at me, but he's so adorable that I knock him out instead of outright killing him. Go to sleep you evil, vicious, fuzzy ball of cuteness.

I grab the steering wheel and aim at the nearest large black and purple ship. Randomly pressing buttons on a console I try to fire the same green blaster cannons they'd used on me earlier. A bunch of sirens go off and I can't tell what I've done, but eventually I hit the right button and the cannons fire.

I watch as the mothership in front of me takes damage. I hit the same button a few more times but have to wait twenty or so seconds for the weapons to recharge. After about a minute of shooting at the other ship it breaks in half then crumbles into large floating chunks. I really wish it had exploded like the Death Star exploded, but instead the ship just kind of anticlimactically falls apart. Oh well, I guess not everything can be super impressive all the time.

The suck thing is that some of the other motherships realize what I'm doing and start firing toward my commandeered ship. I realize it'll only take a couple of blasts to annihilate my ship so I do the only thing I can think to do which is to ram them.

One of the great things about being in space is the lack of gravity, which means you can go faster than you'd think, even in a large ship. I realize that giving it full throttle so quickly will probably damage the ship's engines but at this point it doesn't matter as I'm abandoning ship right-the-fuck-now.

I aim Mona downward, pull the trigger, and start blowing a large tunnel through to the underside of the ship. Dropping inside, I quickly fly down the hole I made and eventually end up out in the vacuum of space. The egg ships that had swarmed around me earlier are now firing at the ship but it's no use, the ship is moving too damn fast. As blaster fire breaks it apart, the massive chunks slam into the other ships, taking out all but three of the large black and purple ships.

The ships I rammed at least had the good sense to send their egg ships out, kind of like shitting their pants with fear. A few thousand ships now form a giant wall around the three remaining motherships. It's kind of crazy to see them stacked up like that.

I realize I haven't heard from Nunya. Not that I could in the vacuum of space but I worry that something happened to her. Thankfully, the Sloths are too distracted with their formation off in the distance to actually be actively attacking me right now. I use my super-vision to look around for her, and after a few tense seconds I spot Nunya's ship.

Flying over, I look inside the cockpit. She seems relieved to see me. I point at her and give her a thumbs up, basically asking if she's okay. She gives a thumbs up back to me. Almost everything on her ship looks okay. One of the guns on the front has broken off, but other than that everything seems to be the way it was.

Nunya does the same thing now that I had just done, pointing to me and giving me a thumbs up. I thumbs up back. She nods then gets a funny look on her face and waves me to come toward the ship. As I do she starts motioning toward the back of the ship so I fly around to the back where the ramp begins opening. I hurry inside as Nunya closes the ramp, doing her best to hold her breath at the same time. Air comes rushing back in and I ask her nonchalantly, "What's up?"

"What's up is that I have a plan. You can either stay onboard or not, but I think I know how to take out the last of the ships without going through that again. It probably wouldn't work a second time anyway," says Nunya.

"It's not like they could stop me," I reply.

"I dunno, it looks like they actually hurt you. You're bleeding from a few hundred cuts all over your skin. Even the layer of fake tattoos is gone so you look like yourself again," says Nunya.

"Probably better that way. Now they really know who they're fucking with and that I'm getting my revenge on them," I reply.

"Well, I've been thinking about that, and it may be a bad thing they know who you are. Because they might know that magic fucks with you. Mac, the member of The Soap Droppers and Blhack Glass, mentioned that the Sloths have magic weapons now. What if they start using them on you? Then you're fucked."

"Shit, you're right. Okay, so what do you suggest we do?" I ask.

"I may have a plan... "

38

"Wait, why did you say 'I may have a plan…' and then just pause like that?" I ask.

"What do you mean?" asks Nunya.

"I mean, instead of just telling me your plan, you literally said 'I may have a plan…' I don't understand why you'd say that. It's like you were transitioning chapters in a book and you were trying to build suspense or something. Or you know, like when a TV show is about to cut to a commercial and wants you to keep watching then ends the scene with 'I may have a plan…'"

"I dunno, it just seemed cool?" says Nunya, shrugging.

"Yeah, well, stop trying to be cool. We're on a suicide mission here and we already have too much damn suspense. Honestly, I'd be a lot happier with less suspense right now. Like, maybe you could tell a joke to lighten the mood or something."

"I ain't telling any jokes right now. Like you said, it's a suicide mission and we need to stop fucking around. The longer we take the better prepared the Sloths will be. So let's go kick some Sloth ass!"

"Okay, fine, but what's the mysterious plan you keep teasing me with?" I ask.

"Don't you worry your ugly little head about it. I got this," says Nunya, steering the ship toward the armada off in the distance.

39

"There, you did it again!" I say.

"Did what again?" asks Nunya.

"The transition-y thingee. Like you're trying to build more suspense. Stop doing that!"

"I really don't know what you're talking about. Just get strapped in."

"Fine, just tell me the plan."

"I'm gonna fly straight at that cluster of ships," says Nunya.

"And?"

"And I'm gonna push that big red button, right there," says Nunya, pointing to a large red button I hadn't noticed before on the dash. How did I not notice it before?

"Okay, I'll bite. What does the big red button do?" I ask.

"You'll see," says Nunya, coyly.

40

"Seriously?" I say.

"Seriously what?" asks Nunya.

"You did it again! Stop transitioning! If I ever write this down in my memoirs you're gonna piss off my readers because they'll have to read a bunch of short shitty chapters that you created because you kept transitioning."

"Well fuck you, and fuck your readers!" says Nunya.

I'm so angry I don't even know what to say. One more snide comment and I'm likely to kill her, so I take several deep breaths and just decide to let it go. Maybe if I don't talk to her she'll stop transitioning.

I sit there in silence, rage building as Nunya flies toward our mortal enemies. And what is she planning? She's planning to push some dumb red button at them. Maybe when she pushes it glitter and tinsel will shoot out at the Sloths and a big banner that says 'surprise' will pop out. Maybe it will launch a bunch of plastic flamingos filled with explosives toward the Sloths, but that seems like it would take a lot of exploding flamingos to be useful. Could also just play really lame music to distract the Sloths but I don't think that would work very well. Who the fuck cares, anyway? I mean, how cool could that big red button possibly be?

Nunya speeds forward, getting close to the giant wall of eggs. As soon as we do, some of the eggs start pulling forward. Nunya immediately pulls back. The eggs go back to their previous positions in the wall. She does this four or five times, poking at the wall then pulling back. Once she's satisfied, she flies down toward the end of the wall and gets close enough to start pulling ships toward her, creating a weird wave of eggs behind us as she flies the entire length of the wall. Imagine that the ships are a giant tortilla and someone started to roll it up. That's what it kind of looks like: a big ass breakfast burrito in the middle of space.

As soon as she has all of the egg ships in tow she hits the reverse thrusters and sends us into the middle of the swarm. The Sloths, most of whom are surprised by the unexpected maneuver, aren't really firing. Those that are firing at us end up shooting other Sloth ships. At the exact moment that we reach the center of the Sloth burrito, Nunya hits the red button.

What happens when she hits the button makes me feel more sick than I've ever been in my entire life. Everything in front of the windshield has become a nauseating blur, as if we are spinning in endless directions. It's like when you get the spins from drinking way too much, only even less pleasant. I have to close my eyes because I can't handle the sensory input and I start to retch. My God it's a horrible feeling. I start counting to myself the seconds that it lasts, eventually hitting thirty before I open my eyes again. Thankfully, we're no longer in motion. The only positive thing about the experience is that I didn't black out, due to the inertia arresters inside the cabin keeping us from feeling the immense g-force from spinning so quickly.

"What in the ever loving fucking name of God was that?" I yell.

"Death blossom," says Nunya.

"Whaaaaaaa... wait, you're telling me that you just fired all our ammo as the ship was spinning, killing off all of the bad guys?"

"Yes."

"What the fuck? And you totally ripped off that 1980's movie at the same time! The Last Starfighter!"

"I wouldn't say 'ripped off'. Maybe more like an homage," replies Nunya, smirking.

"That was... that was... that was so fucking cool! Don't ever do it again!" I say.

"I can't. We're out of ammo, just like you pointed out," says Nunya.

I put my head up to the windshield and look out. Hundreds of cracked beige eggs float around us. Sloth body parts drift in the vacuum, bouncing off each other. It's super disturbing to look at.

Nunya starts tapping away at her touchscreen and a hologram of the remaining ships pops up. It's just the three giant black and purple ships that are left now. No more egg ships come out of them either. Just as I start to say, "I'll take care of the remaining three", we watch as the survivors of their once illustrious armada bug out, jumping to lightspeed and leaving their planet behind.

We float slowly through the debris, coming out the other side to where we can now clearly see planet Showdown. I'm immediately struck by the sight of thousands of other ships leaving the planet, none of them heading toward us. Nunya starts tapping on her touchscreen again.

"Dick, they're transport ships. Should we go after them?" asks Nunya.

I think for a moment. "No. We aren't trying to eradicate an entire species, no matter how horrible they are. Going after them would just be wrong."

"But what if they retaliate? What if they come after you and try to kill you, or destroy your home again?"

"Well, this isn't the only Sloth planet, so even if we killed all of these Sloths we'd still have more Sloths to contend with. Also, if all of that happens, we'd just get to go on another adventure together."

"What do you mean 'we'?" asks Nunya.

"Oh, sorry, I misspoke. I meant 'both of us'," I say.

"You really think you could ever convince me to go on another stupid adventure with you?"

"Maybe. But it's more likely that you'll need my help than I would need yours," I respond.

"Bullshit. I need your help like I need another hole in my head."

"Actually, I've been meaning to mention that you could probably use a few extra holes in that noggin of yours."

"Oh shut the fuck up, Dick. I know you think you're being funny but you aren't. Anyway, I think we should wait for the transport ships to go then head down to the planet so we can collect our booty."

"So, we're pirates now?" I ask.

"Yeah, we're pirates now. Now we get to collect the rich stuff."

"Sounds good to me."

Nunya taps on her touchscreen and the big red holographic arrow reappears. As she flies her ship toward the planet she looks over at me.

"Dick, you okay? You look a bit out of it. I would have thought you'd be happy," says Nunya.

"Yeah, I just wish I'd had a chance to man the rear guns. I wanted to feel like Luke Skywalker shooting at Tie-Fighters."

"Really? That's what you're disappointed about? Not getting to relive one of your childhood fantasies?"

"Yeah, that pretty much sums it up," I say.

"But you just boarded a massive ship and rammed it into a bunch of other massive ships. I mean, you may be the first person to ever do something like that," says Nunya.

"Yeah, but that's pretty normal for me. I just call that 'Tuesday'."

"You need to get the fuck over yourself because you're starting to annoy me again."

"Feeling's mutual, Nunya. The feeling's mutual."

As we head through the atmosphere of planet Showdown I start to realize just how similar the planet looks to what planet Earth Uno used to look like. Only instead of blue oceans and green covered land the water is tinted pink, and most of the ground is an odd red color. If I had a box of crayons I'd probably call the color 'permanent geranium lake'.

Getting closer to where the red arrow is pointing us I start making out buildings. The buildings look pretty normal, actually, just like buildings in a regular city made of gray concrete. I would have figured they'd be more, I dunno, Sloth like. Jagged and dangerous looking like they were going to kill you if you got near them. Instead, it almost humanizes the Sloths because they don't seem too different from the rest of us.

That thought starts bugging me but I quickly ignore it because I know what kind of creatures that Sloths really are. They ambush cargo ships all the time, killing their occupants, innocent people who aren't out to hurt anyone. The Sloths are also actively engaged in wars with a dozen different planets and they are never willing to negotiate or take hostages. Anyone that gets in their way dies. Still, the thought that maybe down on the ground there are schools, hospitals, restaurants, and grocery stores makes me feel a bit uneasy about the whole situation.

Nunya starts her landing cycle as we approach a giant building that seems pretty nondescript but massive. It's maybe ten stories tall and it's really wide and really deep. There's no windows or anything to see through, just one giant bay door that looks like a large spaceship could fit through it.

"So, this is the place?" I ask.

"Yeah, this is the place," replies Nunya.

"Is there any information on what's inside the building? Like maybe what defenses we might run up against?"

"Not that I saw in the information that Blhack Glass gave us. From here on in we're on our own."

"Great," I mumble.

Nunya and I make our way out of the ship and over to the giant bay door. As we approach, I pull Mona back out and Nunya pulls out her magic wand and shield. It's weird, because I feel like we're a couple of cosplayers whose costumes were pieced together from fandoms that have nothing to do with each other. Nunya looks like she's part G.I. Joe and part Game of Thrones, while I look like a pink Incredible Hulk with a laser blaster. I don't think either of us are going to win a prize at Comi-Con.

"So how do we get in?" I ask.

"No idea. Maybe there's a smaller door?"

We get closer to the giant bay door and as luck would have it there's a more normal sized door just to the right of the giant bay door. Next to the smaller door is a 10-digit keypad.

"It'll take me a few minutes to hack the keypad," says Nunya.

"What keypad?" I say, punching the keypad.

"Why the fuck did you do that?" asks Nunya.

"Because of this." With one punch I send my arm through the door then pull back, ripping it off its hinges. Tossing the door aside I look over at Nunya.

"What, I'm supposed to be impressed?" she says sardonically.

"Yes," I reply.

"You're so fucking stupid. Just get inside."

"If I'm so fucking stupid then why did I question the door having a keypad? Sloths don't have fingers, they have claws. How the fuck would they operate a keypad?"

"You think it was a booby-trap?"

"Doy," I reply. She just shrugs her shoulders.

We make our way into the structure and it's completely dark. We both fumble around for a lightswitch near the door. Eventually, Nunya finds the switch and the right half of the room lights up.

My eyes bulge as they try to take in all the information. First, the room is massive. Breathtakingly huge. They could probably fit a couple of spaceports inside of it. I mean, it looked big from the outside but being inside of it is seriously disorienting. Crazier still though is the enormous stockpile of rich stuff that's been heaped into dozens of piles. There's gold, heaps of burgmorps, fancy paintings, sculptures, antiques of all kinds; it's staggering just how much stuff they have all in one place. And weirder still they don't seem to have any security measures here to protect it. Like they think no one could possibly be stupid enough to try to steal it from them. Well, it turns out we're just that stupid.

Speaking of which I start to hear a sound like a low rumbling, kind of like thunder off in the distance. But it doesn't sound like electricity, it sounds more like a creature. Nunya and I turn toward the sound, and in the dark end of the hangar are two massive glowing red orbs, mostly concealed by shadow, that seem to be hanging close to the top of the ceiling.

"What the fuck is that?" I say. "Quick, turn on the other lights!"

Nunya turns back to the door we came in and finds another set of switches. She hastily turns them on. What we see sends shivers down my spine. Of all the things they could possibly have defending this hangar this was what I was least prepared for. They have a Mega-Sloth.

It's so tall that its head nearly scrapes the ceiling. Its claws are the size of small spaceships and they look like they could cut through a mountain like a hot knife through butter. I'm really glad that I took a dump earlier in the day, otherwise I would be shitting myself right now. I look over and notice Nunya has the same opinion, that we may be royally fucked.

The craziest thing isn't that they somehow engineered a Sloth to be so massive. No, the craziest thing is that it seems to have a magic wand of its own, the size of a tree, and it's starting to point it right at us!

"Duck!" I yell, pushing Nunya out of the way while I run and dive in the other direction. A giant ball of pinkish energy comes zooming past us, hitting the ground and sending concrete flying everywhere.

"What's your plan?" yells Nunya.

"I don't fucking know! I've never fought a King Kong sized Sloth before! And definitely not one with a magic wand. If that pink shit hits me I'm a dead man!" I yell, ducking out of the way of another pink ball of energy.

"Yeah, well if it hits me I could be dead too!"

"So don't get hit! That's the plan!"

"Sounds like a shitty plan!"

This time the ball of energy nearly hits Nunya, who barely moves out of the way in time.

"Maybe we should fly! I figure we'll be more maneuverable if we fly," I yell.

"Yeah, okay," Nunya yells back, clearly unsure if it's a good idea or not.

"Oh, and we should probably, like, fire back!"

"On it!"

Nunya starts waving her wand and sends a few fireballs flying toward the Sloth. He uses his wand to dispel the fireballs, harmlessly knocking them out of the air. Nunya switches to lightning and again the giant Sloth is able to deflect the attack, this time by absorbing the electricity into his wand and sending it back at Nunya. She narrowly escapes being hit by the lightning bolt, deflecting it with her shield, but her helmet falls off and her hair is now standing straight up from the electrical charge. It looks pretty silly if I'm being honest, like she was a character on Scooby-Doo who had just seen a ghost.

"Yeah, I got nothing!" says Nunya, as she dodges several pink blobs of energy being lobbed at her.

"Okay Mona, don't let me down!" I yell, as I fire off my blaster. Instead of firing though Mona explodes in my hand, knocking me out of the air and sending me hard toward the ground. The energy released is enough to take the wind out of me, and the shockwave is strong enough to send Nunya flying into a wall. "Mona, you treacherous bitch, you let me down! I should have seen this coming!"

Another pink ball of energy comes flying at me, and as I roll out of the way it actually singes my back. The smell of burnt flesh is gross, and you'd think I'd be used to it by now, except it's the smell of my own flesh burning. If it was someone else's I probably wouldn't care. Since it's mine, I'm disgusted.

I get to my feet as quickly as I can and get flying again. I look over at Nunya, who just dodged another pink blob, and she looks right at me. I turn so she can see my back.

"How bad is it?" I ask.

"Really, really bad," she says.

"Fuck. Then how am I still flying?" I ask.

"You're probably in shock. The good news is you're not bleeding."

"Yeah, thank God for small favors, I guess. So how do we take this thing down?"

"I think we'll need to get closer," says Nunya.

"Are you fucking crazy?" I yell.

"Yeah, apparently I am. I figure if we get closer then maybe we can get the wand out of its hand or something."

"Fuck, sounds like a stupid idea but when has that ever stopped us?"

"Never," says Nunya.

"On three," I start to say.

"Three!" yells Nunya, who starts flying straight at the Sloth.

"Serpentine!" I yell, and I fly straight for the Sloth too.

The great thing is the Sloth sends a barrage of pink energy balls our way and we have to duck out of the way of them as we approach. Evading them probably looks pretty bad-ass. Unfortunately, Nunya miscalculates and gets hit by one of the blasts. Her shield disintegrates as she falls out of the air and she crumples into a ball. Nunya isn't moving.

"NOOOOO!!!" I yell at the top of my lungs. I swoop down and grab for the wand but the Sloth hangs onto it. He flicks it violently, sending me flying back across the room as I let go. The impact from slamming into the wall stuns me for a second then I fall to the ground like something out of a Road Runner cartoon. Thankfully, the next pink ball hits where I used to be, which was up on the wall of the far side of the hangar instead of where I am at right now.

I fly as fast as I can straight for Nunya and scoop her into my arms. The Mega-Sloth seems to have anticipated this and a large blob of pink energy nearly hits both of us as I roll Nunya out of the way. I do my best to protect her as I fly us straight through the nearest wall and out of the reach of the Mega-Sloth.

Setting Nunya down on the ground I roll her onto her back. She looks really badly burnt. I put my hands on her and do my best to heal her. Thankfully, she's still hanging on to life because my healing powers are actually working. Her skin starts to turn back to its beautiful shade of brown instead of the ashen color it was before. Nunya starts coughing, and I imagine part of that is her lungs healing, trying to get rid of the smoke trapped inside them. A few seconds later and she seems mostly herself again. Thank God the adrenaline is keeping me from feeling my back.

Nunya sits up and looks at me. "Thanks, Dick, for healing me."

"Yeah, no problem. Are we gonna try this again?" I ask.

"Yeah. It's a matter of payback now."

"Vengeance? I can work with vengeance. So what's your plan?" I ask.

"We hit it from behind."

"How do you plan on getting behind it?"

"You punch a hole through the wall it's standing up against, surprising it. Then we kick its ass."

"Huh, actually sounds like a plan. Okay, let's do it," I say.

We both get airborne, fly around to the side of the hangar we think is directly behind the Sloth, and just as we're about to burst through the wall I grab her shoulder.

"What is it?" asks Nunya.

"Well, what height should we come in at?"

"Oh, good point. Maybe it'd be better to come in on top of it and aim for the head," says Nunya.

"We can give it a try."

We both move to the roof, right over where we think the Sloth is. I fly up a little higher just to get momentum then come crashing through the roof with Nunya following right behind. We look down and realize we miscalculated exactly where the Sloth was. We're about fifty feet away from it on its wand side. The Mega-Sloth makes a weird shrieking noise then launches pink energy balls at us again.

"Keep your balls to yourself, mister!" I yell really loud. See, you gotta have catchphrases like this if you're gonna be a superhero.

Nunya and I do our best to fly out of the way but being this close is making it hard to maneuver. Instead of going for the wand I fly down and start punching at its chest. The crazy thing is that even though I'm punching it, and even though I can tell it's making the Sloth uncomfortable, it doesn't seem to be doing any real damage. I can punch through steel, but apparently I can't punch through Mega-Sloth.

Nunya tries a different tactic which is to grab onto the Sloth's wand arm. She gets swung around like a ragdoll until she's hanging limply underneath the Sloth's arm, then the Sloth proceeds to slam her into the ground, over, and over, and over again until she falls. Nunya looks like she's unconscious.

I fly up and start punching the Sloth in the face. Its giant eyes narrow but it keeps its creepy smiling mouth closed. The punches don't seem to do much more than anger the Sloth. He turns his wand toward his face and launches a blob of pink energy at me. I realize what he's doing and react just quickly enough to grab a few handfuls of the Sloth's facial hair and pull him toward me. The Mega-Sloth takes the blast right in the kisser and he shrieks, letting go of the wand. I fly down, pick up the massive wand in one hand, Nunya in the other, and fly them back out of the same hole I used when I rescued her the first time.

Nunya is definitely unconscious so I use my healing powers on her again. She pops back awake in only a few seconds; a bit disoriented as I continue to heal her.

"You were knocked out," I say.

"Yeah, I know. You got the wand?" she asks.

"Yup, I got the wand."

"Cool. Are we gonna try and use it?"

"Well, it did seem to hurt it. I dunno. Now that it can't blast us then maybe it'll be less dangerous. Might be good to not use any more magic weapons on it since I'm still kind of vulnerable to magic. Let's just go in and kick its ass the good-old-fashioned way," I suggest.

"Yeah, I think that sounds agreeable."

"Come in from the top again?"

"Nah, let's use the same hole we just went through, like a couple of badasses."

Nunya takes off before I can even react, flying back through the hole. I follow her the best that I can but she's well ahead of me. By the time I breach the hangar wall Nunya's already at the Sloth, pummeling him. It doesn't seem to be doing much good though as the Mega-Sloth bats Nunya away like she's a gnat.

I fly to the back of his head and keep pounding but I still can't seem to damage it. Suddenly, the Mega-Sloth reaches back and grabs me by the legs then starts slamming me into the ground like he's an angry two-year-old and I'm his least favorite action figure. After six or seven slams he lets go. Before I can even react, he uses his claw to slash me, cutting across my gut and sending blood flying everywhere. The pain is intense and I can actually feel it creeping in from my torched back as well. Oh God, I think I'm dying again.

I helplessly watch as Nunya screams then flies right up into the Sloth's face. She punches at its eyes but her fists just bounce off. In desperation she does something really disgusting; she fights her way right up and inside the Mega-Sloth's nose. The Sloth lets out another blood-curdling shriek as I pass out from blood loss and pain.

41

"Dick! Wake up, Dick!"

I can hear Nunya's voice but it sounds super distant, like it's a hundred miles away.

"Dick, wake the fuck up!"

I'm tired. I've never felt this tired in my life. Why do I feel so tired?

"Dick!"

"What?" I try to yell back, but it comes out weak.

"Oh, thank God you're still alive," she says.

I finally open my eyes and look down. I have a giant wad of gauze covering my stomach where I'd been eviscerated. It's dark red now from soaking up a lot of my blood. I also notice I've been strapped down to the meeting table inside of Nunya's ship using cargo straps. I can't really move, not that I'd want to, but it's freaking me out that I'm tied down.

"Why am I tied down?" I ask.

"So you don't fall off the table. Now stop asking stupid questions, I gotta fly us outta here," replies Nunya. She seems super panicked.

I look around and notice piles of gold and jewels and burgmorps all over the ship.

"Hey, you got the goods!" I mumble.

"Yeah, just barely," says Nunya. "But there's a problem."

"What's that?"

"The planet is going to explode in a few seconds."

"WHAT?" I yell. Or at least try to. It comes out more like a coughing sound.

"Yeah. We might not make it."

"How do you know it's gonna explode?"

"Because as I was loading up the ship with loot I accidentally activated a countdown. I think they booby trapped the entire planet to blow."

"Holy fuck, then get us out of here!" I say.

"I'm trying!" yells Nunya.

I look down toward my feet and see Nunya pressing buttons and giving the ship some throttle. The view outside the cockpit's windshield changes from buildings and streets to a beautiful pink sky. Nunya gets us airborne but something doesn't feel right, like somehow we're trapped in molasses. It's like a nightmare where you're trying to run from a monster but everything's slowed down and you can't get away. I hate that feeling.

"Fuck," says Nunya.

"What?"

"We're too heavy!"

"Just go to lightspeed!" I say.

"Can't, need to be out of the atmosphere for that," says Nunya.

"Isn't that rule just to protect the planet you're leaving?"

"No, it's a gravity thing. But shut up, and I'm sorry," says Nunya.

"Sorry for what?" I ask.

That's when Nunya opens the ship's cargo ramp, dumping out all of the gold, jewels, and burgmorps.

"No!!!" I yell. "Not the rich stuff!"

Every single piece of gold, every jewel, everything goes flying out of the back. Everything but me, thankfully. Although, at the moment I'm not feeling too thankful. There goes my ability to pay Nunya back. There goes my ability to pay for my new GT9. There goes my chance at rebuilding my home. Now I don't have anything. Goddamn it!

"Goddamn it!" I yell.

Once the cargo is gone Nunya closes the ramp and we pick up speed. That's when we hear this crazy sound, like some death trumpet blaring at full volume. I realize the planet's exploding. Nunya does her best to keep the ship steered straight but the initial shockwave propels us even faster and completely out of control. We start to spin and I see massive chunks of debris fly past us. As we rotate, I can see where the planet once was but is no longer.

Amazingly, we're flung out past the debris, out into space, but we're still spinning. I have to close my eyes to avoid throwing up. Eventually, Nunya is able to hit a button that suddenly stops us from spinning. She aims the ship toward the nearby space-asshole, and without stopping to talk to security flies through it. It sends us to some far off random location, wherever the previous traveler had flown.

Nunya unstraps herself and comes running over to me. "Do you think you'll make it?"

"If I'm not dead now then I probably won't die. But it's gonna take a fucking long time to heal, even if I heal faster than most humans. How are you? You're coated in some really nasty shit. You need a shower real fucking bad," I say.

"Gee, thanks. And yeah, it's a combination of Sloth snot and Sloth brains."

"Gross! How'd you manage that?"

"Well, I climbed up into its nasal cavity then punched my way to its brain. From there it was just a matter of short circuiting everything. I scrambled his eggs. Then I climbed back out once I was sure it was dead. I filled the ship the best I could with whatever I could carry then I accidentally tripped the countdown and got us the fuck out of their as fast as I could," explains Nunya.

"Sounds like you're the hero then. You saved me, took down the bad guy. Maybe I am just your sidekick," I mumble.

"Damn right you are," says Nunya, smirking.

"I'm just sorry I can't pay you back now."

"It's okay. You tried. But I have a feeling I'll be okay regardless."

"Why?" I ask.

"Because I'm rich!"

"How the fuck are you rich? You just jettisoned all our pirate booty!"

"Not all of it. I only jettisoned your half," says Nunya.

"What do you mean 'my half'?"

"I mean that your half was the half in the lower part of the ship. My half is still above us, in the smuggling space."

"That's great! Wait, fuck, no, that's not great. You're saying that you filled up the ship's attic with rich stuff and none of it is mine because you considered the lower half all my stuff. So even though I went on this whole damn adventure with you, and did at LEAST half the work, you're going to try and fuck me over and lay claim to the full amount of what we have left?"

Nunya blinks a few times. "Yes."

"What a load of fucking bullshit!" I yell. It comes out more like a weeze.

"Calm down, Dick, I'm just fucking with you. We'll split it. 90/10," says Nunya.

"No."

"80/20?"

"No."

"Fine, 70/30, my final offer."

"I'm gonna offer you my fist in just a second," I mumble.

"Yeah, that's not likely to happen. And if you don't quit your bitching I'll unstrap you and jettison your ass out into space. Is that what you want?"

I think about it for a moment. "No."

"Good. Anyway, I think 70/30 makes sense, because let's say you didn't owe me a new bar and we went into it as partners. That's 50/50. But you do owe me a new bar. So you give me forty percent of what you ended up with, which is actually twenty percent of the total. I end up with seventy percent, and you end up with thirty percent," says Nunya.

"Look, I don't really like math, so all of that nerdy equation-y bullshit doesn't mean jack to me. But I understand what you're saying. Fine, you get seventy percent."

"Not like you could stop me anyway. I really could blow you out the back of the ship. And I want you to realize that other people would have left you back there to die."

"Yeah, that's true. Thanks, I guess, for saving me," I say.

"You're welcome. Not sure why I did it, but you're welcome."

"Oh, hey, did you at least get that giant-ass wand the Sloth had?"

"Yeah, it's currently strapped to the top of the ship. It was the first thing I took."

"Nice! Did you already have plans for it?" I ask.

"Not really. Why, do you?" asks Nunya.

"I was thinking we could give it to Steve. He'd probably love it. It'd be a way to thank him for his help."

"Honestly, as charming as he is, he didn't really help us much."

"No, he really didn't. Especially when he gave me Mona. I just wish I'd been able to see into the future and know it was going to explode like that. Yup, that sure blindsided me. I mean, there were definitely no red flags that warned me not to trust it, right?" I ask.

"Sure, Dick. Sure. Anyway, where do you think we should head now?" asks Nunya.

"Well, probably the FIB, the First Intergalactic Bank. We should deposit and convert what we can of the loot then put the money into an interest-bearing account. Might also consider investing in the market, or T-Bills if you're risk averse."

"Wait, I thought you just said you hated math."

"Oh, I do hate math. This is finances. Finances I love."

"What the actual fuck?"

"I get that reaction a lot. So anyway, now that you've got your money, and we're even-steven, can we finally have sex?"

Nunya thinks about it for a second. "Sure."

"Wait, seriously?"

"No! Not seriously at all! Why would you even ask that after all we've been through?"

"Nunya, I was just fucking with you. Because... you're my

friend."

"Wow, you're delirious. We should probably take you to a hospital instead of the bank," says Nunya.

"You know I'm not, so just shut up and pilot the ship to the bank."

"You tell me to shut up again and I'll send you flying into outer space."

"Blah blah blah."

42

It takes a few weeks to fully heal from being slashed open by the Mega-Sloth. I'd wondered just how he'd been able to carve me open like that, and Nunya figured they must have used magic to make the Sloth a giant Sloth, and the remaining magic residue must have made me more susceptible to injury from it. I was like 'sure, makes sense' and didn't question it. Not that I question much of anything. I pretty much just assume life will be crazy, with all kinds of bullshit I can't explain. Better to just roll with the punches. Go with the flow. Take one for the team. Jump on the grenade. All those things.

Instead of going back home immediately, which thankfully I have a home again now that my insurance kicked in and they rebuilt everything, I decide to stay with Nunya for a while. She makes a pretty good nurse, changing my bandages, giving me inappropriate sponge baths, that sort of thing. Okay, maybe the sponge baths thing didn't happen but I definitely dreamt that it did. You can't take that away from me!

With all the money Nunya made she rebuilt the bar exactly like it was. I have no idea why she had it rebuilt the exact same way considering her bar sucked before but I guess she's just a creature of habit. She likes things the way she likes things. Personally, I would have made it really cool, with a mud wrestling pit and a big dance floor with lasers and shit. Maybe even add a few hidden rooms, like an old-timey speakeasy. But no, she made it exactly the same. Once I'm finally able to walk again, and my wounds are healed, I put my tux on and head over to Nunya's bar.

"Nunya?" I say as I walk inside.

"Yeah, I'm back here," she says.

I walk behind the bar and go through an open door I hadn't remembered being there which leads to a stockroom. Nunya's opening boxes of alcohol and doing inventory on them.

"Was this room here originally?" I ask.

"Yeah, it was here. Most people don't even notice rooms like this because it's an area they aren't allowed in. They just kind of block it from their memory."

"Makes sense. So how's business?"

"Pretty non-existent. Had a few cowboys in earlier. At least they were dressed like cowboys. I dunno, maybe they were wearing costumes or something. They kept asking for sarsaparilla and I had to explain we don't carry it like three times. Eventually they just had a few cheap beers then left."

"Cool story, bro. Anyway, I wanted to give you a gift," I say.

"Wait, seriously? You know that even after rebuilding my bar I'm super rich now. Like, I could buy fifty bars if I wanted. Maybe even twice that. And you still got me a gift?" says Nunya.

"Well, I figure you've earned it."

"What is it?"

"I think it's better if I show you. Follow me."

I walk out of the stockroom, around the bar and over to the wall opposite the entrance. Digging into my pocket I remove my trusty bag of ultimate wonders, stuff my hand inside it, and pull out the velvet painting of me. I take down a really lame painting of sunflowers and replace it with the most valuable painting in the galaxy.

"There, that'll class up your joint. You're welcome," I say.

"What the absolute fuck?" says Nunya.

"What, is it crooked?"

"No, it's hideous."

"Hey, I'm giving you the most valuable thing I have, the thing I cherish most. The least you could do is be appreciative of it. And people will come from all over the galaxy to see its majesty," I say.

"That's the last thing I want! I don't care if my bar is successful, I just want some peace and fucking quiet."

"Fine then, I'll take it down." I make sure to say it in a really sad and sulky way.

Nunya grumbles then lets out a deep sigh.

"No, keep it up there. Goddamn it. How did you even get it back?"

"Oh, I got it back from your folks by paying off the GT9. Had it delivered while you were at work yesterday."

"They aren't getting Christmas cards this year," says Nunya.

"From the way your mom talks you don't send them Christmas cards any year. You really should visit them more."

"Yeah, well, I couldn't take time off for vacation before. Now, maybe I'll hire someone to help work the bar. I know I'm gonna regret asking, but do you want a job?"

"As a bartender? Fuck no!"

"Hey, what's wrong with being a bartender?"

"Absolutely nothing, but I can't be pinned down to one place. I'm a lone wolf that likes to do the lone wolfy thing. You know, travel around, killing things. But thanks for the offer. It means a lot."

"Speaking of meaning a lot I have a gift for you too," says Nunya. "Wait here."

Nunya runs back to the stockroom and within a few seconds hands me a large black box. I walk over and set it down on one of the tables. It has a bow, which I have to unwrap, then I pull off the box top. Inside I see the most beautiful thing I've ever seen: two brand new black space blasters, top-of-the-line, with gold triggers. I pull both of them out and notice that one has the name 'Nunya' etched into the side in gold, and the other also has 'Nunya' etched into the side in gold. I start laughing.

"You named them both after yourself?" I say, still giggling.

"Yeah. I wanted you to have the name of the baddest bitch in the whole galaxy on them. That's me. You like them?" asks Nunya.

"I love them," I say. I put the guns down and give Nunya a hug. She's surprised at first, but I'm even more surprised when she hugs me back. I guess it's technically not the first time she's hugged me but it still feels strange.

The sound of the front door opening makes us break our embrace. Nunya turns to say 'come in' to the patrons, but before she can get the words out we hear the familiar sound of space-blasters charging. I look over and my stomach drops because a dozen Unicorns just walked in, armed to the teeth.

"Dick Blowhard?" one of them grunts.

"Yeah?" I say.

"You killed our friends and we're here for payback."

"Aw, fuck no!" yells Nunya. "Not again!"

Special Thanks

Thank you to the following people for making this book possible:

Melissa and Chris Willard
Jessica Warren
Nicole Vesper-Brenner
James "Captain Awesome" Thomas
Hillarie Thomas
Paul Soldan
Michelle Soldan
Connor Riggs
Nicole Ng
Rebecca Miller
Patty McCalister
Greg Manin
Giuseppe Lo Turco
Gary Henton
Christine Frank
Leni and Wes Brenner
James "Doc" Bennett
Jason Anderson
Joe Amon

Read Dick Blowhard's further adventures in the upcoming book

Dick Blowhard 2: Blow Harder

About the Author

If you'd like to know more about T. M. and his other books,
check out www.tmbrenner.com.

You can also find him on Twitter as @TimothyMBrenner,
on Facebook as Author T. M. Brenner,
and on GoodReads as T. M. Brenner.